GW00579414

THORN

First Published by RaspberryRipple Press UK in 2023

ISBN: 978-1-7399237-85

THORN

TINA.R.ABBOTT

This book is dedicated to:
My mum and dad, Rosemary and Charles, to thank them for
all the love and support they have shown me throughout my
life; for being by my side through every surgery and for being
the ones that have always held me up when times have got
tough. I love you both more than words.
It is also dedicated to my son Charlie for being the best friend
I have ever had. For giving me the strength to keep going. I
love you more than I can explain.
And finally, I would like to dedicate this book to the late Mr.
T. R. Morley (orthopaedic surgeon) for literally saving my
life. If God gives anyone wings, it would be you. -X-

Dear Reader,

First, I would like to thank you for taking the time to read Thorn. Although this book is purely fictional, it speaks of a matter extremely close to my heart because, like Violet, I, too, have Scoliosis and Kyphosis.

By writing this book, I wanted to give an insight into the mind of someone who has a physical disability or difference and the effect that the world may have on them. Although this is set in the 19th Century when things were much worse, I have dug deep into my own emotions over the years and portrayed them in the main character.

With this information, I must advise that there are some scenes and use of language that may be upsetting to some (these include ableist slurs, verbal, mental and physical abuse, and abduction). They are not intended for the purpose of upsetting you, but only to make sure that the story is told with the message that it was meant to portray.

However, it is not all doom and gloom. It is a story of love, kindness and hope amongst the twist of a 19th Century Romance, Fantasy and Gothic story.

I hope you enjoy this book and love Violet and all the other characters as much as I do.

Thank you for your support.

Tina.R.Abbott

THORN

PROLOGUE

Kitty Hall nestled under the comforting arm of her husband, James. The scent of his cologne was familiar and strong. His fragrance entwined with the soft aroma of lavender soap upon her skin as she breathed him in. Her fair skin flushed petal pink with happiness. Honey blonde curls cascaded down the sides of her face, framing her beauty. It was not a surprise that James fell in love with Kitty, but it was not only her beauty that he admired. Kitty Hall was kind and loving. A compassionate woman and it was that, more than anything, James loved the most about her.

It had been one year, to the day, since their wedding and, already, they had been blessed with a child. Little Violet Hall cooed, gurgled, and wriggled in the young woman's arms. Her large green eyes stared adoringly at the woman who held her. Warm, safe, and loved. She, too, even at such a young age, knew the extent of her mother's heart. Kitty held her close, breathing in the soft scent of her baby. Her entire world swaddled in ivory fabric. Fragile and vulnerable, protected in her embrace.

"Oh, she's a darling. Truly, she is." crooned a lady dressed in grey silk as she peered over Kitty's shoulder. "You will be a fine mother, of that, I am sure."

"Thank you, Aunt" Kitty beamed. Her eyes sparkled as she acknowledged the kind words.

Kitty's mother approached, clicking her tongue behind her front teeth. The berating noise ticked quietly to avoid the ears of any other but her daughter. "Heaven knows how you are going to cope with a child." she sneered in a whispered breath, "You can barely look after yourself!".

Kitty inhaled deeply. The words crawled over her skin as her heart pounded in her chest. How easily the venom poured from the woman's lips, she thought. Kitty refused to let her mother spoil their joyful moment. She smothered the tendril of pain that threatened to take root deep in her heart, pushing against the ache as she inhaled. It dulled a little more with each, and every, breath. As she tensed, James caressed her arm, pulling her close to him in his protective and reassuring manner.

Kitty's husband did not need to remind Mrs. Bainbridge of whose home she stood in. His bold glare in her direction was all the reminder she needed. The old woman sniffed stubbornly at his authoritative message while James kissed the top of Kitty's head. It was a supportive, silent message of his love. His gentle touch eased Kitty's mind, while she stayed focused on the men and women gathered around them; her attention only on those who offered approval of their beautiful daughter.

'Not much longer.' Kitty thought, eyeing the luggage that lay in wait beside the large mahogany front door. Tonight, their splendid home would, once again, be their own. Kitty's mother was to make her leave.

The old woman, thankfully, resided a fair distance from London and the family that Kitty now treasured. Kitty had spent two months enduring her mother's tongue and, in return, having to hold her own. Mrs. Bainbridge had denied her almost nine weeks of being the mother she knew she could be, leering over her shoulder, correcting her at every opportunity. Kitty was emotionally exhausted. Tomorrow could not come soon enough. It was then she would have her chance. A new beginning. Just the three of them.

The servants had stacked an embroidered valise and a simple leather suitcase neatly in the hallway, at the request of James. He stood boldly as an extension of his wife, and her power within their home, as he had given the order. The bags were a reminder to Mrs. Bainbridge of her demanded departure but, to the woman herself, they were a statement of her daughter's cruel and selfish ways. A statement for the guests to see as they wandered her daughter's home. The old woman would occasionally gaze in the luggage's direction and wipe away a dry tear, deliberately mustering sympathy from anyone who cared to offer it. She would casually inform those who looked at the expensive cases of her impromptu dismissal.

The softer side of Kitty struggled as a sense of guilt itched under her skin. Her conscience teetered on the brink of asking her mother to stay a little longer, yet there was also the part of her that felt emboldened and elated by her bravery at not relenting to the woman's emotional blackmail. In the years gone by, Kitty would not have dared to dream of saying such a thing to her mother. It seemed her own daughter's presence had instilled in her a newfound strength that she found utterly exhilarating.

Mrs. Bainbridge would return to the home where Kitty grew up. A quaint house in the country with a fair amount of land. She would never be alone, Kitty thought, as she remembered the neighbours of her childhood days. She remembered how serene it had been, but its peace often marred by the verbal lashings her mother had inflicted upon her until the day she'd left. Her brother William was a freer soul, the apple of their mother's eye. There was not a time when the woman had scolded him for any misdoing despite there being many. The day Kitty took her leave, she was glad to break free. The shackles of her past fell away as her childhood home faded into the distance and she began her new life in London with her husband, James.

London life was a far cry from the quiet the countryside offered. There was no escape from the noise in the heart of London other than inside the four walls of their home. Smog in the air was depressing. The rattle of wheels over cobbles sounded like thunder. The call of the child trying to sell the Morning Post, harsh upon her ears. Pickpockets, weaving amongst the men and women trying to find anything to sell, worrying. But she was free.

In time, London, and all it offered, became a part of her, and she a part of it. She had become acquainted with women of varying ages and a friend to those amongst the small embroidery group she had founded. Despite the uneasy moments spent with the women and the tension of the long awkward silences, they were, at least, a distraction while she awaited the daily return of her husband from work.

James spent his days adorned in the most expensive tailored suits. A necessary extravagance to assure respect in the houses of parliament. A politician, 'Making London a better place', he'd boasted, and he'd meant it. He was a kind-hearted man and Kitty was confident that he would achieve great things in his role there. He was the subject of almost all her conversations that broke the silence of many an embroidery gathering. She was proud of him as her husband and as the father of their daughter.

Kitty's father had absconded leaving her, her brother, and her mother when Kitty was just six years of age. She often wondered whether it was her mother's ways that had made him leave, but she believed it never offered a reason acceptable enough to abandon his children. Looking at Violet now, so fragile and precious, made it even more difficult to comprehend the working of his mind many years ago and all the years that followed. She did not blame her father for not being strong enough to cope with her mother's vengeful and spiteful tongue, but she could not help but harbour a little resentment towards him for leaving her there. She vowed silently to her little girl that she would always stay by her side, both her and James. Little did she know, for it was a heartfelt promise, she would later learn it was one that she could not keep. Fate guided the wheels of the carriage one cold winter's evening, and Violet was left alone.

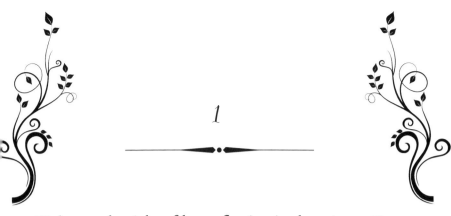

1

Violet caught sight of her reflection in the mirror. Her warm chestnut brown hair braided neatly in a bun, piled upon the top of her head. Her skirts cinched in at her small waist. The colours of her clothes were dreary and lifeless, but they fitted her petite frame comfortably, accentuating her feminine shape.

'If I face forward,' she breathed thoughtfully, tilting her head to the side, and smoothing down the front of her skirts, 'I can't see it. Without it, I think I look quite pretty.' The wooden exterior of the mirror framed her image as she exhaled slowly, trying to cool the relentless burning within her chest. In truth, Violet didn't feel pretty in the slightest. How could she when she was told daily that she was not even human, let alone pretty?

'It would just take one step; one turn and the illusion would fade.' she thought.

A prickling sensation stabbed at the back of her eyes as she swallowed the painful ache squeezing her throat like a savage, vengeful vice. A continuous, deep ache throbbed like a fresh bruise upon her heart. Each time she gazed upon her reflection, she felt the large rough fingers of self-hatred wrap themselves around the pulsating muscle and the ache grew deeper still. Her breath caught as tears pooled in her beautiful green eyes. A river of emotions threatened to spill over and course down her cheeks, stained pink from the emotional pain that burst in her chest with every beat. It felt like punishment for her existence. Her confidence hung in tatters like the hems of her skirts. Her light, dimmed in the darkness of others, hiding in the shadows of her thoughts by the burden she should never have had to bear. 'If only everyone looked at me from this angle,' she thought to herself, 'then they'd never see my curved spine.'

Violet's grandmother burst through the ashen grey door of the room, almost yanking it from its hinges. The clatter as it hit the wall startled the young woman into the present. Mrs. Bainbridge's eyes pierced through the darkness of the grey morning, rage ablaze within them. "Ooh, look at me!" she mocked, her sour face reddening. "I'm so pretty! Turn around, girl. Go on! Please... be my guest... take a good look!" she sneered, gesturing to the mirror. A flicker of the old woman's satisfaction maliciously licked the amber of her eyes. "You are not pretty, girly! You are a monster... A hunchback!" she spat.

Violet flinched at her grandmother's last words. Her heart hammered. 'A hunchback', it was the name that scarred the deepest and her grandmother knew it. Nausea swirled like a tornado in the pit of her stomach.

She swallowed, pushing the sensation back down as it climbed her insides. 'I'm not a hunchback!' she screamed from the depths of her mind. The old woman's ignorance was unbearable. Violet's legs weakened as the pain of her grandmother's words ripped through her insides as sharp as a serrated blade. She gathered every molecule of courage she could, strengthening her legs just to remain standing. Her chest rose and fell as her body trembled in the familiar darkness of the old woman's glare.

Mrs. Bainbridge's grey hair, scraped back tight in a bun upon her head, shifted as her face puckered with spite. Malevolence danced in the deep folds on her forehead and the lines etched around her eyes. Satisfaction and pleasure of the pain she was causing thrilled her. "Violet?" she scoffed. A single blast of air puffed from her mouth as she threw her head back in bitter amusement. "I bet they would never have called you that if they had known what you were! You are far from a flower, you are nothing but a thorn, Thorn!"

Violet's throat felt devoid of any moisture as she fought to contain the mass of destruction flailing inside her like a wild beast. It had been twelve years of name-calling, criticism, mockery, and, worst of all, Mrs. Bainbridge had taken her beautiful name (the name her mother and father had given to her) and replaced it with 'Thorn'. Her body continued to tremble under her thin clothes, all the heat draining from her body.

Violet's name was slipping further and further from her grasp. She couldn't remember the last time she heard the sweet sound of it. Her grandmother gleefully told Violet that the old woman and her mother were beautiful. She told her they were flourishing roses, and Violet was just a simple, ugly thorn that had grown between them. She blamed Violet for the distance that grew between her and Kitty. The one that had festered like an untreated wound. The one she failed to repair before her daughter passed. She blamed Violet's father for getting in the way; for twisting her daughter's mind. Everything was the fault of others and never her own.

"Yes, Grandmama," Violet muttered meekly, "Thank you for taking care of me. I know I am a burden to you." Violet repeated the same words every day, for she knew it appeased her grandmother.

"That's right!" she seethed. "You are a burden to me. It is true. This is the only home you will ever know. No man will seek your hand in marriage. Your mother may have told you differently, but she was wrong! An utter fool for filling your head with such nonsense. You'd do well to remember that, Thorn!"

As the conversation played out, Violet's mind took her home, to her mother and father, and back to the early days of her childhood. She had only known them for eight years, but she missed those days terribly. She missed the scent of her mother's perfume; her long, honey-blonde hair, and oh, how she missed her warm, comforting embrace. She missed her father and the way he used to tease her playfully, reminding her how beautiful she was, no matter the bends and twists of her vertebrae. He would tell her that her curve was beautiful, and she wouldn't be Violet without it. Those were the days she held on to. 'The days I was truly loved.' she breathed silently, the tremors of her body fading as she let the memories wash over her.

Violet stirred her gruesome breakfast of thin, watery gruel. Cooking was the one, and only, chore her grandmother turned her hand to. Although some would assume that it was out of love for her granddaughter, Violet knew better. Mrs. Bainbridge's eagerness to cook was born from utter selfish greed. While Violet struggled to swallow the slop that swam in her bowl, her grandmother devoured the sunshine-yellow of eggs and the succulent fine cuts of bacon. The aroma of the salty cooked meat tickled Violet's senses. Her mouth watered as her imagination feasted upon it. She closed her eyes and, as every spoonful of gruel poured into her mouth, she pictured the bacon in forkfuls upon her tongue.

Her imagination swept her away as she kept her eyes averted from the woman's plate for fear of reprimand. It would be another lecture on how much of a nuisance she was and how she was ungrateful for wanting more than what she had. A chorus of chastising and manipulation to hide the old woman's truth. Violet's truth was that she wasn't ungrateful at all. She was grateful for the fraction of warmth the gruel still had left; grateful for the thin fabric that protected very little of her body from the bite of the autumn wind; grateful for the roof over her head.

She was truly grateful, but she was tired of being punished for just being herself; tired of hiding from the neighbours for fear of what they may say about her; tired of labouring on the land; and tired of her grandmother's wicked ways.

Violet pulled on her coat over her frail body. It was old and worn, with patches at the elbows where she had attempted to repair it rather than her grandmother having to replace it. Its thin fabric did very little to offer her protection from the chilly winds that battled against it.

She fastened the three sporadically placed buttons that remained. The third dangled like a brown dreary bauble from a Christmas tree, reminding her to sew it back on later that evening. She lifted the wayward straggle of cotton and wound it around the button to secure it in its freefall position. 'That should hold it for now.' she told herself, making her way to the front door.

Her muscles ached at the thought of her daily chores on the land but, even though her back would burn with fatigue within just a few minutes, this was the only part of her day that offered her some freedom.

Her grandmother continued to sit at the kitchen table, voicing a list of even more chores she had set aside. 'Everything then.' thought Violet as she pulled on her scuffed boots. She gazed down at them, there were holes worn in at the toes; the material frayed. 'Hat and coat to match, Violet.' she inwardly mused, trying to make light of her poverty-stricken clothing, 'We will make a lady of you yet!'

She couldn't remember the last time she had received new clothes, and it wasn't as though she could idly shop for them either. She wore only old garments that her grandmother had discarded to make way for the old woman's new, far more expensive attire. Paid for, of course, with Violet's inheritance - the money the old woman should have kept saved for Violet's future. Violet's inheritance had dwindled slowly over time, leaving very little left for her. She had nothing unless her grandmother permitted, so Violet went without albeit the crumbs the old woman threw her way. Violet was trapped, caged like a beautiful bird by a woman who despised her.

2

"I have to go to London tomorrow," the old woman announced as Violet eased off her muddy boots. "I trust you will continue with your chores, Thorn?"

"Yes, Grandmama." Violet replied. The mud caked her tired and sore hands. Her knuckles ached from gripping the tools in the bitter winds. Her fingernails were broken to a length much shorter than was bearable to her senses, and her blisters stung at the slightest touch.

"Very well, I shan't be gone long." Mrs. Bainbridge sniffed. Her eyes followed the narrow slope of her nose toward Violet, who sat crumpled in a mess of filthy boots, skirts, and coat upon the damp stone floor. Her hair was a mess of chestnut strands, the bun misaligned after a long strenuous day.

"Why are you going?" Violet asked, her eyes averted from her grandmother's disapproving stare. She cursed herself as the words tumbled off her tongue. Her questioning would not please the old woman in the slightest. She held her breath, pretending to fiddle with the last boot, waiting for the venom, but it never came.

"I have to attend a meeting with your mother's solicitor."

Mrs. Bainbridge replied. She turned her head away from her granddaughter and continued. "I may be gone a few days. You are to stay here at all times. Do you understand? I will not be the subject of the neighbours' idol gossip!"

There it was, that poison in her voice. 'At least it was not as sharp this time.' Violet thought, but she could sense that the woman was withholding something important. There was an air of impatience in her tone. Knowing that even if she knew the truth, there wouldn't be anything she could do to stop it, Violet assured herself that, on this occasion, ignorance was probably a blessing.

"Yes, Grandmama. I understand."

Violet's tired eyes scanned the kitchen, her mind wracked with further suspicion of the woman's secrecy. It was spotless, with not a single item to scrub or clean. This was peculiar and a first for her. Every day, after long hours of labouring, mountains of dirty crockery, cutlery, and pots greeted her as she stepped through the door. They would accumulate in her absence in anticipation of her sore, blistered hands to wash them. In normal circumstances, one would assume that they'd had guests, but Violet knew that the extremity of the mess was deliberate and entirely for the sake of torment. Her grandmother revelled in every opportunity to create more work for her. "No rest for the wicked" her grandmother would smirk, followed by "Idle hands are the devil's workshop!" The glee in Mrs. Bainbridge's eyes glowed menacingly bright. She spoiled for any excuse to banish her to the barn in the pitch black of night.

Violet couldn't fathom the reason behind the cleanliness. Dread swished in her stomach. 'Why is today different? Is this a trick?', she pondered. She chewed on her lower lip, biting back her curiosity for fear of reprisal. Her thoughts returned to her grandmother's impromptu trip to London. 'Surely,' Violet silently wondered, 'I should attend such meetings now that I am almost of age?' She considered that, perhaps, the meeting had nothing to do with her small inheritance (a silver brooch that belonged to her mother and a gold pocket watch of her father's, Mrs. Bainbridge had informed her) and only of importance to her grandmother. Perhaps this was what her mother and father had wanted.

Whatever queries danced energetically in her head, she did not dare encroach on the subject any further. Her fear of retaliation hung over her like a storm cloud waiting to burst open. The gentler side of her grandmother stood in front of her. She did not want to risk waking the beast that hid in her shadow.

"When will you be leaving?" she asked instead.

"Are you trying to hurry me?" the old woman hissed, leering at Violet through squinted eyes. Suspicion clouded the dark crescents beneath them and deepened the lines of rumpled skin scored around her mouth. Her brows furrowed as the beast threatened to move closer.

"No, Grandmama." Violet quickly assured her, shooing

the beast away. "I just thought that you may like a cup of tea before your travels?"

Violet swallowed her temptation to exhale. Such an action would have shown her relief to have thought of such a quick response. She dared not reveal her longing for her grandmother to leave, to leave her there on her own. It would mean days of peace, free from the woman's wrath. A welcome extension of the mere few hours she was used to, as she toiled daily on the land.

"Yes, that would be acceptable." the grandmother replied curtly. The polite response of 'thank you' floated between them but was visible only in Violet's mind as she readied the tea. There was no reason she would expect the two simple words to fall upon her ears and, just like every other time before, they dissipated, unspoken, into the quiet of the room.

For the next hour, the tension grew in a suffocating silence between them. The only sounds that broke it were the tinkle of the floral teacups upon their saucers and the rush of liquid with every sip. The awkwardness hung in the air like the dank stench of mould. Mrs. Bainbridge sat poised, shooting expectant glances toward the door every few minutes. The drawn-out moment festered between the two women.

At last, the sound of carriage wheels upon gravel rattled toward their house. Violet's grandmother's face brightened at the welcome noise. "I am leaving now, Thorn." she began. "Do not let me down. You stay here.

No-one must see you or even hear you. Is that clear?!"
Her eyes widened as they met Violet's.

"Yes, Grandmama." Violet gulped under the heat of her glare.

"I mean it, Thorn, or there will be hell to pay!" At her words, the woman stood, pushing back her chair. The screeching sound of the friction upon the ice-cold stone floor tore through the room, followed closely by the clacking of her heels as she hastened to open the door.

The driver of the carriage stepped forward to collect her luggage, but Mrs. Bainbridge halted his entrance with the palm of her hand. "That's far enough, thank you!" she trilled. She did not want him to discover Violet.

Violet tucked herself into the far corner of the room behind the curtain, hidden in the shadows that pooled there. The old woman shot her a warning look and walked out of the door.

'Suitable for a month's adventure rather than a week.' thought Violet as she watched her grandmother and her luggage board the carriage.

The driver was wearing a creased, unkempt suit. His boots were thick with mud, and his hair drenched in its natural oils. Mrs. Bainbridge's expression was one of disgust as she took in the sight of him. Violet felt a wave of satisfaction at her grandmother's discomfort and, as the carriage drove away, she inhaled her newfound freedom.

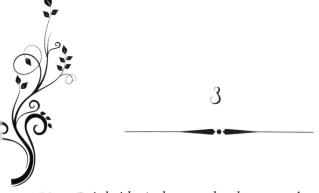

3

Mrs. Bainbridge's bones shook upon the seat of the carriage. The heavy fabric of her coat tucked the warmth in and around her upper body. A thick fur collar nestled against her neck and under her chin. The old woman's legs, kept warm under the heavy ruched skirts and petticoats that flowed down from her waist. Patent leather carriage boots peeked from underneath the hems. She oozed an unmentionable wealth, but it was wealth that did not belong to her.

Mrs. Bainbridge drew back her shoulders and sucked in her stomach muscles under her rigid corset. She pushed the heels of her boots firmly against the carriage floor. Her body fought against the involuntary movements as it jolted and rocked with the incessant juddering of the carriage, travelling over every cobble, stone, and piece of grit that pathed the way. Its framework creaked at every impact, no matter how small.

The carriage lamp swung above her head, the only light for miles in the depths of the ink-black and starless night. She was exhausted, but she would not sleep. Her eyelids fluttered, wavering between this world and the world of dreams as the rattle of the vehicle's wheels enticed sleep upon her.

Violet's grandmother tsked loudly as the driver whistled merrily behind her. Her face soured at the tune he blew upon his lips. His merry nature irritated her. Her blood roared with a poisonous, contained anger, pumping loudly in her chest. A small whisper of a growl rumbled in her throat, releasing the pressure within her. It echoed her annoyance at his presence. She could not see him, nor he see her, as they sat within and upon the Hansom Cab, and she was glad of it. She revelled in the privacy as it permitted her to relax, letting go of the mask she wore when in the company of others.

The old woman squinted at her reflection, the barrier upon the glass between her and the dark scenery, as they made their way through and away from the countryside. She may not have been able to see beyond the carriage door, but her vision of the next few days was crystal-clear as it played over in her mind. She knew what she had to do. There was very little money left and she must request more. 'How is an old woman to live without it?' she thought to herself, 'That girl owes me everything after all that I have done for her!' Her thoughts kept her company for the rest of the journey, spurring her on in her endeavor. She convinced herself that they were her moral guidance and justification. She had created a perfect veil between her lies and the truth.

"Here we are Mrs. Bainbridge." the driver announced, his London accent thick upon his tongue. He pulled the carriage door wide open for the woman. His shoulders drawn back as he stood to attention, behaving as though she was the queen. Violet's grandmother turned toward him to depart from the warm leather seat.

"I 'ope that your journey was pleasant, Madam?" he continued, bowing low, then offering a broad and welcoming smile as he stood and faced her.

"Quite satisfactory." she lied. A thin-lipped smile sliced across her face. One that did not meet her cold, ungrateful eyes.

The driver offered to help her down. The light from the carriage threw itself upon the man's outstretched, hard-working, calloused hands. Mrs. Bainbridge sniffed as her eyes fell upon the rough skin that covered them. She leered at his short, unkempt fingernails, clean but jagged at the edges. Reluctantly, she placed her hand in his, stepping down onto the solid pavement.

As she stood upon the cobbles of London, her disgust at the kind man slithered beneath her mask. Her struggle to maintain her composure was tiresome, but necessary. She inhaled the frosty night air as she averted her gaze to the house in front of them, fiddling with her gloved fingers, flicking away the memory of his touch.

"Mother!" Mr. Bainbridge boomed, as she stood in front of him in the hallway. He wore a suit of the deepest black against a crisp white shirt. His bowtie grasped his neck, taught like the rope of a noose. He pulled at his collar to loosen it. His face reddened as he did so, displaying his discomfort and his apparent love of sherry. His chin doubled as he pushed his head back against an invisible wall and tightened his jaw in a welcoming smile. "How marvellous to see you!"

"Oh, darling!" the old woman crooned, her features softening at his warm welcome.

William Bainbridge cleared his throat. "Is Violet not with you?" he asked, peering behind her as if his niece hid within the folds of the woman's skirts like a small, nervous child.

"No William, I'm afraid not," she said, her regret of Violet's absence falsified upon her lips. "She is rather unwell. I have had to leave her in the care of her nurse." Another lie. Each one poured off her tongue as smooth as warm honey.

The man rocked back and forth on his feet, one hand tucked into the pocket of his waistcoat and the other clutching a small glass of sherry. "Ah well, best if she stays where she can get better." he offered, relief laced in his words.

"Yes, quite." his mother replied, trying not to show her annoyance at the sound of the girl's name. "Where is my beautiful granddaughter?" she added, hastening to change the subject.

"Grandmama!" a young woman beamed. She walked toward her, dressed in the finest lilac silk. Ivory lace trimmed the neckline and cinched the garment in at her slender waist. She threw her arms open wide and closed them around her beloved grandmother, bestowing her love and warmth upon the woman she believed her to be.

The old woman smiled, deepening the lines around her mouth. Most would have assumed such lines were born from joy and laughter over time, but the years of scowling with bitterness and bad temper had left marks, like scars, deep within her skin. "Isabelle, you grow more beautiful every time I see you." Mrs. Bainbridge simpered, gently cupping her granddaughter's hands in her gloved fingers. "Oh Grandmama, you are too kind." the young woman replied. "Such a shame Violet isn't with you." She squeezed her grandmother's hand and kissed her cheek.

Isabelle often wondered about Violet, but in all the years she had known of her, they had yet to meet. She had always been told Violet had health issues that prevented them from spending time together. Isabelle's desire for her to meet and spend time with Violet never dulled. She longed to know her as much today as she did as a child. They were cousins and, perhaps, maybe they could be more like sisters, she'd thought. Isabelle had always wanted a sister.

Mrs. Bainbridge swallowed as her face hid behind Isabelle's gesture of affection. The act she forced herself to maintain thoroughly exhausted her. "I'm tired." she offered abruptly. A sharp edge caressed the tone of her voice. "If you could show me to my room?"

The curt announcement hardened William's face as he looked from his daughter to his mother. His mother looked troubled, and his daughter seemed taken aback by the old woman's unexpectedly sharp tone.

"Let me show you, Mother." he said, gesturing to the servants to carry her luggage to her room. He glanced sideways at Isabelle. They looked at each other uttering unspoken questions at the unusual manner of the woman. If Violet had been there, she would have thought the old woman to be most polite, considering her true nature, but the company she kept now had never seen that side of her, and Mrs. Bainbridge was adamant they never would.

"Thank you, darling. I am so very tired," she replied softly, trying to eradicate the tension that hung in the air. "Although I shall miss Violet dearly, it is quite exhausting caring for someone with so many needs."

William placed his arm around his mother's shoulders. "You are a good woman, Mother." he said, "Kitty would be so very proud of you. You have loved and cared for her child when others would have, most likely, sent her away with her being a... well... you know..." He leaned in close and whispered, "... a curiosity and all." Violet's grandmother nodded to communicate her understanding as William straightened to his full height once again. "Please don't be offended, Mother, when I say I know it cannot be easy caring for someone as poorly as she. I believe you are doing an excellent job of taking care of her. In fact, I have no doubts, what-so-ever."

Mrs. Bainbridge nodded again, this time her movement more pronounced. "Thank you, William," she muttered. "After a little rest, I am sure I will be as right as rain."

The deep red and gold décor gave her room the essence of luxury. A large bed with a dark mahogany frame, adorned in the same rich tones. Gold fillagree patterns etched deep within the wood. The exquisite detail, suitable for royalty. A fireplace roared, filling every inch of her sleeping quarters with a warmth that soothed her. She exhaled as her eyes roved over the elegance of it all. 'I will have all of this soon,' she thought, flames of determination licking at her soul, 'I will want for nothing!'

As she rested her head upon the thick, comforting pillow, she drifted into a deep sleep. Thoughts of the following day turned over like the pages of a book, filling her dreams as she slept.

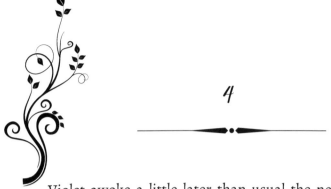

4

Violet awoke a little later than usual the next morning. She had no-one to scold her for her 'tardiness' or drown her in a heavy dose of manipulation. It was just her, alone and free for the first time in, what seemed like, forever since she had lived there.

The low sun peaked through the mud-splattered window, warming the side of her face. She could hear the gentle chirping of the birds as they sang to one another beyond the glass pane. She listened to the peace that resounded throughout the house and inhaled its soothing energy.

"What shall I do today?" she wondered aloud. She turned her head and gazed at the small daguerreotype on her bedside table, as if the three figures within the image could advise her. The sun flickered off its silver frame as the only reply. She studied her mother and father, who sat there, unmoving, smiling back at her. A little girl sat on her father's lap. It was Violet. Even at such a young age, she had shown signs of change in her posture, but the smiles upon her parents' faces showed only love for their daughter. "You loved me." she whispered to the image as a ragged breath emanated from her lungs, "I know you did."

She folded back the thick blankets that had kept her cosy and warm throughout the night. With her grandmother away, Violet had seized the opportunity to make use of the warmest blankets in the house. She convinced herself that if she washed them and put them away before the old woman returned, her grandmother would be none the wiser.

It was the first morning she had ever awoken without the cold seizing the muscles in her back. The tension that would normally ache profusely, with every move, did not creep over her as she loosely rolled her shoulders to check. Nor did it make itself known when she slowly twisted her torso from side to side. 'I could get used to this.' she breathed happily, making light of the thousands of nights she had spent, freezing, under the thinnest blanket her grandmother could find. It was her 'punishment for being different' and 'inflicting such shame upon an old lady.' She knew it was no use trying to explain that the affliction that bent and twisted her spine was not deliberate. She would have done anything to make it go away. It was pointless, as her grandmother was adamant in her belief that it was Violet's fault. She believed there was a demon within her granddaughter, and nothing could make her see otherwise.

Violet swung her legs over the side of the bed, her pale feet upon the ice-cold wooden floor. She tensed her toes as the chill spread like frost under the soles of her bare feet. Violet clenched her teeth with the pain that seared through the flesh, permeating the bones underneath. There was neither a carpet nor a simple rug to offer her some kind of relief from it as she readied herself for the day ahead.

She selected her warmest clothes, as thin as they were. Holes dotted in her skirts from ash that had scattered from the hearth, and the hems frayed from the paths outside. They spoke of a measure of poverty that you would not see in her grandmother's attire.

Apart from being too cold, Violet wasn't concerned by what others may think of her shabby clothes. 'No-one will see me, anyway.' she thought. "It is neither here nor there, Violet." she told herself. "You must remain hidden at all times!" she continued, mimicking her grandmother's selfish words.

The thought of the old woman sparked an idea. It sizzled like a fuse in her mind as she slowly pushed back the door to the old woman's room. She held her breath, as if she expected to find her grandmother on the other side of it, readying herself to be berated by her sharp tongue, and slung out to the barn to sleep amongst the hay bales. She felt foolish as she gazed upon the silent, treasure-filled room. She had been in there many times but now that it was just her, alone in the house, the tension that would usually stifle the air, as she placed tea and cake on the woman's table, had dissipated along with the tray of food she would have been holding. In its place, there was an aura of tranquility. The silence washed over her in glorious waves as she pulled back the door to her grandmother's closet.

She gasped at the array of fine clothes neatly aligned before her. Some hung upon hangers while others were folded neatly upon shelves. Emerald greens, an exquisite deep blue, luxurious creams, earthy browns, velvets, satins, and silks. She knew that these would, one day, be hers, but she also knew, by the time they found their way to her, their quality would be far less remarkable - worn and washed to a ghost of their former glory.

She laid her hand upon the sapphire blue velvet cape. Her fingers brushed against its soft fibres. She noted the soft silver trim matched the satin lining as she draped it across the inside of her arm.

Guilt for helping herself to her grandmother's garments smoldered in her chest. She pulled back her shoulders and inhaled, snuffing out its embers, and made her way out of the room, hugging the cape against her body. Confidence, fuelled by resentment toward the old woman, hit hard upon the wooden floor with each step.

The aroma of bacon filled the kitchen as it spat in the pan upon the open fire. She'd grabbed one of the two rashers, both wilted at the edges, and fried it alongside a broken egg. She breathed it in, both the fragrance and the warmth that radiated as it turned from a dark pink, almost maroon, to a paler pink that curled and rippled in its own fat. The clarity of the thin liquid albumen of the egg bubbled into a solid white, a golden sun at its centre. Her mouth watered in anticipation.

Carefully, wrapping a thick cloth tightly around her hand, she removed the kettle of hot water from over the fire and filled a teapot. She craned her neck away from the steam as it threatened to scold her face, rising in a stream of opaque white plumes that mingled with the sweet aroma of the tea. The hot water drenched the leaves and absorbed their flavour as it filled the floral teapot.

It was Mrs. Bainbridge's favourite crockery, with its golden handle and trim, framing the bouquet of chrysanthemums delicately painted upon its smooth, glazed ivory colour. Violet lifted the delicate item and poured a little of its contents into a matching teacup. A hue that resembled smokey quartz trickled from the spout.

The only milk from the pot was turning. Thick lumps congealed in the white liquid. The odour was more of sickness than milk. Violet wrinkled her nose as the pungent odour flooded her sense of smell. The muscles in her throat flexed as she tried not to heave. Violet refused to add it to the cup. Instead, she cooled her tea with a little cold water and placed the teacup next to her plate of egg and bacon.

The salt bounced across her tastebuds as she savoured the meat. It tasted as good as she had imagined on all those occasions when it had been denied to her, perhaps even more. It was harder to swallow than her usual gruel but, it did not matter, she would 'chew for a thousand years', she thought, if only for the taste alone. The sunshine yellow yolk wobbled as she placed her elbows on the table, but as she pierced its centre with the prongs of her fork, it oozed across her small plate. It attempted to fill the empty spaces but, as she mopped it with the chunk of stale bread she'd found in the pantry, the ivory porcelain peeked through.

Violet inhaled the fresh morning air. It felt crisp as it caressed her pale skin. Her cheeks flushed with its touch. But underneath her grandmother's cape, she felt warm for the first time. She stood in the open field, staring out at the forest. It seemed to call to her. Its whispers carried upon the breeze, tickling her ears and tousling the loose strands of her hair. She had only ever ventured as far as the edge of the land and stood on the brink between the grass and the trees. The forest was the border, and the trunks of the trees were the bars to her prison. A wicked sentence inflicted upon her. Her only crime was her existence. Her grandmother was her jailer as she screamed and yelled for Violet to remain within the four corners of their land. The pitch of the old woman's scream pulled her back every time. But now, here she was, alone and free; free to do whatever she pleased.

5

"M-m-morning Mrs. Bainbridge." the young girl stuttered at the door. She twiddled her fingers nervously as she made her presence known. "M-m-master wanted to know whether you will be j-j-joining him for b-breakfast, M-m-ma'am?"

The girl's delicate stutter irked the old woman. "Yes, wretched girl!" she snapped. Violet's grandmother's eyes stabbed through the low light of the bedroom as she shot the servant girl a look of disgust. "Why must I always endure people like you?" she spat.

"P-people like m-m-me, M-m-ma'am?"

"M-m-morning!" the old woman mocked. The air hissed as she sucked it through her teeth, her displeasure with the girl building within her.

The gentle and timid young woman choked back her tears at Mrs. Bainbridge's mockery. Her speech difficulties haunted her since she was a little girl. She had thought, or at least hoped, she'd found peace at Bainbridge House. But as Violet's grandmother spoke, the old woman's words fractured what little confidence she had. Feeling small and broken, she hurried out of the room. "Tsk, pathetic." Violet's grandmother mumbled.

"Miss Everleigh?" William Bainbridge stopped the young girl as she hurried to the kitchen. "Whatever is the matter?"

"N-n-nothing Sir" she whispered; her eyes tinged with the look of someone who had been crying.

"Why are you crying then?" he asked. His brow furrowed with concern.

"S-s-something in my eye, Sir." she lied.

He removed his hand from her quivering shoulder, confused by her obvious distress. Miss Everleigh quickly excused herself, putting an end to the conversation, and scurried down the hall as fast as her legs could carry her.

Upon her shoulders and heavy upon her heart, she took with her the burden of shame inflicted upon her by the old woman's ignorance.

Mrs. Bainbridge greeted her son as she entered the grand dining room. The silver cutlery shone as the low autumn sun streamed in and caressed it. She lowered herself into a deep mahogany wooden chair padded with rich red velvet cushions.

"Good morning, Mother!" William beamed, tucking his napkin securely into his collar. "I trust you slept well?"

"Yes. Thank you, darling," she replied, sipping her tea. "It was most restful. Most restful indeed." Violet's grandmother felt a flush of excitement at the day that lay ahead of her. The thought of her soon-to-be wealth thrilled her. Her stomach fluttered with anticipation.

Convincing the solicitor would not be an issue, she

assured herself. He was a dear friend of the family and had dealt with many of their legal requirements over the years.

"Have you met Miss Everleigh?" William asked, gesturing to the young woman as she entered the room. At her master's words, Miss Everleigh stopped walking. She lowered her head, avoiding eye contact with Mrs. Bainbridge. She was sure that the old woman would deride her once more with no hesitation. Miss Everleigh was not sure she could cope with any more unkindness. Earlier that morning, their encounter had ripped her emotional scars wide open.

"No, I don't believe I have." the woman lied, wiping her mouth with her napkin. "Good morning, Miss Everleigh" she smiled, her mouth pinched with the effort.

Miss Everleigh gasped inaudibly at the woman's lie, then quickly regained her composure. "G-g-good m-morning M-ma'am." the young woman smiled. She surmised she had caught Mrs. Bainbridge at a critical moment before breakfast. Her heart lifted a little and relief oozed across her face. The cosmetically kind words of the old woman before her, partially painted over the cracks of the hurt their encounter had caused. She curtsied and left the room, feeling a little brighter than a few moments ago while the old woman swallowed her revulsion of having to be courteous.

Violet's grandmother focused on the plate of her usual bacon and eggs. The bacon looked more appetizing and

and sumptuous than what she was used to. Perhaps it was because she found herself in a more luxurious setting, and the company she now kept was more to her liking, she thought. It made her mind slip back to her usual dwellings, to the memory of Violet. She masked her unwavering hatred for the girl.

"I have an appointment this morning," the woman chimed, "At Darlington and Darlington Solicitors."

"Oh?" William looked up from his paper, a curious expression on his red face. "Is anything the matter?"

"No, darling," she crooned, "Violet has asked me to visit them so that she may access her inheritance, that is all."

"Oh, I see," he said, lifting his newspaper and folding it. "I hope some of that inheritance is being put to use regarding her care, Mother?"

"Oh, goodness!" The woman placed her hand over her stony heart in an act of pure shock. "I wouldn't dream of such a thing! Kitty and James wanted the inheritance for Violet." she sang from under her disguise, "She is a young lady and requires many things. The money is very useful for that purpose as intended. I have a little money put by, so we manage just fine as we are. Please don't concern yourself, darling."

William nodded in acceptance. A look of annoyance flitted across his eyes, sickened by Violet's assumed selfish manner, then dwindled away, softened by his mother's false kindness towards his niece.

The chill and smog of London filled Mrs. Bainbridge's

lungs. She coughed as it irritatingly trickled down her throat. She was not used to the density of the pollution.

A concoction of voices, the rattle of carriage wheels, and the clopping of horseshoes upon the pavement drowned her thoughts as she walked precariously over the cobbles in her new carriage boots. A child wailed the daily news, his hand high in the air waving the ink-stained paper. She flinched in disgust as a child ran past her, uttering sharply to herself about their lack of manners and consideration but, as she ascended the steps leading to Darlington and Darlington, a glimmer of greed twinkled in her eyes.

Her lips pursed as she smiled at the young gentleman who graciously held the door open for her. He removed his hat and tipped his head in greeting. She looked him up and down, noticing his lack of wealth in his poor attempt to fool otherwise. His face was handsome, she mused, but as she thought of Isabelle, she prayed her granddaughter would never make his acquaintance. The possibility of them being a match would be nothing short of ludicrous, she thought.

She turned her focus toward Mr. Darlington's office door. Her heavy skirts rustled as she walked, determinedly, towards all that stood between her and Violet's inheritance.

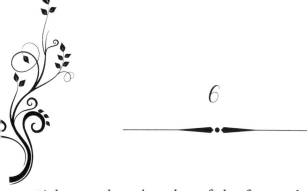

6

Violet stood at the edge of the forest, deliberating her next move. Her heart fluttered nervously as she stared up at the trees looming over her. Apprehension bubbled in the pit of her stomach, unsure of who or what she would meet amongst them. The trees huddled together before her as if considering the young woman who, so bravely, dared to enter their world.

Her grandmother's words played over and over in her memory. They tugged at her conscience, preying on her insecurities. An invisible force pulled her back toward her home, but her determination pushed her forward. The depth of her desire to explore the forest sang like a bird fluttering in time with her heart. It was ferocious and eager. Her mind, thirsty to discover what else life could offer.

She had seen so little of the world in her twenty years. The absence of experience had instilled in her a sense of vulnerability and fragility. However, amidst the nerves and the chaos of her fears, Violet possessed a hidden strength that sparked and flickered with all the tenacity of a raging fire. She had spent twelve years confined to the four walls of her grandmother's home and its restricted land. 'Far away from the prying eyes of humankind. No-one needs to know I live with a freak!' Mrs. Bainbridge had sneered at an eight-year-old Violet.

'Humankind', the term baffled Violet. She did not understand how the two words fitted together and rolled off the tongue so sweetly, as if it all just made sense. Her grandmother had taught her that human nature was not to be kind at all. She could not think of a more misleading word. In truth, she believed it to be an outright lie. A fabrication upon the lips of every man, woman, and child.

The scent of pine drifted upon the wind. An enthusiastic stream of air whipped up the leaves from the soft, moss-blanketed forest floor. It carried them, swirling, battering the trees. They scraped against the brittle bark as though they were trying to return to where they had once flourished. Vibrant orange, gold, red, and rustic brown leaves danced in circles around her boots. Some, perfectly formed in the shape of hearts, while others curled in at the edges like rolled parchment. The wind whipped them from the earth, flicking them at her legs like a playful pup greeting their owner after a long-drawn-out absence.

The excited breeze placed its invisible palms at the small of her back, gently pushing her forward, deeper into the forest. She made tiny, hurried steps at its persistence. Her feet scurried through the crisp, crackling leaves, lain heavily in her path. Luscious forest-green shades garnished generously by autumn's delicate embellishment. The trees towered above her, peering over. They stretched and bent. Branches coiled and tangled as they curiously paid attention to their new guest.

Waterfalls of silver etched in scores, deep within the bark of trees. They flowed down and out in tendrils of roots upon, and buried within, the soil. Beyond the bare branches, proud and magnificent, stood the evergreen display of pine, fir, and cedar. Pride enriched their colours. Their appearance, majestic and powerful as kings and queens.

Violet drank it all in. The fresh clean air filled her lungs. She exhaled and, in that breath, she released all her emotions. Tears streamed down her face, but not those of sadness. They were tears of relief and joy. She had left that world behind. It seemed a million miles away. She let go of the house in the distance; it's four walls that contained her; the land that hid her from dangerous eyes and the days of labour forced upon her. Her muscles screamed at the memory. Her breath blew away her grandmother's vicious words until they were all but a faint whisper. She sent them far beyond the edge of the forest, where they could not touch her. There, amongst the foliage and the beauty, Violet did not need to hide.

Her eyes fell upon a tree. It twisted and bowed, a graceful contemporary dance, frozen in time. She marvelled at its beauty, its individuality. Each tree differed from the next, each one was intricate and unique. She realized how easier her life would have been if she'd been a tree instead of a woman. For if she had, with all the twists and bends her body made, nobody would have told her she was ugly or peculiar. Artists would have painted her upon canvas or paper, the memory of her existence preserved for generations to come. People would have admired her image displayed on the walls of famous galleries or in the homes of the wealthy. They would have appreciated her for who she was.

Violet walked, weaving in and out between the trees. Her hands caressed the dry, cracked bark of each trunk as she passed them. At their touch, she steadied herself against the uneven earth beneath her boots.

A bird glided, silently, from a branch of one tree to another, his eyes fixed on Violet. "If only you could talk to me..." Violet mused, looking up at the bird, "First you would tell me why you are following me." she chuckled, "Surely I'm not that interesting?" Violet smiled as she looked at his sweet, petite little face. His eyes were bright and beady. He looked enthralled with his unknown visitor as he angled his head from side-to-side listening. The bird chirped a short melody in reply as though he had thought about every word she'd spoken.

"Come on!" she called up, waving her hand, beckoning for him to follow. She knew that he would have followed her despite her invite, but somehow it made her feel a little less alone and more in control of the company she kept, even that of a bird.

Other than her new feathered friend that, devotedly, followed her, and the lone squirrel picking and gathering the fallen acorns as it scurried about, there seemed very few signs of life within the woodland. She didn't know why, but she assumed that there would be more. 'Maybe my presence worries them.' she thought.

She watched the squirrel stop, his little paws grasping and turning an acorn over and over whilst its teeth eagerly nibbled and cracked it open to reveal the prize within. His bushy tail quivered. It was a warning for her to keep her distance from him. Violet didn't want to frighten the sweet little creature, so she slowly and diligently ambled past. The bird stretched his wings and followed her.

Violet could not fathom the time. The sun grew as weary as her body as it descended beyond the forest border. Sunlight faded into grey mist around her, drawing in the evening. The moody tones, broken only by the flickering glow of gold between the bare branches of trees. Its warm honey hue danced off the ripples of a babbling brook that cracked the forest in two. Violet hitched up the bottom of her skirts as her foot sank into its shallow water. Diligently, she waded through its gentle flow. The snap of a winter-kissed cold soaked through her boots to her feet. It flooded through the holes in the soles where they had worn away. Her breath hitched at the sensation but, with it came an overwhelming sense of exhilaration, rippling through her in surges of elation. She had never felt so alive.

1

"Ah, Mrs. Bainbridge," the man said, standing up as she glided into his office. His words slid through the air like a snail across a lawn, slow and drawn out. His voice was a deep, croaking rumble with each extended sound. "Please have a seat." he said, gesturing to the dark, soft leather chair opposite him. He lowered himself back down into his own, his eyes firmly fixed on Violet's grandmother.

He considered the woman before him. They had met several times, over the years, concerning the matter of Miss. Hall but, each time she sat across from him, a sense of unease crawled beneath his skin. There was something about her that didn't sit right with him, something unnerving. He shrugged it off and cleared his throat, trying to hide his distaste for the woman.

"Perhaps a cup of tea?" he offered.

"No, thank you." Violet's grandmother responded curtly.

Prophesying further wealth, excitement roiled in her stomach. The greeting the man bestowed upon her was not one that suggested she was welcome. She knew falsities when she encountered them. Fear of refusal marred her optimism. She buffed off her displeasure at his manner, straightening her posture, giving the man the impression that she was not to be messed with.

"How can I help?" Mr. Darlington asked. He looked concerned by the woman's obvious impatience.

"I am here to request further funding for my granddaughter, Violet." she began, poised and still.

"I see." he drawled. The man rolled a fountain pen between his fingers as he listened. His silence gave way for the old woman to continue.

"As you are aware, she requires much assistance, what with her being a curiosity." Mrs. Bainbridge allowed a whimper to escape her lips, then raised a handkerchief to her eye, wiping away a dry, imaginary tear.

"Quite." the solicitor uttered in agreement. His brain whispered a million doubts all at once. His gaze was one of concern, but not for the woman that sat across the desk from him.

"I would require an extra two hundred pounds of Violet's inheritance." she stated, her eyes meeting his. "I do not like to request such a thing from my granddaughter, but I am an old lady of very little means, and it is the only way that I can provide care for her... to keep her well, you understand?" she sniffed, accentuating her distress of the meeting.

The man leaned back in his chair. His fingers smoothed down his thick, bristling, grey moustache. He placed his pen on the paper that lay gently scattered in front of him. His hands were on his chest, fingers laced. A perplexed expression pulled at his features. Mrs. Bainbridge lowered her gaze to her lap as she waited for him to speak.

As the silence stretched out, she raised only her eyes to get a measure of the man. His delay puzzled her. She inhaled deeply, cooling the irritation at Mr. Darlington's aloof manner. "Is there something the matter, Mr. Darlington?" she asked. Her voice remained sweet, as heat spread up the back of her neck. It was a mixture of fear that he would refuse, and anger at keeping her waiting. The anger engulfed her fear, snuffing it out. 'This was supposed to be simple,' her thoughts hissed. 'What is taking this fool so long to answer?' She knew that a request for two hundred pounds was excessive, but she had quashed any doubt, telling herself that it was necessary to keep her in the life that she had become accustomed to. After all, she had 'given the girl a home!'

Mrs. Bainbridge did not want to have to live as Violet did. That kind of life was for creatures like Violet. The life she already had was far more than the girl deserved, the old woman assured herself. The young woman's inheritance was the key to the life Mrs. Bainbridge should have had and one she had earned.

Kitty and James Hall had not entrusted Violet's inheritance to the old woman willingly. Mrs. Bainbridge secured that power the day she expertly forged a letter to Darlington and Darlington, in her daughter's name. She had practiced Kitty Hall's writing until there was no possibility that anyone could doubt the authenticity of it. Full control of Violet's finances landed blissfully in the old woman's hands. 'Why should I be subjected to such poverty? Everyone knows that the money should have been passed directly to me rather than her!' she'd seethed quietly on the day of the will recital. Her belief was unfounded, cruel, and ignorant, yet the dialogue of her thoughts was, to her, the only confirmation her belief required.

Mr. Darlington leaned forward, placing his elbows firmly on his desk. "Mrs. Bainbridge," he began, "Unfortunately, Miss. Hall's monetary inheritance currently stands at zero."

"Whatever do you mean?" she asked, stunned by the man's words. Her fear rose like a cobra, its venom swirling in her stomach as its body dropped like a heavy weight, making her muscles tense.

"You have used it all, Ma'am." he responded.

The old woman's throat dried in disbelief. "All of it?" she asked, wondering whether she had misheard him.

"Yes, Ma'am, all of it."

She could have sworn she saw a glitter of glee in Mr. Darlington's eyes as he delivered the news. "How?... It can't... It was Violet, wasn't it?" she demanded.

"No Ma'am. How could that be when she is... err... how do I put this... when she is... err... as she is?" There was an air of satisfaction as he watched the woman unravel in front of him. His suspicions about her true character simmered on the surface.

"She must have!" she snapped. Her cheeks flared red against her shocked, pale skin. She grappled for words, anything, to make this horror end.

"I can assure you, Mrs. Bainbridge, I have never spoken with Miss. Hall. The only correspondence I have ever received, other than your own, is that which your late daughter provided via yourself... The letter that provided you with control over your granddaughter's money. I am extremely particular and have an excellent memory. I do not make mistakes!" A stern tone coated his words. His distaste for Violet's grandmother was slowly festering into hatred.

The old woman's face drained as pale as milk at Mr. Darlington's response. She was not used to being the one in receipt of such anger.

Seconds felt like minutes and minutes like hours as the distress of the news flitted back and forth across Violet's grandmother's mind, warping the lines on her face. The reason for her expression was obvious.

Mr. Darlington watched and waited patiently for her to absorb the information he had delivered so fervently. Her eyes shifted from side to side, her mind racing for ideas, any way to obtain the finances that she longed for as if her life depended upon it.

"All that remains is the property that Mr. and Mrs. Hall bequeathed to their daughter." the solicitor said, breaking the silent tension.

Mrs. Bainbridge looked up at him. Malicious hope festered in her eyes. "The property?" she questioned, innocence and shock falsely laced in her words as though she truly believed he had not noticed her behaviour during the entire meeting.

"Yes, Ma'am," he replied, "The house where Miss. Hall lived with her parents."

"Perhaps we can sell it?" Violet's grandmother suggested. Her tone was eager, desperate. "To help pay for her care, of course."

"I'm afraid not, Mrs. Bainbridge." he said, firmly.

The woman's chest tightened at his refusal. "Why ever not?" she said, her words accusatory and defiant.

"Because, Ma'am, Mr. and Mrs. Hall requested that, upon their death, the property is to be sold only by Miss. Hall, herself. I cannot grant such a request from yourself."

"Did you not read the letter that I... Kitty wrote? It clearly stated that I was to handle all of Violet's inheritance?" Her patronizing tone curdled her voice, treating the man as if he was an utter buffoon.

Mr. Darlington's moustache twitched as he held back the words he knew he would regret in an instant. He slipped a neatly folded piece of paper (the letter Mrs. Bainbridge had forged) out from the already opened envelope, sitting amongst the paperwork, and slid it across the deep, polished, mahogany desk toward him. His eyes followed every word on the paper whilst he silenced the rage at her disrespect toward him. He read every word once and then once more; closely and diligently, careful not to miss even a dot of the ink, making sure he was entirely confident in his understanding. His satisfied gaze lifted to meet Mrs. Bainbridge's eyes. "I'm sorry Ma'am, Miss. Hall's letter omits any mention of the property, but only of cash and coin. I cannot allow you to act on behalf of her concerning the property in question. It would go against my deceased client's wishes and Miss. Hall's."

Violet's grandmother sat rigid in her stance. "That little bitch!" she seethed. The woman froze as the words flew from her lips. Mr. Darlington did not hear her outburst. His enthusiasm to remove the woman from his office distracted him. He decided he would offer her some further legal advice that may appease her, "If Miss. Hall was to attend and sign the required documentation, we could proceed with the sale."

A slick, strained smile twisted his moustache at the ends. While he waited for her reply, he couldn't help but notice the anguish on Mrs. Bainbridge's face. He wondered whether he had initially misjudged her. Perhaps she truly did want to help her granddaughter. Perhaps she only seemed stand-offish because it was a stressful matter. He could not decide between the seventy percent of him that suspected her to be a wicked, bad-tempered, rude woman or, the thirty percent of him that hoped she was just a concerned and stressed grandmother, giving her ample excuse for her apparent absence of manners.

"She cannot attend. As I have explained previously, she cannot travel." The woman pinched the bridge of her nose, highlighting her exasperation, "I need the money now."

Sensing the woman's aggravated, prominent disdain for him, Mr. Darlington sat up straight and pulled back his shoulders into a stubborn posture. He wanted to exude clarity, yet he did not want to add further suffering to what may be a very fragile woman. "Sorry Ma'am. There is nothing else I can do." His body language and stern expression magnified the authority he held.

The skin around Violet's grandmother's lips puckered and pinched into white, as her face turned to a contrasting shade of searing red. Her mask cracked as she glared at the man. "How can a creature like Violet be expected to care for a house, let alone sign the documentation?!" she roared. "Just like my pathetic daughter and son-in-law to have left their home to a freak!"

The solicitor's eyes widened at the old woman's words. In the last few moments, she had confirmed all his doubts about her intentions. He had seen her ability to change from a doting grandmother to one that overflowed with vengeance. He pushed his chair back and forced himself to a standing position. "I believe it is time I bid you good day." he barked, glaring at the old woman.

Speechless, she stood up, turned on her heel, and stormed out of the office and back on to the streets of London.

8

As Violet's foot touched down upon the other side of the babbling brook, the moss green and the earthy browns of the forest floor disappeared under a thin layer of ice. It crunched and cracked under the thin sole of her boot. 'That wasn't there a moment ago,' she thought as her heel found grip under the broken shards of ice that lay like blades. 'So strange.' she mused.

The air felt icy as its fingers gripped her airways. She shuddered, observing the stark difference between the two sides. Violet knew very little about the rest of the world, let alone the rest of England, but this felt peculiar to her. A strangeness that she would never have thought existed. "Is this what the world can be like?" she asked, gazing up at her curious friend. The bird ruffled his feathers, making him look plumper and softer than before. His eyes did not tell stories of any peculiarity. His new appearance spoke only of the vast change in temperature. "Perhaps it is what the world can be like." Violet smiled.

Violet's education drew its last breath the day her parents met their untimely end. Her mother had taught her to read and write, but Violet despaired at her penmanship. Her handwriting was illegible to anyone else but herself, and she thought her spelling atrocious. She did not have enough time with her mother for many reasons, and learning to write was one of them. She couldn't even remember the last time her grandmother had permitted her to write. "The pen is a dangerous weapon." she warned her. The old woman's face had hovered inches from Violet's. Her breath, hot and sour, upon the girl's face. "Such a weapon is meant only for those who are the norm," she spat, "Not for someone as pathetic and odd as you!"

As for books, Violet was too afraid to ask. To make such a request from her grandmother would only have proved to have been futile, much like every other request she had made.

She craved books almost as much as she craved the bacon upon the old woman's plate at breakfast time. Violet did not just want books, she felt she needed them. Perhaps she would have been able to teach herself how to write and spell. She would have been able to dive into the worlds that existed amongst the pages. Ones that would carry her far away from her own when it became all too much.

With every step she took, the ice gently thickened into a blanket of snow. She looked back as the vibrant autumn colours of the forest faded from her view into a simple, glorious memory. Large flakes of snow drifted gently down between the gaps in the trees. They reminded Violet of tiny, soft feathers. Pure white intricate patterns settled in her hands as she held them up, palms facing the clear blue winter sky. 'There's something so magical about snow.' she thought, as she twirled under the flurry of white, her head tilted back, her eyes closed. The world spun inside her head, faster with every turn. Her heart blossomed like a flower in the morning light. She basked in the tranquility of this new, wintery world. The thrill of an overpowering sense of joy spilled from the young woman's lips as she squealed in delight.

The harsh breeze stung her face, but the thick, warm cape enveloping her, protected her slight frame from the wind's relentless, gnawing teeth. She regretted leaving the muffler on her grandmother's bed. It, or a pair of gloves, would have been perfect to warm her winter-nipped fingers. They were bordering on sore and numb as she tirelessly rubbed her hands together. The quick movements created a gradual rise in heat between her palms that spread outward. The stiffness in the bones of her hands gently subsided. She tucked them inside the cape, to ward off the sting of the winter breeze, and continued forward, ignoring the chill of cold that crept up her legs.

Time passed as she trudged tirelessly through the forest. Her boots were heavy, weighed down by the clumps of compact snow clinging to them. Each stride ripped through the pure white clouds of unmarred snow, creating deep scars in its beauty. They followed her, remaining until a flurry of snowflakes filled each one, denying all knowledge of her journey.

A cabin appeared just before the last trees of the forest parted company to make way for the land beyond. It stood quietly at the side as though part of the forest itself. Snow had lain heavily upon the rooftop. It glistened under the moonlight that caressed it. Water poured down over the edge, freezing into blades of ice. Beauty and danger danced at the sharp tips of the frozen daggers. They hung over the entrance like guards protecting their kingdom.

There was something truly majestic about it, Violet thought. The cabin looked weathered and beaten, yet quaint and magical, like those in the fairytales that she knew. This was the closest Violet had ever been to any other home than her own. She lived in isolation as her grandmother had intended when she purchased the property, keeping people away from the secret Violet had become.

Violet approached the cabin cautiously. From a distance, she tried to see through the darkened window, desperately searching for any signs of another within. There was no movement, not even a glimmer. She felt braver, inching further toward the inviting premises. Finally, at the front door, she reached out her hand and laid her palm against the damp wood. It creaked on its hinges at her touch.

Her heart raced as she pushed back the door. Her touch was delicate, afraid the noise it would make would wake the entire forest. She blinked, slowly adjusting her eyes to the gloom. The force of her boot on the floorboards released a creak that ripped through the silence. She held her breath, her heart thumping loudly in her ears. She waited for the roaring accusations of her grandmother to rise above the pounding of each pulse. Nothing came, not a single word or sound met her ears. She took another step until the gloom of the cabin swallowed her in its shade. She had crossed the threshold.

Her chest tightened as she battled her rapid breathing against the choking, musty air, engulfing her. The thick scent filled her nostrils as she reached for the small table.

Gripping its smooth edge, she allowed it to steady her. She closed her eyes and thought of the adventure through the forest. She pictured the scenery, the array of golds, reds, and oranges, and the little bird's sweet face. The tension in her body fell away to allow deeper and slower breaths.

In the darkness's obscurity that filled the cabin, Violet could see the outline of a small vase on the table. The shape of a single flower was displayed in the middle. "It can't be," she whispered to herself. Curiosity took over as she rummaged upon darkened flat surfaces for a candle and a friction light to burn its wick. Her fingers prodded and poked at unrecognizable shapes. Her fingertips eventually fell upon a smooth cylindrical, glossy stick of wax, a perfect, untouched wick at its tip.
Her hands moved a few inches further along the rough wood where they (whether it was luck, deliberate, or pure coincidence) stumbled upon a friction light. Taking her

chance, she quickly lit the candle.

A warm glow flickered in time with the flame. Shadows pooled in the corners; her silhouette stretched up the wall. Violet's eyes met with the centre of the table where a single Violet sat in a small vase. Its pleasant hue, fresh as though it had recently been plucked from the earth. She leaned forward and secured the candle into a holder, then turned her attention back to the flower.

The powdery scent of the Violet was sweet and familiar. A memory flashed in her mind like a photograph - a vase filled with the same flower, sat on top of a piano as her mother played for her. It was a time that she had forgotten, but the memory was bittersweet.

The flame continued its dance at the tip of the candle's wick as the wax dripped slowly down the sides and onto the holder where it sat. The flame threw its light upon the hearth of the fireplace, seducing the kindling wood with its power.

As the fire roared, its amber glow poured into the room, oozing out, like thick honey, over a lonely armchair. The fabric was a deep chocolate brown. The dust had settled and knitted into its fibres. A floral rug brightened the earth tones that filled the new surroundings she stood in. Its pattern broke apart the monotony of the wood beneath her feet. Shadows drew back, frightened of being burned by the fire. They hid under a small bed, pushed neatly against the far wall. The cabin was small but cleverly equipped for one person. It was simple, quaint, and ideal.

Violet's desire for a home of her own had always followed her, playing over and over in her daydreams. Here it brought it to the front in vivid, ideal images. 'This would be perfect,' she thought, gazing around.

'But it's not yours, Thorn!' a voice in her head reminded her. The stern, imaginary voice of her grandmother made her heart plummet with the truth.

She slumped down into the chair. Her tired body nestled firmly into its padded embrace. Dust flew up in clouds, making her cough as it hit the back of her throat and there, she let the world fall away as she, herself, fell into another.

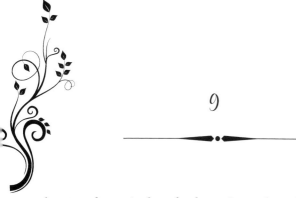

9

The London air brushed against the old woman, her expression taught with indignance. The natural crimson rouge of fury settled in scattered blotches upon her face. Its vibrant shade fought against the stiff wind that tried to pale it - a battle lost. They began to fade as the cool autumn breeze swept over the exposed skin on the back of her neck.

She remained still at the top of the harsh stone steps leading to the solicitor's office, her mind reeling from the conversation she'd just had. She strained to soften her hardened features as her anger simmered within her. 'How dare he?' she seethed silently. 'How dare he deny me what is rightfully mine! What use is a house to that little bitch?!'

A passerby tipped his hat at her. He was a tall, well-dressed young man with a cheery disposition. His hair was as vibrant and rich as autumn leaves and his eyes were a deep, comforting brown. Unaware of her temper, he offered an upbeat "Good morning!" and a dazzling broad smile that creased the corners of his eyes. His merry voice sang out, snapping Mrs. Bainbridge out of her inward venting. She lazily raised her gloved hand to wave - the polite response. Her lips pursed in a strained smile. The man was in far too good a mood to concern himself with the spiteful look of distaste she gave him. He hurried along, bestowing his joyful nature to as many as he could.

Mrs. Bainbridge repositioned the strap of her reticule, settling it in the crook of her elbow. Her hands, now flat against her stomach, shoulders back, head high, she carried on down the steps and onto the cobbled path below.

Violet's grandmother had considered returning to her son's home directly after her visit to Darlington and Darlington, but the furnace had been stoked in her fierce, unforgiving eyes. She was beyond vexed. She was seething at the very thought of Violet - pinning the entire blame, for the morning's outcome, solely on her. As her blood raged in her veins, she knew it would be unwise to return immediately. She did not have the gumption to explain her attitude or, perhaps, even have to admit her true reason for her visit to London. She would have to wait for the strength of her emotions to pass before she did so, avoiding all discussion on the matter. As her mind wandered, her feet did the same.

The rattle of carriage wheels upon the rough stone burned through the chatter amongst the city's people. Clouds of white billowed from the mouths of horses as their hooves beat gloriously upon the street where they cantered. Drivers sat upon the Hansom Cabs with perfected postures. They emanated a regal air to those whom they passed, advertising their services. Women in fine clothes, from pastel shades of pink, blue, lilac, sage, and cream to deep rich tones of burgundy, plum, emerald, and sapphire blue. Newly forlorn widows in black satin, heartbroken from loss. They all appeared to glide like angels, their feet hidden by their skirts. Bonnets were upon the heads of the more mature women while the young ladies were adorned with the latest fashion of wide-brimmed hats.

Their attire reeked of wealth, while the poorer folk seemed to merge with the dull and damp tones of the city. Their hair was brittle from smog. Skin raw and dry, weathered from the relentless winds as they swept through the streets. Obvious signs, to those who cared, of the absence of heat in cramped homes, homelessness, or, worse still, because they were slowly dying amongst them, cast aside like the waste and the rats that filled every nook in London.

The ignorance of the rich was a highly contagious, uncontrollable epidemic inflicted upon the poor folk as they were dismissed and ill-treated by those who were rich in education but poor in empathy. Violet's grandmother was one of them, possibly even more cruel. She only saw those who were wealthy as her equals, and those who suffered the harsh hand of poverty as vermin. Her heart was as hard as the cobbles her heels clacked upon. 'They need to work if they want what we have.' she hissed under her breath, her nose wrinkling as she stared down at a boy no older than five. He was shivering as he sat on the ground, a worn hat upturned in front of him in the hope of a coin. 'They have only themselves to blame for their downfall!' She grimaced at their dismay. 'Worse than rats!' she spat, her eyes glaring at the child who recoiled at her words.

Mrs. Bainbridge's feet had found a steady stomping rhythm as she, without care, charged through the people. She strode at speed, unaware of her destination, but, as her eyes fell upon the welcoming wrought-iron gates of the park ahead, she deemed it as good a place as any to spend some time attempting to clear her mind.

Just as she assumed it would be, it was much more peaceful in the park. The calm ambience slowed and softened her heavy steps. The distant sounds of the city hubbub seemed to be muffled, pushed far behind her to a dull mumble. She welcomed the escape from reality as she took in the view.

A young mother, dressed in a pearlescent rose gown, pushed her baby in a perambulator. Another small child walked by the woman's side. The little girl's golden ringlets bounced in time with her tiny steps as she chatted excitedly, pointing her little finger at everything she passed, encouraging her mother to look.

Violet's grandmother settled herself upon a bench on the opposite side of the path which divided the park into two like a frozen grey river running through it. Two enormous oak trees stood stripped bare of leaves, their branches like long, thin fingers, clawing and stretching over her in menacing shadows. Their leaves strewn on the grass, the green faded into browns and blackened at the edges from the smog that filled each pore.

She watched the ducks idly glide upon the water of a pond, occasionally bursting into a race when a morsel of stale bread hit the glossy surface. Circles rippled around the hardened dough as the ducks submerged their beaks to steal it from the water's depth.

The young mother nodded her head toward Mrs. Bainbridge in acknowledgement of her. The old woman smiled profusely. Her forced smile was thick and sickly.

"Mama!" cried her little girl, distracted. Her small, outstretched index finger pointed to a sheet of paper attached to the trunk of the tree. "Mama!"

"What is it, Petunia?" the mother asked, intrigued, walking her daughter closer to where the little girl had been pointing.

Mrs. Bainbridge shifted upon the bench. She pushed her spine hard against the wood as its shape responded by pushing back into her flesh. She inched away from the approaching family, trying to give us much space between herself and them.

"It's a show, Mama, with funny-looking people! Please, can we go?" the little girl begged.

"We will have to ask your father," the mother replied, "although some of them look rather frightening." she added.

"Please, Mama?!" the girl begged in a whimper, tugging on her mother's skirts.

"We will see. Come now Petunia, we must go." The woman unravelled the little girl's hand from her skirts, turned, and led her away from the vibrant lithograph, while Mrs. Bainbridge's eyes flickered with the excitement at what the little girl had discovered.

The old woman's mask had restored itself to its former perfection. 'The walk has done wonders' Mrs. Bainbridge mused; her eyes fixed on the inviting, tantalizing scene upon the lithograph. A feeling of triumph swelled in her chest. She gave a short groan as she eagerly pushed up from the low bench. Gathering herself and reaffirming her posture, she sashayed toward the wondrous image. Curiosity had peaked within her at the little girl's words - 'Funny looking people.'

Mrs. Bainbridge adjusted her spectacles, reading the printed words slowly and carefully so as not to miss any details. It read:

'Carson's Creatures of Curiosity
Perfectly Peculiar
Frighteningly Freakish
Come Ogle the Oddities
A show of wonder and Surprise!'

The old woman slowly turned her head to the left and then again to the right. She glanced nonchalantly around the park to assure all eyes were averted. When she deemed it safe, she removed the lithograph from the tree and promptly tucked it inside her reticule.

The façade of the meal that evening was a nuisance to Mrs. Bainbridge. It prolonged the impatience that ravaged her insides. She was desperate to look further into Carson's Creatures of Curiosities. This could be the answer to everything she required, she thought, the answer to all her problems folded neatly, upon paper, inside her bag.

Her curiosity gnawed away at her as she sat feasting upon the meal the household cook had prepared, diligently and with care, for her master and his daughter, as well as his guest. A delicious chicken pie surrounded with an array of vegetables and covered with thick, perfect gravy sat upon her plate, but Violet's grandmother still found fault with it. It was nothing disastrous, she supposed, just a slight bitterness to the vegetables, but, as eager as she was to retire to her room, she could not refrain from critiquing those who had failed to meet her standards.

Whilst William and Isabelle discussed matters of the day in the parlour, the old woman headed for the kitchen, considering it her duty to scold the cook. It was carried out perfectly in her usual secretive and sly manner, reducing the cook to the brink of tears (never too much, but just enough so that it stopped there at the kitchen door; Mrs Bainbridge's cover remaining intact).

As she sat on her bed, she smoothed her hand over the

crumpled lithograph, displaying it upon her lap. A show in three days, it read. Curiosities, it had stated - people that did not meet the belligerent rules of society. They were part of humanity, yet the ignorance of others denied them. The cogs in Violet's grandmother's brain whirred into life as she placed the mental image of Violet amongst the men, women, and children on the paper.

"Yes," she breathed, hope lifting her voice, "I think I will pay this Mr. Carson a visit."

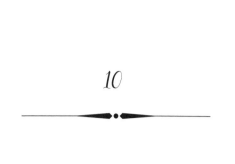

10

Eyes of peridot green peered down, a face hovering above her own. They looked at her intently, as if they had been waiting for her to rise from her slumber. Violet's breath caught as she used her arms to drag herself away from under the intensity of their gaze. Her knuckles pressed against the coolness of fresh linen, sending alarm and panic through her core. Where was the chair from the cabin with its rough fabric? Where were the dark wooden walls?

"Where am I?" she asked. She kept her head down, avoiding eye contact with the person in front of her.

Although she still wore the clothes she had on yesterday, she felt naked under their watch. The curve in her spine felt prominent, as if she was on display for everyone to gawp at. To her, it was the only thing they could possibly see. She was petrified of who they may be, or what they may be capable of, especially with regards to someone with her affliction. Her stomach swirled with nausea as her mind swam with insecurities. She wanted to hide from them; vanish into thin air; cease to exist. Anything to hide her body.

In twelve years, as she grew older under her

grandmother's watchful eyes, she had not been allowed to socialize with anyone outside their home. Mrs. Bainbridge had taught Violet that the young woman was ugly and not to be beheld by the eyes of others. She would be beaten, cast out, ridiculed, and caged by strangers if they'd found her, but here she was now facing that very prospect.

"Please don't be afraid." said a man, his tone soft.

Violet brought her knees up in front of her chest, curling her body into the smallest size she could become. "Please don't look at me." she begged.

The sound of scraping of wood upon more wood filled the room as the man dragged a chair toward the side of the bed. Violet stayed huddled; her head tucked down as if that would somehow make everything and everyone disappear.

"Violet, please look at me." came the voice, pleading.

Hearing the kindness in the man's voice, she raised her head a fraction until her eyes met his. The man's ink-black hair framed his face. Subtle kinks of waves rippled in each strand. His waistcoat of sapphire blue draped over his broad shoulders. Small buttons of a brilliant gold cascaded down the front, punctuating the waistcoat's deep, bold shade and smoothing the fabric against his toned abdomen. He wore trousers as dark as the night and a shirt as white as snow. The button of his collar remained open, revealing his smooth skin. Violet thought the man was beautiful, but it only made her feel more subconscious as she sat there in front of him.

"My name is Emil," he began. "You do not need to be be afraid of me."

"How did I get here?" she asked, her voice a mere whisper.

"Now that is a puzzle." he replied.

"What do you mean?" Violet lifted her head until her entire face was revealed. Emil's eyes lit up as she showed him her soft, pretty features.

"Well, I'm not entirely sure how to explain this without appearing a little dishevelled in the mind..." he mused out loud. "The truth is we discovered you, asleep, in the armchair. Well, when I say we, what I really mean is Eliza, the household cook, found you. I never knew she had such powerful lungs! In all my days, I do not believe I have ever heard a woman scream like that before!" A smile tugged at the corners of his mouth as he remembered the exact moment. "It is as though you just appeared in the parlour out of thin air. Poor Eliza almost fainted." A smile of pure delight spread across his face. His fun nature, evident in the twinkle of his eye.

Violet thoughts distracted her. She did not know how she came to be in this man's home, but, most of all, she did not know how she had ended up in the bed. Violet paled as she let her mind wander. "I'm so sorry!" she gasped, trying to scramble out from under the sheets. They twisted with her every movement, tightening and blocking her escape.

"Please Violet, there is no need..."

"You keep saying my name. How do you know such

details?" she asked, confused.

"Ah, forgive me," he said, "you were mumbling it in your sleep. You seemed very persistent that you were only to be called that, so I just assumed it was correct."

Violet stopped fighting with the blankets, their strength undeniable as they twisted over her feet and coiled around her legs. She relaxed her posture on the mattress in defeat. It made sense to her she would probably dream of, what most would assume, something so trivial. They would not know how it feels to have been denied their own name and there were no words to help her explain it.

As she drifted inward, swamped by her thoughts, her mind stumbled upon her current situation. This man had not said a word about her appearance. He had not laughed, mocked, or questioned it.

"Do I not seem a little different to you?" she asked, looking up at him. She tried to gauge his reaction.

He looked puzzled by her question. "I don't understand." Emil's eyebrows furrowed with genuine confusion. "We are all different, are we not?"

"I suppose so." Violet said. Her mind seemed to separate from her body as she listened to her own words and the words of this stranger before her. The man seemed to have a very different outlook and perception from that of her grandmother.

"Are you referring to your spine?"

"Yes." Violet muttered. She wanted to scoop the blankets up over her head and hide again as a sense of shame washed over her in tidal waves.

"Why would that make me treat you any other way than I am now? Did you choose to be born with such conditions? No, you certainly did not. So, Miss... erm... err..."

"It's Violet Hall."

"Thank you, Miss Hall. Yes, as I was saying, I see no reason, what-so-ever, to inflict more harm on you than what, I am sure by your current demeanour, you have already suffered."

Who was this man? Where did he come from? Were there other people like him? Why had her grandmother told her otherwise?

Emil watched her, her thoughts visible in the subtle twists and frowns that formed and shifted across her face. He watched as she questioned everything he'd said. Her self-loathing was vicious and strong-willed. He suspected she had known little love in her lifetime. Her confidence was minimal, he thought sadly. "If you don't mind me saying, Miss Hall, I think you are a very attractive lady. Your spine does not alter that fact." Emil's face reddened at his bravery. He didn't dare tell her he thought she was the most beautiful woman he had ever seen. Her name was perfect, for she was as pretty, petite, and delicate as the flower.

Violet looked up at him, her face flushed as pink as a rose in full bloom. Her heart thumped inside her chest alongside a most peculiar feeling. She had never felt such a way before, but it was almost exciting, she thought, as it battled against the scars of her grandmother's words.

Emil's eyes studied her face as she studied his. She was

searching for a crack in the conviction of the words he was speaking. "It is no good trying to find fault in the truth I am telling you, Miss Hall. There is no doubt of your beauty." Heat crawled up his neck as he spoke. There was something about her that made his thoughts flow freely into words. He couldn't stop. "It would do you well to remind yourself of that. The opinions of others are no concern of yours. Their ignorance is their burden, not one that you should have to bear."

Violet's lips could not move. His words had rendered her speechless. She thought her heart may explode with the amount of kindness he was showing her, Violet Hall; a curiosity; one labelled most strange.

Silence spread between them. Moments ago, Emil couldn't stop talking and now, as regret crept up upon him, he wondered whether he should have. The glittering eyes of the young woman in front of him were brimming with wonder as his words fell upon her like rain. He hoped she would take heed of his words and the conviction in them, or would he despair as she let them slide away like drops of rain upon a window? He prayed, with all his heart, that it would not be the latter.

A maid entered the room. Her footsteps, a gentle tapping in the quiet. She coughed, no louder than a whisper, a subtle announcement of her arrival.

"Ah, good morning, Miss Allen." Emil smiled at the woman. "I trust you are here to help our new guest?"

"Yes, Emil" she replied. Miss Allen's eyes smiled as the

corners of her mouth curled upward to reach them. She beamed as she looked at Violet. "Good morning, Miss".

Miss Allen was a mature woman with silver hair, curled loosely into a chignon. Her features were warm and kind, nothing like those of Mrs. Bainbridge. Her cheeks were a sweet pink against the twinkle of her blue eyes. Violet felt immediately at ease in her company.   .

"Good morning, Miss. Allen." she replied.

"Oh, there's no need for all the formalities, duck, you can call me Rosie!" she grinned.

Emil looked at Rosie, his eyes playful. "Well now, I don't know whether I should be offended." he laughed. "You've never let me call you Rosie."

The woman's eyes glittered in response. "That's because I have known you since you were knee-high to a grasshopper... and you've never asked!"

Emil rocked back and forth on his heels, chuckling to himself.

"Now, let's get you dressed for the day ahead!" Rosie suggested, looking at Violet. "I believe young Emil here may have something special planned. It's not every day we have a guest!"

With that, Emil turned and left the room. "Bye Rosie!" he called cheekily, leaving Violet and Rosie alone to listen to him laughing happily to himself as he walked away.

11

"I only have these clothes." Violet blushed, embarrassed by the shabby fabric, stark against the luxuriance of the room. Her nerves were getting the better of her as Rosie looked her up and down, assessing her attire.

Violet's fingers fumbled at the tatters of her skirts. She twiddled at a singular hole in the washed-out, dreary cotton. Over time, it had grown from the size of a farthing to that of a shilling, entirely the fault of the nervous habit that had snuck up on her with the greatest of stealth. She did not know when or how it had first started, but once it took a grip, she could not relinquish the new form of comfort. It had been a welcomed distraction when in the tangled web of her grandmother's unnecessary and unwarranted chastising, and, she realized, it appeared again when under the scrutiny of strangers. At first, she would pinch the fabric together so that the hole would pucker between her closed fingertips, gently squeezing and twisting at the bunched cotton. The more nervous she became, the more she would twist it until the material grew taught under the pressure of her actions. Over time, the edge of the hole slowly, and silently, frayed. It gently tore and stretched until it was big enough to put her finger through.

Now, as she watched Rosie, her finger rotated, twitching at the knuckle, teasing the material until it wrapped around her digit like a scarf around a neck. Her skirt hitched slightly, revealing the upper of her old, worn boots.

"Don't you worry about that, duck," Rosie said gently, eyeing the poor state of Violet's clothes. "Leave it to me. I think it's about time you were treated like the beauty you are, Miss!"

The apples of Violet's cheeks flushed a soft shade of pink as her mind absorbed the word beauty. "You can call me Violet." she offered. Her voice wavered with an air of doubt, contemplating whether the kindness of these new people was real or a forced politeness to put her at ease.

"Very well, I shall call you Violet, Violet." the woman smiled.

The tension in Violet's shoulders dissipated as she looked at Rosie. The woman's expression was as warm and sweet as milk and honey. Violet, appreciatively, drank it all in as it slowly chipped away at the invisible wall she had built for her own protection.

Rosie turned to face the wardrobe and eased the door open to its full capacity. Violet stretched her neck, trying to catch a glimpse of the clothes hung neatly on the rack but, no matter how much she tried, it was to no avail. The maid's simple grey dress was far more elegant than her own, Violet thought, and she would have been delighted with the same, but she could not help but wonder what else could be in there.

As she waited patiently, Violet was privy to only a few clues, the occasional gasp from Rosie followed by a sigh, and then the "Oh, that will never do!" the woman muttered to herself.

As Rosie took her time making what the young woman assumed was a very difficult decision, Violet's gaze wandered around the room. She took in all the rich colours that surrounded her. Thick and luxurious plum coloured drapes framed the sash window. Their fabric trimmed with a vibrant gold to match the gold leaf etched into the carvings on the dresser table. The bed sheets were a thick cool fabric under the tips of her slender fingers as she run them across their flat surface. The pillows were plump, propped against the head of the bed. Her boots pressed into the soft carpet beneath her feet.

Violet avoided the image in the mirror. She already knew that she, in her drab clothes, looked very out of place. She wanted to forget the way her spine twisted and curved, even just for a mere few minutes. Moments like those were extremely rare but, when they were hers for the taking, she grabbed them with both hands, never wanting to let go. It was a freedom that others took for granted, but one she could only pray for. Little confidence existed within her, always struggling under the weight of her insecurities.

As she waited, her desire to want to believe in the kindness of these new people grew, but she reminded herself to be cautious. They were practically strangers, and it would be foolish to trust so soon. To think such a way felt ungrateful, she thought, especially as they seemed so genuine. Violet wanted to trust them, but she couldn't help but feel a little afraid.

"Aha!" Rosie exclaimed, startling Violet from the incessant chatter of her thoughts. The woman turned on her heel, holding the most beautiful gown Violet had ever laid her eyes upon. Seeing Violet's face, Rosie's chest expanded with pride and satisfaction. "This will fit you lovely, this will!" she beamed.

Violet's eyes were wide with rapture as she took in the exquisite detail of the gown. Surely this could not be for her? she thought. "Oh, I couldn't possibly," Violet gasped. "It's too beautiful."

"A stunning gown for a stunning gal!" Rosie replied. "We will have none of that doubt in this house, Miss. Violet."

The dress was a lavish green satin, as rich and as vibrant as emeralds. The fabric shimmered in the sunshine that poured through the bedroom window, sparkling off the crystal-cut vase on the table. An intricate pattern of lace trimmed the skirts and neckline. Even her grandmother's wardrobe could not have produced such elegance.

Violet's breath caught, panicking when she took in the detail of the corset Rosie had produced for her to wear. She thought it looked painfully rigid.

"Now, don't you go worrying Violet, this will be a perfect fit. I'm known for my eye for detail, and this is the perfect corset for you." Rosie said, as if she could read Violet's mind. "Now let's get you dressed!"

Violet stood trembling as she removed her old clothes. She wrapped her arms around her body, covering as much of herself as was possible. Any other hands than her own had never dressed her before. It felt bizarre to have someone help her into her clothes, but she knew she could not put that incredible gown on alone. She feared, if she did, it may take her a few days at least.

Violet cringed, cursing the shame that always brought her to the brink of tears as Rosie's hands touched her back, but the maid did not criticize her or make her feel inadequate, she just continued to dress her as she would have done for any other; her manner was constantly considerate and kind.

The comfort of the corset surprised violet. Despite the extra curves in her spine, it only proved to offer her the support she had not known she needed. It pushed up against her ribs like gentle hands holding her up. Her muscles sighed with relief as they rested against it. The crinoline petticoat rippled in layers of ivory fabric, one upon the other, as they cascaded down to the hem. It was simple, yet she could not deny the gracefulness of it.

She stood in front of the mirror, her face turned toward the image of her body for the first time since she had, somehow, found herself amongst these new people. She watched the transformation unfold and, as the emerald-green fabric poured down her body, covering every inch of the ivory petticoats, Violet's heart beat wildly. These kinds of moments were not meant for someone like her, Violet told herself as she turned in front of the looking glass, but she couldn't dull the thrill that fluttered in her stomach as she looked, admiringly, at her reflection. She twirled in pure joy at the woman, who copied every detail of her movement, both smiling profusely at one another.

"Well, you like it then?" Rosie asked with an all-knowing smile. Her eyes twinkled as she, too, watched Violet's reflection.

"It's exquisite!" Violet gasped, holding back a squeal of delight.

At the breakfast table, Emil sat waiting for her. He couldn't understand the sudden onset of nausea, ruling his stomach like a turbulent ocean as the muscles tightened against it. "Good heavens, Emil!" he told himself. "What on earth has got into you?" But, as Violet entered, he did not need to answer that question.

"Oi! It's not polite to gawp at a lady!" said Rosie, chuckling and snorting to herself. She had known Emil his entire life and she could tell him his own emotions before he could draw breath, long enough to understand them himself. It brought her great joy to see the young man so enthralled with their new guest.

"Yes, of course. I apologise Miss. Hall, for my awkward manner." Emil cleared his throat. "Please have a seat."

Violet walked precariously up to the chair which Emil gestured for her to sit upon. Her steps felt awkward as her feet adjusted to the snug fit of her new boots. They were patent black leather adorned with a scalloped edge and silver eyelets. She adored the heels, despite the wobble as she tried to find momentum. They gave her an extra inch or two of height. The entire new ensemble had instilled a sense of pride she had never known before.

Breakfast was a feast of cinnamon and all-spice pear butter thickly spread upon delicious waffles. The flavours danced upon her tongue in bursts of fruit and simmering spices. Violet, reluctantly, refused a second helping for fear of appearing gluttonous.

Emil talked easily with her as she sat on the chair only a few inches away from him. His company was comfortable, as though she had known him for a lifetime, as she listened to the stories he told of his childhood.

"What about you, Violet?"

"What do you mean?" she asked, taken aback. How could she tell him that her grandmother thought her so hideous that she would hide her from the rest of the world and, if she told him, would he then start to notice and think the same?

"Your childhood? Do you have any fun stories to tell?" The green of Emil's eyes was vibrant with anticipation.

"Nothing as exciting, I'm afraid," she replied. She took a deep breath and, without further ado, let go of her inhibitions. "My grandmother does not care for me that much." The words spilled rapidly from her lips as she gestured to her physical form.

The smile on Emil's face plummeted with sadness. He recognized the hurt that glistened in the tears pooling in Violet's eyes. It baffled him how anyone could not care for the young lady before him. He grew an instant dislike of the grandmother she spoke of. "I hope you don't mind me saying, Violet, but your grandmother is an utter fool."

"Here, 'ere!" Rosie piped up from the corner of the room as she fussed with the decanter sitting neatly on a small table. "I'd like to 'ave words with her!" she grumbled.

Violet was silent, not knowing what to say.

"Well, let us not dwell on the ignorance of others this fine morning, Violet. Today we shall make glorious memories with people that adore you and your company, and you shall start with us!"

Violet blushed at his enthusiasm. It was exhilarating, she thought, as the tension in her body melted away.

12

Violet sucked in her breath and held it as she took her first step over the threshold and into the light of the day. Apprehension of the reception, she assumed she would receive, squeezed at her throat. Emil quickly took her hand and looped her arm through his to offer his support and reassurance. "You have nothing to fear, Violet." he whispered in her ear.

The softness of his breath tousled her hair as his fingers grasped her trembling hand. At his touch, she remembered to breathe. Her breaths were slow and controlled. A wave of emotion tickled her as his thumb caressed the back of her hand. She inhaled three short, staggered breaths at the sensation flitting wildly through her. A feeling, like no other, played out within her chest - a butterfly fluttering its beautiful, tiny wings. The soft, rapid beat of her heart was not that of fear, but something else, something she had never experienced before. Although it was strange, she could not say that it was terrible. It did not make her feel melancholy but uttered whispers of new beginnings, animated with the feeling of hope.

Keeping her focus on her feet, Violet gripped Emil's

hand tighter as he led her down the remaining steps and onto the cold, grey stone path.

"Look up, Violet." Emil encouraged.

Violet raised her head slowly. She couldn't bear the thought of the awkward stares of strangers. If someone called her a name, she thought she would perish on the spot, out of shame, in front of Emil and Rosie. But, as she took in the hustle and bustle of the street before her, nothing came. There were no names spat at her; no laughter ridiculing her appearance, and no lengthy stares that made her feel utterly worthless. She was amazed at the random flashes of white teeth that smiled in her direction from passersby; the onyx black top hat that swivelled in a gentleman's hand as he bowed heartily in greeting towards her. The kindness shown, both breathtaking, and powerfully sweet upon the sun-drenched autumn air.

"Come!" beckoned Emil softly. "There is more I must show you."

The carriage wheels rolled upon the cobblestones. Violet watched the world pass from her window. She could sense Emil's eyes fixed on her. If he had not made his opinion of her appearance known, then perhaps she would have felt only unease, but the looks he gave her were kind and appreciative. Heat spread across her chest and up over her pale skin at the awkward silence between them. She fumbled in her mind for something to say. The words wouldn't come.

Emil shifted upon the seat as his inner voice berated him for allowing such silence to grow between them. For the first time in his life, he had lost the ability to speak in the presence of a woman.

He had been watching her as she looked dreamily out of the window. Her face flushed, her eyes glittering. He wished he had been privy to her deepest thoughts so that he could find the right words to spark up a conversation, destroying the void they now endured. His thoughts were ebbing and flowing like a tidal wave, nonsensical babbling instigated by his heart in the presence of Violet. His eyes would not move from the vision she was as she sat less than two feet away from him. He had tried, but it was no use. She was poised, beautiful, and utterly radiant. Her deep emerald-green gown enriched the chestnut hue of her hair; it highlighted the vibrancy of green that swam in the irises of her eyes. He could not understand how she thought so little of herself. He inwardly seethed at her grandmother, and any other person, that had moulded her mind to believe such preposterous lies they had told her.

"It's so quiet in 'ere you could 'ear a pin drop!" Rosie announced. She had been noting whatever was growing between Emil and Violet. Their stretched-out silences would just not do, she thought. Her eyes flitted between them, scrutinizing. She had seen how Emil looked at Violet. His emotions, splashed across his face. She had never seen him look at a woman that way before. Hope surged through her body until she feared she may burst from it. By chance, the worlds of two young people had intertwined. The future fizzed with excitement, she thought happily.

Violet pressed her lips inward, clenching them between her front teeth. She held her cheek against the cool glass that provided relief from the relentless heat in her face. Now, she could not feel just one set of eyes on her, but two. The young woman couldn't take it anymore. She was growing more flustered by the second. Violet turned to meet their gazes. Emil looked thoughtful, his cheeks flushed as though a lady's rouge had attacked him. Crimson blotches clung to his ears. His eyes glazed, but soft, as they met hers. A knowledgeable smirk filled Rosie's face; her eyes alight with mischief. That was all it took as the corners of Violet's mouth tugged profusely. Any fear she had once had of their thoughts of her shattered as a laugh expelled from deep within her throat. She felt alive, so much more so than when she had been alone at the cabin. This was so new, thrilling, and indescribable.

Emil practically bounced into the tearoom. He took huge strides of pride, walking with Violet close by his side. Violet could not have held back from entering, even though she wanted to. His proud stance gave her extra strength, a feeling of protection. Although she had yet to experience anyone like her grandmother in Emil's company, the scars of Violet's memories continued to breathe life into her insecurities.

A man walked forward, gesturing for them to approach a table. He wore a charcoal-grey tailcoat and trousers. The jacket lapels were a deep black velvet. His waistcoat, bold ivory against his stark white shirt and cravat. Over his arm, he carried a cloth of the same white hue. The man's greeting was warm and welcoming without fault. Violet felt at ease in his presence.

Emil pulled out a chair for Violet, inviting her to sit. A million thoughts ran through her head; what if she tripped up?; What if she sat down the wrong way?; What if? What if? What if?

Once she'd sat comfortably in the chair, she shook off her internal embarrassment at such foolishness. In its place came pure delight as she looked upon the table before her, laden with the finest crockery and silverware. Tall cake stands decorated with miniature sandwiches, scones with preserves and cream, slices of Victoria sponge - in honour of the queen herself; Battenberg with its sweet pink and yellow commemorating the wedding of Queen Victoria's granddaughter to Louis of Battenberg. Violet had known this because her grandmother had felt it was her duty to inform Violet of such events. It gave the old woman the opportunity to remark on the lives and happiness of the 'normal' young women (as she referred to them) while soaking up the hurt that radiated from Violet. But, as she looked at Emil and Rosie, the kindest people she had ever met, the memory of her grandmother's gloating was erased and replaced with the present. This moment would soon be a memory, she thought, one she would choose to hold on to and cherish.

An aroma of bergamot, rosemary, and rose blossoms filled the air as the hot steamy liquid flowed from the teapot into each teacup. The sweet intoxicating scent was a glad alternative to the strong, and somewhat pungent, aroma she knew. "Get this down you." Rosie said, filling Violet's plate with a piece of each cake. "Don't you go being shy around us, Miss. Hall."

Violet was grateful for the woman's intuition. Her own reluctance to dive into the food was a burden that she could not seem to get past, even though the food was deliciously enticing. She had never seen a more inviting table.

A memory of her mother wriggled to the forefront of her mind as she took the first bite of a decadent scone. The mixture of jam and cream burst into life upon her tongue. A picture of her mother laughing, whilst trying to teach Violet how to hold a teacup like a lady, sprang into her mind. Violet had giggled alongside her mother, as they falsified extravagant, well-to-do accents; her little finger extended, accentuating their status in society. They had always known that they were of the wealthier class, but she remembered how her mother had found all the rules and regulations stuffy and restrictive. Violet couldn't help but long for those rules and regulations now as she sat across from Emil. Maybe in time, she would become more lax in adhering to them but, for now, she wanted to blend in with these incredible people. The thought of being part of something new excited her.

Violet held up her teacup the way her mother had taught her and brought it to her lips. The steam of the Earl Grey tea rose over the brim, dampening her cupid's bow and the tip of her nose. A loud, long slurp bubbled from Emil's direction, grabbing Violet's attention. Mischief glittered in his eyes like a naughty child as he stared at her from over the brim of his cup. His grin was infectious, she thought, as the corners of her mouth twitched. Rosie followed suit, as another loud slurp growled from her direction and then Violet knew she should do it too. Throwing all caution to the wind, Violet took a sip of her own, drawing air in at the same time. The liquid bubbled upon her lips and tongue as her successful slurp could be heard from across the table. As they laughed, Violet could have sworn she heard her mother laugh with them.

13

In a small shop on Oxford Street, Violet perused the aisles, immersed in rows upon rows of books. Their leather-bound covers were immaculate and refined. Letters, gilded with gold, pressed lightly into their depths, formed titles of fantastical stories. Each one delved into brand-new worlds, far beyond her imagination.

As she opened the first book, she breathed in the smell of leather, paper, and ink. Her fingertips caressed the pages, turning them over, one at a time, revealing the next, and the next, and the next. 'One day I will buy so many books,' she thought, 'I will need an entire room just to keep them.'

"For you, Violet." Emil said, holding out a package to her.

"For me?" she asked, shyly.

"Yes, for you. Open it." he smiled.

Violet carefully pulled at the string. The tightly wrapped brown paper relaxed around the gift in her hands, gently falling open, revealing a deep, rich chocolate brown leather book. Its title and author, etched in gold like many of the others in the shop, but this one was far more exquisite, Violet thought, with ivy leaves curled up and around the beautifully written words 'A Christmas Carol by Charles Dickens'. The pattern formed a festive wreath around them; a golden bow, finishing it perfectly at the bottom.

Heat warmed the back of Violet's eyes as she softly gazed at the book. A ball of emotion grew in her throat. It was tight and hard to swallow as she tried to push it down. His kindness had taken her by surprise.

"Are you alright, Violet?" Emil asked. He had never meant to upset her, yet there she was, on the brink of tears. He wished he could take it back and make her happy again. "Please, I did not mean to upset you."

Violet sniffed as she wiped away a tear snaking down her cheek. Her emotions had got the better of her. She didn't know what to say as much as she didn't know why this incredible gesture had brought her to tears. She threw her arms wide open and wrapped them around Emil. "Thank you, thank you, thank you!" she sobbed into his chest. She could hear his heart thump within it as she nestled into him.

Emil's concern vanished as the warmth of Violet's body embraced his own. He pulled her closer still, breathing in the fragrance of her shampoo, his chin resting upon her head.

"You are very welcome, Violet."

Rosie smiled to herself as she watched them from behind a bookshelf a small distance away. Her heart ached for Violet. It was clear the young woman had received very little, so far, in life in the way of possessions and love. She hoped that she and Emil could change all of that for her. They were long past wondering where she came from. Rosie was more concerned that Violet may leave as suddenly as she had arrived. Losing her would be hard to bear, she thought, and, by the way Emil held the young woman, she knew he could not bear it either.

Rosie never thought she would meet someone she would approve of; someone who she thought deserved the love of Emil. She looked at him as if he was her own son. Despite her role in his life, she felt protective of him, but there was nothing about Violet that made her uneasy or caused her concern. She couldn't think of any other more suitable and worthy of his time and love. Silently, she gave them her blessing and prayed her hopes for them both would come to fruition.

"I'm just off to catch up with a friend," Rosie called as they exited the bookshop together. "I'll meet you at the carriage later on!" she finished quickly, scurrying away, allowing them no time to enquire of her plans.

Rosie was aware she was not very good at hiding a lie, but how else could she have given Violet and Emil time alone? she wondered. She knew she should have, perhaps, stayed to chaperone the couple, but no-one would question Violet's status; they would simply believe that she and Emil were a young married couple. 'Who would doubt it?' she mused, turning around briefly to look at them. 'Look at them," she assured herself, "they've grown awfully close in such a short time. There's no way you'd think otherwise. Besides, it's none of their business, anyway. Bloomin' nosey parkers!' she huffed to herself, striding faster along the cobbles.

"Okay..." Emil looked confused by the woman's departure. "I did not realize that Rosie had other plans today. Where shall we go next, Miss. Hall?"
"It is such a beautiful day," Violet replied. "Perhaps we can just walk and see where it takes us?"
"That is a grand idea, Violet." he beamed.

Violet's teeth clenched at the burning sensation in the muscles of her back. They ached with fatigue, but she would not allow them to put an end to such a beautiful day. She exhaled slowly after each breath she took, imagining the pain dulling within her body. It allowed her to keep up with Emil and, in time, with his leisurely pace.

They strolled past the windows of many a shop. The glorious smell of the bakery drifted out into the afternoon air. The tantalizing aroma of freshly baked bread made their tastebuds beg for a bite. Their stomachs growled in agreement despite already being satisfied. The city was bright and clean. It spoke nothing of the man that had carried her grandmother off to London in his Hansom Cab. His dirt-stained clothes, grubby face, and hands spoke only of smoke and filth. There were none like him in the London street they now strolled upon. It was as if there were two versions of the city.

As she thought about where she was, the possibility of bumping into her grandmother hit her like a boulder to the stomach. Her eyes searched, nervously, as they walked a little further, subconsciously gripping Emil's arm tighter.

"Is everything okay, Violet?" he asked, a little startled by her strength.

"I-I-yes." she replied. What was she to say to him? How could she tell him? She was trying to forget her grandmother, but she knew it would not be wise to withhold such information. Instead, she revealed to him just enough to help him understand her dilemma and the truth of her past.

With every word that rolled off Violet's tongue, Emil fought the anger building gradually inside of him. He could not show his anger, he thought. It would only serve to make Violet feel worse or, possibly, even afraid of him. He wanted neither of those things to happen. Emil took both of her hands, turning her toward him. "I assure you, Violet, while you are in my company," he said, his eyes looking deep into her own, "I will not let another hurt you. They will not even touch a single hair upon your crown. You are safe with me, I promise."

His words were a comfort to her. She imagined her father would have said something very similar. However, she knew he would not have looked at her the way Emil did in that moment. Emil's pupils were a large, perfect drop of black ink that pushed back the green of his irises until there was only a thin peridot, glittering outline remaining. Her body shivered under the intensity of his gaze, the energy between them caressing her skin. A warmth radiated across her shoulders, travelling up her neck and resting in the apples of her cheeks. She bit her lower lip and looked away. Insecurities about her appearance rose and receded with every breath. The very notion that the man who was now walking again, arm in arm with her, could ever feel any type of love for her seemed thoroughly implausible. She thought herself a fraudster for even considering it.

There were many beautiful young women gliding along the cobbles of the town. Tall, elegant, perfect bodies. Beautiful straight spines. She could not deny that she envied them. Her life would have been so much easier if she had been like them, too. Perhaps even her grandmother would have loved her how the old woman loved Isabelle. Yet Emil did not look at another. He doted on her, even after such a short time of knowing her. She held on to her last thought. It kept her grounded in the truth and not swept away by the self-doubt that riddled her brain like a parasite.

They gazed in the windows of florists, another bakery, and a shop that sold silk threads and the finest fabrics. The alluring aroma of coffee poured onto the streets amongst the roar of voices from a coffeehouse. Finally, Violet stopped abruptly at a window displaying a gown that looked as though they had created it from the fabric of dreams. The dress was a deep cerulean blue. Its neckline and sleeves were trimmed with ivory lace. A pattern of wild roses grew up the skirt on extended stems, climbing onto the bodice and up toward the neckline and over the shoulders. The fabric sheen made the dress appear to glow, almost as much as the light in Violet's eyes as she drank it all in.

"Would you like it?" offered Emil.

"Thank you, but please don't. You have done so much for me already." she replied, kindly. She could not bear the thought of this incredible man doing any more for her than he already had. He had gone above and beyond, she thought but, what she truly desired the most, was his company. Emil did not push the matter further, for fear of making her feel uncomfortable. "I understand." he answered softly.

Emil's mind had wandered. Thoughts tugged at his heart, wishing for Violet to stay with him. He had tried to push them away but, the more he grew to care for her, the more they plagued him. He did not know what would happen to her, this young woman who just materialized out of nowhere. Despite discussing it several times, none of them had known how she'd just appeared in their home. They had rehashed every detail of her arrival, but even Violet could not enlighten them. How could he be sure that she would stay? How could she even know? Emil sighed. There was simply no point in torturing himself with questions he could not answer. It would only prove to use up the precious time they had left together, and he would let nothing mar that.

Rosie stood waiting at the carriage, a pleased, all-knowing smile tugging at the corners of her mouth as they walked towards her. Her eyes, almost disappearing behind the fullness of her cheeks as she watched them so enthralled with one another. Emil and Violet waved to her, both expressions the same but hidden from the other. Their inner secrets reciprocated yet not spoken aloud.

The driver helped Rosie up and into the carriage, where she waited patiently for the young couple so they could return home together.

14

By morning, there was a particular air about Mrs. Bainbridge as she walked grandly into the parlour. Silver grey fabric oozed over her body in the form of a dress. Her grey hair looked dull against its hue. Her body was rigid, confident, proud, and expectant. Had Violet been present in that room, she would have thought the woman's stance utterly strange. Her grandmother's unfamiliar energy would have unsettled her to her core.

"Good morning, Mother!" William sang, eyeing her, bemused by how she stood. The smile that stretched across his mother's face was one that even he, himself, found to be a rarity. He studied her expression. A fragment of curiosity pinched and furrowed his brow. "You are very chipper this fine morning, Mother. Pray tell, what is the news?"

"Good morning darling," she beamed, "Can your mother not be happy just to be with her precious son and beautiful granddaughter?" she replied, avoiding the truth entirely.

"Why yes, of course," he smiled, "as we are happy to have you with us as well."

The old woman caressed the side of Isabelle's face,

cupping her chin as she passed her by. "Good morning, Isabelle" she gushed, lowering herself into the chair.

"Good morning, Grandmama." The young woman smiled, a slight giggle escaping from her lips at the joy of her grandmother's mood. "Grandmama, I was thinking of a little shopping today. Would you care to join me?" Isabelle asked, hopefully.

"That would be delightful." Mrs. Bainbridge replied, "I had intended to return to poor Violet today, but I have received word that she is faring rather well so, I do not see any reason I may not stay a little longer if your father permits?" she said, looking at William for confirmation.

William looked up from his morning paper to see all expectant eyes on him, "I did not know we had received mail but, yes, of course, Mother." he replied cheerfully, "You are most welcome to stay as long as you would like."

"Thank you, darling." Mrs. Bainbridge crooned, winking playfully at Isabelle. She did not dare to stretch out the discussion any further for fear of having to explain when and how the supposed letter had arrived.

'Perfect!' the old woman thought triumphantly as she tucked into the banquet of food on the table. She was mindful of herself, her expression detached from the words that played in her head. 'I will stay another five days.' she thought, 'That will give me enough time to get rid of that little wench, and, in return, I shall receive what I am owed without the help of that useless, blithering fool, Mr. Darlington.'

Isabelle stood in the doorway, dressed in a sweet buttercup-yellow gown. Her carriage boots were ivory cream to match her gloves. Her hair, softly drawn back in a chignon, blonde curls hung loosely at the sides, framing her pretty face. Pearls draped around her neck, displaying her wealth. Her eyes glittered as she watched her grandmother approach.

Mrs. Bainbridge now wore a gown of blood-red. Its colour was a hint of the evil that lurked behind the sweet mask of a doting grandmother.

"Do have fun, Mama, and try to relax." William prompted, as he stood at the door watching them leave. "Don't worry about Violet. I am sure she is in very capable hands." Mrs. Bainbridge nodded; her quiet seething, mistaken for concern. Impatience bubbled inside the old woman as the image of the lithograph flashed behind her eyes. The day she would attend Carson's Creatures of Curiosity could not come soon enough.

She now had new plans for Violet that relied on any conduct with Mr. Carson. Mrs. Bainbridge knew she would have to be direct, firm, and precise with the man. The price was not up for negotiation. She knew what the young woman was worth to a man so despicable. As she sat in the carriage, she could almost feel the money sifting between her fingers.

"Is everything alright, Grandmama?" Isabelle asked. She, too, had noticed the faraway stares that adorned the woman's face.

"Why yes, dear Isabelle." Mrs. Bainbridge replied, "I was

just thinking about Violet, that is all."

"Oh, you are good to her, Grandmama." Isabelle crooned. "I am sure you have left her in perfectly capable hands, as Father said. You really have no need to concern yourself."

Violet's grandmother nodded, once again, in response. No-one could know what she had planned for Violet. Violet would not be the ruining of her. "Sadly, with Violet as she is, I cannot help but feel concerned to have left her." she said, strengthening the lie.

"Come, Grandmama." Isabelle began, taking the old woman's hand. "We shall have to take your mind off matters."

Mrs. Bainbridge walked the high street tirelessly, pandering to Isabelle's delight in shopping. They had spent two hours in the dressmakers while they had measured the young woman for a ball gown she would require in a few weeks. She had rattled off all her requests with fervour, ensuring the seamstress was aware she would not be happy with any colour that wasn't of a pastel hue. She wanted to 'exude a certain type of femininity', Isabelle had stated, much unlike her friend Harriet, who was getting quite the reputation for her rather vibrant attire, according to the young woman. "The men are nothing more than simple bees around a honeypot when she dresses like that," she told the woman, kneeling tirelessly at her feet; altering and pinning the hem of her dress. "I do fear for her reputation," she lied, soaking in the glory of the gossip, spilling into the seamstress's ear, "because these bees are not the honourable type. Quite possibly, one might say they are more likened to wasps!"

The dressmaker remained quiet, listening to Isabelle tittering at her own words. She gripped sewing pins snugly between the clamp of her tightly closed lips and nodded her head occasionally in acknowledgement of her customer's words, so she would not appear rude, but it was all the fuel that Isabelle's fire required to continue her chatter.

Violet's grandmother sat thoughtfully on the designated chair, waiting for the dress-fitting to cease. She was becoming impatient as the time dragged. The first thirty minutes were bearable, the other thirty felt like hours rather than minutes. She thought the last hour would never end. It had felt more like five days, she thought, rather than two hours. She was exasperated.

The old woman's irritation gnawed deeper as she eyed the luxurious fabrics that were on display. Her hunger for the money, which was only days from her grasp, was unsatisfiable. If she had it, she could have afforded the luxury of shopping alongside her granddaughter. The fabric she desired would have been hers. She had already envisioned the pearlescent sage-green gown the seamstress would make, adorned with a paisley pattern embroidered into its weave. She would be back, she told herself, as they made their leave.

The smog filled the old woman's mouth as she took her first breath outside of the dressmaker's. Half swallowing and half coughing, she was suddenly more appreciative of the four walls which she had just exited. Her tongue felt dirty at its touch. Tension grew, sending a shooting pain across her scalp, as she took in the filthy streets. The threat of a headache loomed.

Smoke stained the buildings. Blackened air gathered, layer upon layer, strengthening its hold. Mrs. Bainbridge was a little surprised at her feelings towards the city where she had spent her childhood. She wasn't sure whether it had always been this way, and she had simply forgotten, or whether it had changed in quite a momentous way throughout the time she had been absent. She would have returned to the city's depths, had it not been for the shame of having a granddaughter like Violet, she thought. It was one more thing to blame her granddaughter for. Violet's list of guiltless misdemeanours grew with every second that she breathed.

The city dwellers paid no heed to what Mrs. Bainbridge noticed, and disliked, about their city. She assumed they had merely become immune to its downfall. After all, they did not have any other place to make such a comparison. She sniffed at the poorer community among them. 'Another blight upon London.' she thought, 'I may have to reassess where I shall reside once I get rid of the girl.'

"Come, Grandmama!" Isabelle sang, leading the way into a coffeehouse.

All the colour drained from Mrs. Bainbridge's face as she watched her granddaughter walk confidently through the door. "Isabelle!" she croaked, "We mustn't!"

It was too late. The young woman was now firmly across the threshold and mingling amongst the crowd. The old woman took a deep breath, trying to remain calm and dignified in a situation that startled her. She had never known a coffee house to allow women into their establishment. They had always been male-occupied premises. For women to enter was unheard of, yet there she was, witness to her granddaughter breezing through the door without a care in the world. She stared, unmoving. Isabelle turned and watched her grandmother absorb the scene in front of her. She quickened her pace, tottering around people and tables, towards where the old woman stood gawping.

"Grandmama, are you alright?" she asked. She took hold of her hand, guiding her toward an empty table. A gentleman moved aside, allowing them to pass. His eyes focused only on Isabelle, as if she was a glowing angel among them. He tipped his hat and wiggled his eyebrows at her. Mrs. Bainbridge caught sight of his advances. She glared at him until he had no choice but to move from her line of sight.

When Mrs. Bainbridge finally found her voice, she looked directly at the young woman. "We should not be in here, Isabelle." she remarked, "It is most undignified and unheard of!"

"Honestly, Grandmama!" Isabelle replied, "You would

think I had brought you to a house of..." she began, then whispered, "ill repute."

"Isabelle!" the old woman snapped. She quickly looked over each shoulder to see whether anyone had heard. Isabelle giggled, amused at her grandmother's reddening cheeks.

A waiter placed two cups of aromatic coffee on the table. The bitter fragrance filled their senses, washing away the disagreeable odour of the street outside. The old woman's beady eyes looked to her granddaughter for answers.

"I assure you, Grandmama, ladies are most welcome in this establishment. Things are moving forwards for us ladies. You'll see, one day, we will be welcome in all the places that gentlemen are and I, for one, am most looking forward to it." Isabelle beamed.

Observing more women amongst the crowd, and listening to Isabelle, Mrs. Bainbridge relaxed a little but kept watch for any male that approached, ready to shoo them away. She sipped cautiously at her coffee, her body twitching and shuddering from its bitterness as the hot, somewhat vile, yet soothing, liquid washed over her tongue and slipped down her throat.

15

It was the cold that hit her first. She screwed her eyes closed, too afraid to open them and look. The temperature against her skin did not tally with the warmth of Emil's home. The noise outside was entirely different. Rough fabric beneath her fingers unsettled her. She knew where she was even though she still clung to the hope that she wasn't. She hoped that if she waited for just one minute or, possibly, two, she would hear the familiar sound of Rosie's feet shuffling toward her bedroom door to bid her good morning.

The minutes passed, but still there were no familiar sounds that gave her hope. She inhaled deeply; an ache clenching, like a fist, around her heart. 'Dear God, please don't let me back here.' she whispered. She didn't want to leave Rosie and Emil behind but, deep down, she knew they weren't there anymore.

Were they even real? she questioned herself. Doubt upon doubt, building a wall between them. How could she be there one minute, deliriously happy in a world that showed her nothing but love and kindness, and then, the next, in a world that terrified her? Violet curled her legs up onto the chair, wrapping her arms around her knees.

The cabin, and all its contents, closed in around her. A tear rolled down her cheek as she held on to the life her dream had teased her with. 'It had to have been a dream,' she told herself. 'You cannot simply be in one place and then suddenly in another. That would be impossible.' Her breaths, ragged as her tears flowed. "Stop it, Violet!" she snapped at herself, her forearm swiping over her eyes, wiping away the tears, "If you want things to change, you will have to do it for yourself!"

Her limbs dragged with the weight of her longing as she walked back to her grandmother's house. Disappointment tainted with grief coursed through her veins. She berated herself with the reminder it would do her no good to dwell on something she could not remedy. She had to focus on everything she was capable of, and how she was going to achieve it. The cabin was her future now.

As expected, the house was empty. Violet was glad of it. She wouldn't have been able to explain away the tear-stained face to her grandmother. The old woman's mockery and snide jibes at her misery would have proved to only drown her voice.

Violet had no appetite. Her sudden loss, of those she'd grown to love, had snatched it from her. She turned her mind to the details of how she was going to escape from her life with her grandmother. Violet began searching the house for useful items she could pack up and take with her. She opted for the older utensils and tools as she rummaged at the back of cupboards, where they lay discarded and forgotten. The old woman wouldn't know of their absence for quite a while, if ever. She took the crumpled blankets from the bottom of the ottoman, then cleared her room of all her items. The latter part did not take long as there was hardly anything at all (just one other dress, undergarments, a shawl that had seen better days, and a hairbrush). As she folded them neatly into a pile, she thought about how cold it had been in the forest and decided she would keep her grandmother's cape. It was the least the old woman owed her after years of torment.

The hessian sacks that held her newly sourced items were heavy and bulky, bruising her legs as she attempted to carry them, so she began loading them upon a small wooden cart hidden at the side of the house. She hauled the last sack up and over the top of the vehicle, ensuring nothing would spill from it. All the sacks sat huddled together, perfectly snug and secure.

Her grandmother would not notice the absence of this cart, she thought. Violet, very much, doubted the old woman knew the little wooden contraption existed. Violet's nimble fingers and artistic mind had created it many years ago with the spare parts and tools she'd discovered abandoned in the barn. It had taken the strain off her back on many an occasion, and to her, it had become an old faithful friend.

Violet dragged the cart over the field. Its wheels

struggled as the sodden soil pulled it back and down into the grasp of its squelching grip. Pain gripped her spine as she tugged against the earth's hold on the contraption. The subtle limp of her left leg, exaggerated with the motion. Her palm grew hot against the friction of the rope as her toes curled within her boots as they, too, threatened to pull her down.

By the time she had reached the drier land beneath the shade of the forest trees, she was exhausted. The cold of the autumn would not release the humidity, tacky against her skin, as sweat trickled down her neck and underneath her thin blouse. Her back throbbed deep within the muscles as fatigue set in. The pain was as deep and sore as a thousand lashings. 'I've come this far,' she thought to herself, 'I'm not going back now.' Violet lowered her body to the floor, using the trunk of a tree to guide her down gently. She needed to rest.

The branches of the trees swayed in the wind, reaching toward her. This time, they did not seem curious. Their movements were those of an old friend reaching out to welcome her home. She listened to the breeze as it caressed her face. It played with her loose curls, bouncing them against the softness of her skin. Her chest heaved against the tightness within it as she fought to inhale the cool, clean air. With each breath that followed, her lungs yielded a little more.

The earthy tones of the forest only added to the wonder and thrill of her freedom. 'I could sit here forever.' she told herself but, even though she would have gladly stayed seated amongst the autumn leaves, she pushed herself up from the floor and stretched away from the pain that remained.

Heaving the cart over the brook proved difficult despite several drawn-out attempts. An invisible barrier appeared to stand firm between both sides of the forest. The cart was not welcome to cross it. The forest was adamant in its decision and there wasn't a chance Violet could change its mind, so she collected up the two heavy hessian sacks and hauled them over the water, careful not to wet them. As she placed them on the frozen ground, she realized her efforts had been in vain. The snow melted into the fabric, depleting all the attempts she had made to keep them dry. Undeterred and undefeated, Violet gripped the sacks. Her knuckles turned as white as the snow, the weight of her belongings struggling against her grasp.

Dusty footprints, as reminders of her presence, walked across the cabin floor. The single violet in a vase stood lonely on the table. There were no other traces of movements, life, or of hope. It seemed foolish to hope but, still, she did. She longed to find something that told her Emil was real; that it wasn't just a dream.

Dust clung to the hessian fabric as she placed the sacks down on the floor. Her arms seemed to almost float, briefly, as she let them go, noticing the release in the weight that had been pulling them down. The curtains swayed as a breeze brushed against them. The sunlight flickered between the gap; dust motes danced in its glow. Violet reached towards the curtains, pulling them wide open. She raised her arm to cover her eyes as the light flooded her vision.

Stepping out from its glare, she placed her arm by her side once more, carefully studying the furniture that filled the room. There was a small bedside cupboard that she hadn't noticed before. A stormy grey wood with a rough, beaten appearance, as though rot had taken root from the damp swept in with the cold. The small door drooped where the bottom hinge had worked itself loose. There was no handle, just a hole where it had once been. She placed her finger into the hole and hooked it until she had enough grip, then tugged. The door popped open.

Carefully, she extracted each item from the sacks. One by one, she placed them inside the tired-looking cupboard. 'Old items for an old cupboard' she smiled to herself, 'but they are all mine. A new start.'

As she worked, the fire in the hearth warmed the cabin. She pushed away the memory of Emil as she listened to the popping and crackling as the flames writhed upon the timber. The taught tug at her heart of her feelings for him surfaced, beautiful yet agony with his absence.

The daylight had faded into dusk when she finally ceased her chores. She sat on the bed, creasing the fresh, untouched linen beneath the blankets. Her stomach rumbled as her teeth bit into the apple, plucked directly from the tree on her journey there. A small token, the forest offered her, simple yet precious.

Violet eased herself back onto the bed. The flock mattress pushed against her spine like firm hands, soothing away some of her pain. The pillow felt thin under her head, something hard beneath it. She slid her hand underneath its cool dry texture, her hands searching for purchase of the mystery object. Her fingers brushed against long edges and protruding corners. It feels like a book, Violet thought, as she lazily dragged the item out with one hand. She gasped; her breath lodged in her throat. Between her fingers she held, as she had suspected, a book. It was not just any book; it was a replica of the one Emil had gifted to her. Its deep chocolate cover was unmistakable. The exquisite gilded finish shone against the light of the fire.

Her hands trembling, afraid to believe the impossible, she turned the front cover over, and there on the first page was a message:

Dearest Violet,
With Much Affection
Your Emil

'He's real!' her mind screamed. 'He has to be real!'

16

Emil sat in the parlour, a newspaper held high, covering his face, attempting to read the daily news. He read and re-read sentences as his stomach roiled with nerves, distracting him. Time ticked loudly upon the wall. A large brass clock glared down at him. The wait was debilitating.

"Ah, Rosie," he smiled, as the gentle woman entered the room, "Have you seen Violet this morning?"

"Not this morning, duck," she replied. Her brow furrowed. "She should be here by now. Don't you worry, I'll fetch her."

"Thank you, Rosie."

Rosie trotted out of the room. The poor girl must have overslept, she thought, exhausted from their day out yesterday, or, perhaps, it was just a simple error of the maid who may have forgotten to wake her.

Rosie scrunched the fabric of her skirts in her fists, hoisting it above the toes of her boots. Her skirts had got the better of her on many occasions, frightening her as she'd catch the tips of her boots in the hems followed by a tumble of her ankle or a twist at the knee, but 'not today!', she thought.

Outside Violet's room, she held her breath, listening for any sounds of movement from within. She knocked several times on the door, but her knocking proved only to be fruitless. The rapping of her knuckles against the wood met with nothing but the sound of her own breath and the swish of her cotton dress sleeves.

Rosie pushed against the cold, flat surface of the door. It creaked open at her touch.

"Violet, duck?" she cooed, "Are you awake?"

No answer.

"Violet?" she cooed, again.

Silence, not even the rasp of slumber. Curtains covered the windows as though the night continued within the room, ignoring the day beckoning beyond the glass. The darkness flooded the room with deep shadows and mysterious shapes. Rosie's eyes adjusted to the gloom as she crept toward the window, where she drew back the curtains.

The sunshine washed away the deep shades of black and grey, pushing them into the corners and under the bed, throwing light into the richly decorated room. Rosie turned on her heel, happy, and expectant to see Violet tucked up, warm, under the blankets, but the bed lay empty and cold. The bedclothes lay ruffled, strewn carelessly, where her body once rested, but Violet was nowhere to be seen. A thread of panic tickled Rosie's chest. Her eyes darted, briefly, toward every corner, and every wall, of the young woman's chambers, wondering whether she had failed to see Violet the first time she'd looked. There were no traces of her anywhere; no clues to where she might be. Hurriedly, Rosie made her way out of the room and down to the kitchen.

"Have you seen Violet?" she panted, staring at the young cook's back. Rosie leaned against the wall, trying to catch her breath.

"No, Ma'am." replied the cook. The steam billowed from the kettle as the boiled water trickled into the teapot and soaked the tea. "I ain't seen her or 'eard her at all this morning."

"Oh, good grief." Rosie whimpered, fraught with worry.

"Can I 'elp at all, Ma'am?"

The house was of a fairly generous size, large enough for one to get lost in. Rosie crossed her fingers, hoping Violet had taken it upon herself to explore the many rooms it held, and would show up at any minute. The grim possibility of having to tell Emil that the young woman had vanished made her shudder, not of fear, but of dread of seeing the disappointment upon his face. He seemed more merry and light-hearted since Violet's arrival, and it had lifted her heart to see him that way.

"Right, you check the gardens," she ordered the cook, not unkindly, "and I'll check the library."

"Right you are, Ma'am!"

Rosie and the young woman parted company, searching their designated areas. The back garden was quite small, requiring no more than a glance from the doorway. The library was a little larger but needed only a few minutes of perusing; Corridors, abandoned; Other rooms, untouched.

Rosie's stomach knotted with anxiety. She was at a loss as to where Violet could be. Words tumbled, and tripped, over themselves in her head, trying to find the right ones to tell Emil the news in the kindest, and most considerate, way possible. Rapid swirls of nausea spiraled inside her. There was no easy way to deliver such news, she thought, absent-mindedly chewing at the tips of her fingernails. She huffed loudly. There was nothing more she could do. There was no use in delaying the inevitable any longer.

The detailed carving on the parlour doors curled and stretched, teasing her as she stared at it. She closed her eyes, steadying her nerves in preparation for what the next few moments would hold. Taking a short sharp intake of air, she turned the brass knob, and then quickly exhaled.

"Violet?" Emil called, hopeful.

"Sorry Emil, it's only me." Rosie responded quietly, stepping further into the room.

As she stood in front of the young master, he eyed her composure. He thought it unlike Rosie to be as quiet as she was. The subtle slouch in her shoulders as she curled in on herself, and the twiddling of her fingers, did not offer him much hope of good news.

Emil was reluctant to enquire further, fearful of the answer he knew would come. The unspoken words hung in the air, unwanted like a pungent odour.

"She has gone, hasn't she?" he asked. The colour of his face drained; The light in his eyes dimmed.

"Yes." Rosie shuffled on her feet, looking down at them. A terrible pang of guilt twanged at her heart to deliver such a cruel blow to the young man.

"Did she leave a letter or say why she was leaving?"

"No," Rosie began, "but that's the thing, Emil, I don't think she just left." Her eyes were now cast upon him, searching for the light he held for the young woman.

"What do you mean? How can she not leave yet be nowhere to be found?" Emil looked perplexed at the woman's statement. "How could Violet be gone if she had not left the house, Rosie?" he said, reiterating his question another way.

"Well, her bed is as though she slept in it. Her bedclothes, dishevelled; curtains were closed; and the chamber door shut tight. No one saw, or even heard, her leave. We would surely have heard her movements."

"That's impossible!" Emil snapped. He did not mean to be so abrupt with Rosie, but the ache in his chest was uncomfortable, stubborn, pushing vehemently against the struggling pulse of his heart.

The young man screwed his eyes shut and buried the tension on his face in the palms of his hands. His elbows propped on the table. He focused on his breaths, pushing back into his face in small puffs of warm, moist air, as he stared into the darkness behind his eyes. Violet's face painted across his memory, reminding him of how they had met. It then dawned on him that if she had just appeared in his home, then perhaps she could have just disappeared, too. The idea would, once upon a time, have sounded ridiculous and utterly implausible to him. He would have laughed at such a foolish suggestion but, the more he thought it over, the more it made sense. Her smile, the laughter, the way she looked at him? She could not have chosen to leave... She would not have chosen to leave. "She would never have returned to her grandmother." he mumbled.

"Pardon?" Rosie asked.

"She would not have returned to her grandmother," Emil announced, louder this time. "There was nothing there for her except misery. You are right, Rosie, she did not leave us. Think about it! She just appeared here. None of us know where from. That means the opposite is also possible, does it not? That she may just disappear? Which, in turn, would mean that she may also appear again."

The chair slid across the floor toward the bookcase, behind the table, as the back of his legs pushed against it until he had found his feet. "I must get everything prepared for when she returns."

Rosie watched Emil stride out of the parlour. She felt admiration, blemished with pity, as she watched him fight back his sadness with the hope of Violet's return.

"I will be back later." he called and stepped out into the world. All Rosie could do was watch him leave.

Emil walked that morning, a carriage ride would only

hurry his endeavour. He needed time alone, in abundance, to gather the chaos of his thoughts and emotions as they fought amongst themselves. A walk would give him the time to sort through them and put them all in order so he could think more clearly.

The autumn sun hung low in the sky. The trees were scantily clad with leaves that burned a brilliant shade of red against the golden orb. Emil's feet kicked at the myriad of crisp, rustic, orange leaves, sliding slowly along the path as the wind blew movement into their seasonal dance. He pushed the notion that he would never see Violet again, far back into the darkest depths of his mind. It would not do to dwell on such negative thoughts, he told himself. He refused to relinquish all hope, for, if he did, he feared his heart may snap in two. Falling in love with her had been simple. Letting her go was unthinkable. He had never known a woman like her before, and he knew he would never meet one like her again. As a breeze swept across his face, he silently prayed for her to return.

17

"Emil!" came a cry. A female voice she recognized. "Emil, come quick!" It was Rosie.

Violet's eyes shot open, exhilarated to hear her familiar melody once again. She was back. Tears of happiness pricked her eyes; her breaths, squeezed in and out of her chest amongst the excitement fizzing there. A smile stretched wide across her face until her jaw ached as Rosie stepped back into her chambers.

"Hello, duck!" Rosie beamed. "We thought we'd lost you for good." The woman sniffed, blotting away a tear. "We were so worried."

"Oh, Rosie, I thought you were all a dream." Violet replied, "I felt utterly lost without you."

"We're no dream, Missy." she smiled, "We are as real as you are. Besides, you ain't getting rid of us that easily." she chuckled.

"I never want to get rid of you, not ever!" Violet replied. She wiped away her own escaped happy tear at the sound of a gentle knock on the door.

"That will be Emil." Rosie said, "He's been trying to be so positive that you would come back, but I know it's been hard for him, poor lad."

"Violet?" Emil's voice drifted through the gap in the door.

"Just one minute!" she called, standing in her old, tattered nightclothes. "Rosie, please can you help me?" she asked, gesturing to her clothes.

"I know the perfect dress!" she replied, turning to the wardrobe.

"I'm so sorry I left you both." Violet apologized.

"What are you saying sorry for?"

"You said that Emil..."

Rosie turned from the wardrobe to face Violet. "Oh, I didn't mean it like that, duck," she said, cupping the young woman's face in her hands. "Now you listen here. You're a good girl, Violet. Any fool can see that. Don't you go feeling any guilt over what you can't control. I only said that because I want you to know that Emil thinks the world of you. Nothing more than that, duck."

"Now let's get you dressed."

Violet emerged in cerulean blue, roses weaved like vines from the hem of her skirts to her lace-trimmed neckline and up over her shoulders. Her chestnut curls, loose, flowing freely down her back. Long, silk ivory gloves stretched from her fingertips to just below her elbows.

Emil's mouth fell open as she stepped out onto the landing. Words snatched from him as his eyes fell upon the young woman. The dress looked beautiful in the shop, but on Violet, it was far beyond that. She was dazzling, he thought. She was more glorious than the roses woven upon her attire. Her eyes sparkled more brilliantly than the brightest star in the night sky. Emil lost himself in them. He did not speak. His gaze was soft, and revealing of his admiration for her. Violet blushed under the warmth of the looks passed between them.

"Thank you for the beautiful dress." she whispered, "It was extremely kind of you."

"No, thank you, Violet. It gave me the distraction I desperately needed." Emil replied, "I was afraid you wouldn't return, so anything that would fill my time was a blessing. The dress allowed me to believe you would come back."

Emil gently took her hand and pulled her close in an embrace, kissing her chestnut crown. A fusion of bergamot and lavender filled Violet's senses as she stood in his shadow. "I am very glad to be back." she whispered against the hardness of his chest.

As the clack of horseshoes upon stone came to a halt, so, too, did the carriage. Violet peered out of the window, her eyes wide and her mouth agape at the size, elegance, and majestic air of the building. Its dome-like structure stretched for miles. A grand arch welcomed guests as a sweet symphony bled out onto the streets. A frieze stretched the hall's circumference, illustrating offerings from all over the world. The building looked young, clean, and vibrant, much like its guests as they streamed into its belly. Violet felt positively tiny in comparison as she stepped out onto the cobbles in front of its giant structure.

Emil, ever the gentleman, held her hand. His hair, the colour of midnight under the moonlight, gleamed like silk in its glow. The shadows of the night sharpened his jawline like an artist perfecting their work. Wisp-like shivers tickled her skin at his magnificence.

Violet could not remember a time when she had seen so many people all at once. The hall was teeming with finely dressed men and women. Their warm bodies bustling amongst one another, all focused on where they were trying to get to. Her grip on Emil's arm tightened, making their way deeper into the throng.

A young woman, dressed in carmine red, flowed on her partner's arm; a rose nestled in her auburn curls, and her skin kissed by the sun. Another woman in Sapphire blue, onyx black hair, olive skin with eyes as blue as the ocean, curtseyed to a gentleman who eyed her keenly. Two women gazed lovingly at one another; one tall, with hair like ribbons of gold; the other, curvaceous with hair as deep as mahogany. A kiss snatched between them as they giggled and blushed, the invisible barrier forever broken. Love is beautiful, Violet thought. It gave her a sense of peace, allowing her to relax amongst the crowds.

As Violet took in the individuality of as many of the guests as possible, the crowd seemed to disperse. The room appeared larger; her breathing was less capricious as they drifted further in. The striking chandeliers glimmered overhead, perfectly apt as they hung poised above the gathering of men and women flowing with finery to the music. Diamonds adorned the necks of women as though the stars had settled there to rest.

Violet felt clumsy as she tried to keep in step with Emil. The click of her shoes upon the marble floor was lost in the chatter and song. She had never danced before, yet her body absorbed the melody, seemingly to unlock her rhythm. She was thankful, for it allowed her an ounce of dignity despite losing count of how many times she had stepped upon Emil's toes.

Violet's hand brushed against Emil's chest as he pulled her closer. With one hand, Emil clutched hers, his other rested upon the small of her back. His touch, warm on her spine, reminded her of how it curved and twisted a few inches from his thumb. Her body stiffened. She felt exposed under his touch. Heat grew in her chest, somewhere between fear and shame. But as his hand caressed along the path of her vertebrae, and lingered upon the area she detested the most, his forehead rested upon hers. "You are perfect." he whispered. The heat in Violet's heart subsided as she let his words sink in. Tears threatened to spill as she allowed herself to believe him, to believe in herself.

The gold, red, and ivory of the room blurred as Emil spun Violet around, then pulled her back in. The scent of orange blossoms in her hair was intoxicating, Emil thought, as her head rested upon his chest. He wished to escape the crowds and take Violet with him. His heart thudded beneath his ribcage. He never wanted to let her go.

As the music died, he led her through the people and

away from the floor.

"Where are we going?" she asked. Her feet took two steps to a single one of his as she tried to keep up.

"Do you feel that, Violet?" he asked as they stepped out into the open air. Stars burst through the bruised black sky, eager to watch the night unfold.

The glossy exterior of parked carriages mirrored their beauty. The cool breeze rushed over the bridge, engulfing them. Violet noted the stark contrast between the cool night air of autumn and the humidity of the hall. The air folded around them. It's chill, wonderfully soothing.

"It feels wonderful!" Violet sucked in the crisp, clean air, raising her head to the night sky. The wind tickled her skin. As she closed her eyes, she listened to the sweet sound of the violin floating softly from the hall, the music greeting all who cared to listen.

"Walk with me, Violet." Emil pleaded, offering his arm. "It is a marvellous evening, too marvellous to be missed."

Emil and Violet walked side by side, fingers laced together as they took in the scenery. Lamplights burned bright as they wandered the paths of London. A lamplighter passed them by, whistling merrily to himself. The young man lifted his cap, "Evening!" he called. A knowledgeable smile of the couple's bond stretched from one ear to another across his face; a wink punctuated the end.

Quiet swept the street in the absence of others. Their conversation swept away with it. Emil stopped and turned to face Violet. "Violet, I..." he started. He thought it would be easy, but the words were stuck on the tip of his tongue. He scratched the back of his neck awkwardly, then took a deep breath. A cat's tail coiled around Emil's leg, distracting him. The cat's head nudged against his shin; his body weaved between where the young couple stood. The black, grey, and beige stripes of the cat's fur rippled as he prowled lovingly around them.

As the cat strolled away contently, Emil and Violet turned their attention back, once again, to each other. Eyes locked, waiting for the other to speak. Emil moved towards her. She could feel the warmth of his body radiating against her skin. She breathed in the fragrance of his cologne, his body close. Violet's breath hitched as the tip of his nose met hers. He traced it over her cheek, his lips hovered over her ear. "I love you, Violet." he breathed, his whisper running its gentle fingers down her neck, "I think I've always loved you." Flutters of desire caressed Violet's skin, her throat dry with emotion. "I love you, too." she replied, her breathing ragged.

Gently, Emil placed his thumb and forefinger on her chin and tilted it upward so that her gaze met his. His green eyes hungrily absorbed every inch of her face and lingered on her lips. The brush of his fingertips ran steadily along her jawline and caressed behind her ear. The palm of his hand rested at the back of her neck. His fingers weaved within the strands of her hair as his chest rose and fell in exaggerated bursts. Their bodies moved closer. Electricity bristled at the brush of his lips against hers. An explosion of sparks fizzed, exploring her flesh.

Violet's body trembled; his touch intoxicating. All Violet's inhibitions faded away; her mind and body, swept up in the moment. Everything she never knew she had wanted was right there in that glorious pocket of time. Her heart soared with ecstasy as the world around her ceased to exist.

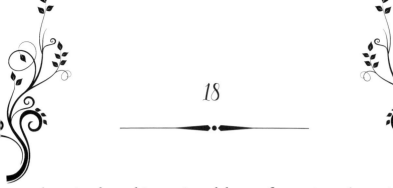

18

Alone in the cabin, stripped bare of security, plunged deep into the world she hated. Violet had been ripped from Emil's arms, her hopes and dreams cast into the shadows. She slammed her fists down into the subtle softness of the mattress in unbridled frustration, clueless of how to get back to Emil, not even knowing whether it was a possibility. She cursed fate as he waggled his finger in her face, taunting her with his secrets and power.

Violet stared at the ceiling as though it was fate, himself. A stand-off between them. A battle of wills. Violet fighting for her right to return to Emil. She despised the vast, impassable void between them. Time was the only path she appeared to tread, but never the same distance with its turns, swoops, and sudden drops beneath her feet. She hugged the book to her chest, pulling the memory of Emil close to her. It reminded her he, and the world she had visited under the cover of night, were as real as the object in her arms. 'Perhaps this is the nightmare.' she sighed, 'My very own personal nightmare. Perhaps Emil is where I should have been all this time?'

Violet rolled onto her side and curled into a ball. An

emotional bruise bled in her stomach, dripping with grief. The gap between her and the man who had stolen her heart widened by the waking hours.

Violet refused to move from under the blankets for the rest of the day, other than to agitate the dying embers in the hearth. The grip of sadness was strong and unrelenting. Thoughts of Emil whittled away her time alone until a tidal wave of sleep washed over her, taking her home.

Emil's jawline appeared sharper. His forlorn features, dotted with stubble. Shadows darkened the crescents beneath his eyes. His posture slumped defeated in a chair. To Violet, she had only been gone for one day, but the man sitting at the table told a story of prolonged loss.

Violet pushed the door open, inching forward. Her tread was soft upon the floor. The same waistcoat he had worn the first day they'd met hung loosely over Emil's shoulders. "Emil," she called, her voice drifting into the room.

Emil turned quickly. His eyes were wary, as though he'd stared into the brilliance of the sun. He studied Violet, wondering whether grief had snatched his sanity from him. Three weeks had passed with not so much as a whisper. She had vanished without a trace. He had never wanted to lose hope of seeing her again - the guilt of it riddled him - but each day his destiny appeared to mould and squeeze into that particular, dreaded, unwanted prospect as it dragged him down with it. She had been slipping through his fingers like sand between the throat of an hourglass.

"Violet? Is that you?" he asked, getting to his feet.

"Yes, Emil. How long have I been away?" she muttered, assessing the distress apparent upon his face.

"It has been weeks, my love." he replied, moving closer to her.

"How can that be?" she pondered aloud. "It has not even been an entire day for me." Her fingers twisted the fabric, pinched between their tips. It didn't make any sense. Fate was toying with them with its cruel, twisted games.

"If I am honest, Violet, I do not understand any of this either, other than I am relieved and overjoyed at your return. All I have ever been able to do, in your absence, is pray that you would find your way home to me and, when you do, you will never leave again."

Claws dragged and pinched at Violet's heart as she listened. Guilt struck her despite her innocence in it all. She quickened her steps, hurrying to embrace him.

"I'm so sorry," she said, wrapping her arms around his neck. "I promise, I do not choose to leave you. I would never leave at all, but I do not know how I am to stay here. This is as much a mystery to me as it is to you."

Emil pulled her close, his cheek against hers. His hands slipped firmly across her back and down to her waist. His face nestled into her neck as he breathed her in. "You must not feel sorry, Violet. I know you would not just leave me. Let us be glad you are home now, and for however long the heavens allow. Let us not waste a moment." Emil smiled, taking her hand, and leading her out of the room.

"Ah, good evening, Sir!" A tall, sombre man filled every inch of the doorway. Both hands cloaked in white gloves. One hand spread beneath a silver tray as it balanced upon his touch. The other hand, tucked neatly behind his back. A jet-black suit tapered from his broad shoulders, narrowing gradually, to the hem of his trousers that swung over the tops of his buffed leather shoes. The colour and fit of his clothes exaggerated his height as he peered down his nose at Emil and Violet.

"Good evening, Charles. I apologise for our tardiness."

"Not to worry, Sir." Charles began, "Truth be told, the cook is quite relieved you are a little later than planned."

"Oh, why is that?" Emil asked, puzzled.

"She burnt the cake, sir." The corner of Charles' mouth twitched as he released his thick cockney laugh. He cleared his throat, correcting himself, regaining control of his restrained upper-class British drawl.

Emil grinned secretly to himself as he, and Violet, stepped over the threshold of the grand manor. He was as fond of Charles as he was of Rosie. Both of whom were, coincidentally, married to each other. His grandmother, although she had played her role as a strict, wealthy lady perfectly, found the odd slip of Charles' authentic voice quite amusing. She paid no heed to it in the man's presence, letting Charles believe she had not noticed the minor cracks in his well-rehearsed act. The game tickled her as she chuckled to herself behind closed doors and out of earshot as soon as he exited the room.

Charles and Rosie had always been in Emil's life, as much as his grandmother had been. He remembered little of his mother and father. They had hardly played any part in his upbringing, and their time with him faded with every year as he grew. He could never quite decipher whether he resented their absence or whether he was grateful for it. Surely, the memories he now held would be nothing but stale thoughts of a stranger if they had played their supposed roles. The very idea bothered him greatly, for with his parents in his life, he would never have had the wonderful memories with his grandmother, Rosie, and Charles and he knew he wouldn't change a single moment.

Violet's boots clacked against the polished wooden floor. Golden mist clouded the surface of the chandelier, dangling over their heads. The staircase coiled up like a giant snake, twisting and turning, reaching higher floors. A pair of Royal Vienna vases rested regally on display. Their bases perched on either side of an ashen-black brass clock. Eyes pierced the hallway from a painted portrait, a woman with a young boy at her side. Two faces loomed down on to all those who entered, watchful and intrigued. The peridot green irises and the ink-black hair of the young boy revealed his identity with clarity. The woman was much older, perhaps in her fifties, but the deep black silken chignon had yet to fade. This was the first glimpse of Emil's grandmother Violet had so far. She looked a kind woman, she thought. Laughter lines softened the intensity of her gaze. The delicate blush of pink resting, for eternity, upon the apples of her cheeks.

"Would you like some Champagne, Miss?" Charles asked, lowering the silver tray.

In all her twenty years, Violet had only tasted two drinks, water and tea. The thought of trying something new thrilled her. She gently wrapped her delicate fingers around the fluted glass and lifted it from the tray.

"Thank you." she rasped as she twisted the glass, studying its contents. Tiny, busy bubbles danced within the golden liquid. They popped against the tip of her nose as she sipped warily. A bitter taste tingled on her tongue. She was not sure whether it was pleasant or simply vile. The decision seemed to hang patiently between the two options. Emil chuckled to himself as Violet tried to soften her expression of disgust at the flavour. She was desperate not to offend, fearing it would portray a dreadful first impression to the family of the man she thought so much of. "It is an acquired taste, my love. Do not worry, you will not offend anyone here if it is not to your liking." he assured her, his fingers laced between hers.

"No, really, it's lovely." she lied, but, as the mischief dancing in Emil's eyes coaxed out the truth, she couldn't help but relent. "I'm so sorry." Violet said, handing the glass back to Charles. Her face and neck, pink from the awkward truth.

"Do not concern yourself, Miss. I am more of an ale man me-self." he smiled, then coughed to clear his throat to start over, "One means, one is not partial to champagne either." he drawled, winking at her.

Rosie and Charles were like tea and biscuits. One without the other was never quite the same. Both oozed such kindness and warmth. She imagined how they must be in their own home. The comfortable silences and cosy evenings together. She dearly hoped it would one day be the same for her and Emil.

Violet consciously lowered her shoulders and directly faced Emil's grandmother. Silently, she berated herself for trying to hide the only body she had. She could not hide it forever, but that critical voice of shame in her head would not leave her alone. As if sensing her fears, Emil squeezed her hand.

"Grandmother, this is Violet." Emil said, introducing them to each other. The lady smiled warmly. Her eyes were as gentle as the painting had portrayed. At her feet, a small King Charles Cavalier sat. Her tail beat against the chair with the excitement of new guests.

"It is a pleasure to meet you dear girl." she began, "This is Maizie." she said, stroking the dog behind her ears. "We have heard such wonderful things about you."

Mrs. Meriwether continued addressing Violet as she walked over and wrapped both of her hands around Violet's, gesturing for her to take a seat. Emil blushed at his grandmother's confession. Violet glanced at him, a smile tugging at the corners of her mouth.

Maizie toddled over, tail wagging profusely as it beat against the furniture. The little dog's behind wiggled, curling to the right as she walked excitedly toward their new guest and sat firmly on the toes of Violet's boots, fearing her new friend may up and leave. Violet tickled Maizie's chin and gently caressed her soft floppy ears while her large brown eyes looked up lovingly.

"I believe you have Maizie's approval and, of course, she is my esteemed advisor. I rely solely on her opinion." Mrs. Meriwether beamed as Violet relaxed in their company.

Violet had expected the manor to feel more formal. The living room was much smaller than she'd imagined, and the décor felt welcoming. Flames danced in the hearth. A brass bucket filled with coal sat beside it. A mirror hung over the mantel, adding more depth to the room. The sofa complimented the shade of the carpet and of the walls, a plush sage against a luxurious and rich forest green. The small table sat in the middle of a large rug, decorated with a bone china tea service. A deep midnight blue surrounded the floral design encapsulated in a gold cloud upon the teapot.

Violet shifted in her seat, one foot buried under the weight of Maizie. The little dog was determined not to be moved. Emil passed Violet a steaming hot cup of tea. 'This drink I am safe with.' she thought, remembering the champagne. The hot liquid swam gloriously down her throat.

Mrs. Meriwether was glowing, Violet thought, as the woman reminisced, enthusiastically, about Emil's childhood.

"Really Grandmother, do we have to bore poor Violet with such stories?" Emil blushed.

"I love listening to your grandmother." Violet teased. Her eyes glittered playfully as a wicked look simmered on their surface. She encouraged Mrs. Meriwether to recall more of her memories.

At Violet's side, Emil shrank further into his seat, calmly melting into the joyful conversation. It flowed as fluently as the tea. Cups of tea, filled to the brim, were supped; slices of decadent, rich cake, consumed. Maizie lapped up the crumbs fallen at Violet's feet. Her sweet, short, repetitive snorts amused Violet as she watched her hunt between the fibres of the carpet for more.

Emil's grandmother was the exact opposite of her own, Violet thought. The differences between them were clear and sharply defined. Mrs. Meriwether was everything a grandmother should be, while Mrs. Bainbridge was the leading example of what a grandmother should not be. It was a sad confirmation of her grandmother's spiteful ways, yet it did not deter her from spending time with Mrs. Meriwether again. It had been a glorious and refreshing experience.

"Thank you for inviting me." Violet smiled.

Mrs. Meriwether pulled her toward her in a warm embrace. She kissed her sweetly on the cheek. "It was an absolute pleasure to meet you, Violet." Mrs. Meriwether replied, "I do hope you will visit us again."

"I would love to." Violet beamed, overjoyed at the invite.

Mrs. Meriwether gently squeezed Violet's hand, then turned to Emil, "Darling, please could you escort Charles to yours? It is getting rather late. He and Rosie will be much safer walking home together."

"Yes, of course." Emil smiled.

The clock ticked loudly in the hallway as Rosie and Charles bid Emil and Violet goodnight, closing the front door behind them.

Wind whistled under the door, bringing with it an icy chill, signalling the turn of the season. The sound of Emil's feet shuffling nervously brushed against the floor. The cook had retired to her dwellings, leaving them with only each other as company.

The night was present. Emil's thoughts were frantic. He was terrified Violet would disappear again. Her soft hands brushed against his to calm him. Their fingers entwined. Emil exhaled, slow and deep. He didn't want to wait any longer. There may not be another time, he thought. Slowly, he lowered himself onto his left knee.

"Violet..." he began, as he fumbled in his pocket and pulled out a small box. The box creaked open as he pulled up the lid to reveal a sparkling green sapphire ring. "Violet, I can't describe how much I love you. I want to spend the rest of my life with you. With that being said, I want to ask you one thing... Violet Hall, please, will you marry me?" he asked.

Violet noted the air of nerves that ran through him. They seemed to replicate her own. Their hearts raced in unison. "Yes! Yes!" she cried.

Emil slipped the ring onto her finger, then wrapped her in his arms. All she had to do now was stay.

19

Impatience leaked in bitter drops of poison from her mind into her blood, seeping into every cell as they rushed through her veins, rumbling against her bones. Two days of unnecessary frivolities had passed, and the time had seemed to drag tremendously. Irritation scraped against her insides with every movement she made. A deep lust for money preoccupied the woman's thoughts, knowing she could soon be a much wealthier woman. This Mr. Carson had the means to change her life, her financial status, and give her the freedom she craved from the granddaughter she despised. No matter the effort she applied, she could not shake these delicious thoughts. They were as loyal to her as her own shadow.

Conversations played out around her, drowned out by the internal dialogue, isolating her entirely. This did not perplex her, but the tedium of waiting did. She chewed at the inside of her cheek; the pain anchoring her to the reins of control of the mask she'd created over the years.

She bit back her desire to tell Isabelle to hush. The young woman had begun to vex her. The pitch of her voice, like needles pricking at the old woman's ears. She did not want to jeopardize the bond they had by revealing her true nature. Unlike her feelings for Violet, she truly loved Isabelle. She would not let her mask slip, not even once. So, on the morning of the third day, she feigned a migraine, skipped breakfast in the dining room, and refused all visitors. Her granddaughter had tried to see her, but the old woman replied with an exaggerated whimper, complaining of the pain, although she'd assured the young woman she would be 'perfectly fine within a few hours'.

Time passed slowly in her chambers, her pacing footsteps muffled by the rug beneath them. Mrs. Bainbridge's pale knuckles clutched, possessively, at the lithograph until it crumpled within her fingers. The ticking of the clock resounded heavily amid the silence, inching slowly toward three o'clock.

When the hour finally arrived, the maid tiptoed nervously around Mrs. Bainbridge, assisting the woman with her ablutions and preparing her for the evening ahead. As the maid was finishing her duties, the soft rapping of knuckles upon the old woman's chamber door interrupted them.

"Come in!" Mrs. Bainbridge sang.

Isabelle entered, looking surprised at her grandmother's miraculous recovery. "Are you feeling better now, Grandmama?" she asked. She leaned over and kissed the old woman on the cheek.

"Yes, thank you darling." she smiled.

Mrs. Bainbridge picked up her reticule and placed a

handkerchief inside. She had generously laced the cotton cloth with lavender oil, a perfect remedy for foul odours. She could only guess at the intensity of the terrible stink she would face in a place teeming with curiosities and poorer folk.

"Are you leaving us, Grandmama?" Isabelle asked, watching the woman busy about her chambers.

"My dear friend Barbara has invited me to supper." she lied, turning to meet her granddaughter's questioning gaze. Mrs. Bainbridge's posture demanded trust, yet she still searched Isabelle's face to find it. "You don't mind, do you, darling? It's just that it has been many years since I have seen her, and it would be so lovely to catch up."

"No, of course not. I hope you have a lovely time, Grandmama. You will be back though, won't you?"

"Of course, my darling. Do not fret about that. It is just supper."

Isabelle breathed a sigh of relief. The strain of their relationship the past two days had been apparent, although she had not spoken of it for fear of upsetting the woman. She suspected the migraine was her grandmother's not-so-subtle method of avoidance, but she did not like to think that the woman would lie to her.

"I shall leave you to it, Grandmama. I hope you have a lovely evening."

"Thank you, darling." the old woman crooned.

As the door clicked behind Isabelle, Mrs. Bainbridge smiled with satisfaction at the ease of the lies she had told.

Violet's grandmother's lips pinched, puckering at the edges, as she pushed through the crowds. She held her head high, peering down her nose at the men and women, who seemed to invade every inch of proximity. The heat of their bodies bristled the fine hairs on her arms. A man's hot sour breath huffed on the side of her face. She scrubbed at the repulsive, invisible, moist blemish he had left on her skin, but, no matter how much she scraped with the rough fabric, she could still feel him. His touch angered her. Mrs. Bainbridge scowled, drawing her arms across her body.

The circus crowd jostled the less wealthy around, while the gentry waded through unscathed. Top hats and colourful, rich fabrics lost in a sea of browns, greys, and ivory. Men walked proudly in their flat caps, dark coats, trousers, off-white shirts, and ties. The women wore their best dresses, hiding years of repair, with their bonnets they saved only for Sunday church and occasions such as this. Mrs. Bainbridge clutched her reticule tightly, assuming the merry crowd was there to rid her of her possessions.

The promise of steaming hot, thick-cut chips drifted out into the chilled grey evening. The heat of the stall offered comfort against the harsh whip of the breeze as the crowd patiently formed a queue. One by one, the vendor tucked the food into parcels of newspaper, cravings fulfilled in exchange for coins.

A man on towering stilts loomed over the excited crowd, walking precariously among the people. Children ran beside him, demanding answers as to how he could be so tall. A young man threw down a hammer, attempting to impress his fiancée. The metal clanged against the bell at the top, signalling his strength.

The crowd slowed. Mrs. Bainbridge stared at her desired destination, 'Carson's Creatures of Curiosity'. A large tent of red and white stripes sprawled over the land. The filthy black smudges of soot across the canvas dirtied the colours.

At the left of the entrance, their idea of entertainment stretched across a stage. A sign with the words 'Strange People' emblazoned in bold font across it. Mrs. Bainbridge eyed the people standing on the make-shift display. She studied them from the tips of their toes, searching upwards over every inch like they were nothing more than simple ornaments perched on a table. Her face contorted with every ignorant thought. Their bodily differences incited sniggers of disgust. She failed to see the dark curtains of humiliation that fell over their faces; the trembling as the young lady with dwarfism felt exposed in her compulsory, mocking costume. To the audience, these were not people, they were just things. Fingers pointed at them, mouths agape as guests pushed through the heavy fabric doors and disappeared.

Violet's grandmother perched her bottom on a seat. Her skirts filled out enough space for three. She preferred it that way because, with two practically empty seats on either side of her, it discouraged further human contact than was necessary.

"Mama, the lady's dress is on my seat!" a little girl whimpered loudly, but Mrs. Bainbridge ignored her. She shot a threatening look at the mother, who quickly grabbed her little girl.

"You can sit on my lap, darling." the mother assured her daughter.

Once the child had settled, Violet's grandmother returned her attention to the stage. The tent teemed with excited onlookers. Some had to stand, but she would not relinquish the seats her skirts had claimed. Children's heads peeked under the circus tent, trying to watch without parting with coins. Bodies stretched to see over the tops of tall hats. It was chaos, but as the acts began, silence reigned over the people.

The young woman with dwarfism she had seen outside was the first to stand under the intense glare of others. They paraded her around the arena, for all to see, on the back of an elephant. Both looked exhausted, yet the crowd cheered for more. Some were excited where others screamed words such as 'Freak!' The young woman closed her eyes, placing her trust in the elephant, her faithful companion, beneath her. The darkness hid the tear that trailed from the corner of her eye.

As the night wore on, Mrs. Bainbridge grew ever more excited with her plan. The show was perfect for Violet. She was sure Mr. Carson would wish to buy her. The old woman fidgeted with overjoyed anticipation. Her manner practically mirrored the children as they watched fire being consumed, clowns juggling, and a young man with hair that grew over his face. They had cruelly named him 'The Dog-Faced Boy' and stripped him of his identity.

When the last act was complete and the people made their way out, she waited patiently for Mr. Carson.

"Excuse me, Mr. Carson!" she called, watching the man pack away the apparatus from the show. He looked up and scanned the tent. The light from the torch flames blurred his vision.

"Over here!" she sang, sweetly.

"Err Can I 'elp ya?!" he asked. He looked her up and down as she came closer, wondering why a woman so finely dressed would want to converse with him.

"Yes, but it is a rather delicate matter." she whispered, nodding her head toward the others who loitered nearby. She did not want them to hear what she had to say. This transaction was to be swift and secretive.

Mr. Carson's wagon rocked as they stepped up into it. He cleared away the clutter and brushed down a seat, gesturing for her to sit.

"No, thank you." Mrs. Bainbridge said, rebuffing his generosity. There was no time for such informalities. "I have come here today," she sniffed, eyeing the mess that surrounded her, "to offer you something that I believe you will not be able to resist."

The man's eyes widened at her confidence. What on God's earth could this woman have that he could want? he thought. She was much older than he was. In fact, she was well beyond his years. Her wealth was the only attractive thing about her, he'd thought.

As if she had read his mind, her face turned scarlet. "Mr. Carson!" she screeched, "I believe you misunderstand me entirely!"

The man stepped back as her voice threatened to perforate his ear drums. "Please elaborate..." he suggested to her, his finger deep in his ear pushing at the wax. "Perhaps I may learn to understand what it is you propose." Mr. Carson had adopted a lighter, upper-class accent as though it was a new language, one that she would understand and respect.

"I have a curiosity for you," she announced. "Her name is Violet. She has lived with me for twelve years and, quite frankly, Mr. Carson, she is an absolute burden upon someone my age."

The man gulped at the malice in her voice. He realized then that her lady-like demeanour of only a few minutes ago had simply been an act. "And what exactly is it that makes her a curiosity, ma'am?"

"She is a hunchback." she growled.

The man's eyes gleamed. He did not have one of those. She would be an extra attraction for his show. "Ooh, a right little gold mine! 'ow much d'ya want for her?" he asked. His finer accent was lost in his excitement. His eyes squinting, awaiting her response.

"£200." she snapped, "It is not much considering what you will earn from a freak like her."

"Cor, £200 is a bit excessive, ain't it?"

"No, Mr. Carson, it is not excessive. It is extremely reasonable."

The man tapped his chin, then run his fingers across the stubble splayed in many directions upon it. His actions exuded confidence. He was a businessman and negotiations such as these, required careful consideration. "I'll 'ave to 'ave a look at it 'fore I decide."

Mrs. Bainbridge huffed loudly, "As you wish, but you will need to travel out of London. My home is not here."

"We're travelling out tomorrow anyways." he said. "Hows about we meet first and discuss the matter? I can't talk 'bout it 'ere... walls 'ave ears, if ya know what I mean?"

Mrs. Bainbridge tutted at the nerve of the fool, implying she may not understand what he was telling her. However, she agreed to his terms to secure the ending she hoped for.

20

The resounding noise of the inebriated men rolled like thunder throughout the public house. The woman behind the bar leaned over and joined in, her breasts heaving over the cut of her dress. She threw her head back in time with the regulars as they roared with laughter. Ale sloshed over the sides of tankards, wetting the already damp floor panels at their feet. Ash fluttered slowly down from the ends of cigars. Their sweet, sickly aroma, stinging eyes and noses. The pungent smell of alcohol, unwashed and overworked bodies, and smoke filled the establishment.

Mrs. Bainbridge's entrance drained the pub of its raucous sound. All eyes darted to the woman who had entered willingly into their world. Her clothes did not match those who supped their daily; the skin on her hands, soft and supple from a carefree life. The way she walked reeked of delusional grandeur. Underneath her façade, the woman was desperate to find Mr. Carson. She did not want to be in a public house. She felt it was beneath her to be somewhere where the poorer folk attend. Her eyes searched the room for any sign of the man. The stilled faces that glared at her caused panic to rise, squeezing at her lungs. Her lips puckered as she tried to maintain her composure.

It had felt like an age before Mr. Carson had made his whereabouts known. "Ah, Mrs. Bainbridge," the man snivelled, moving closer. His hat rested against his chest. A dirty hand held it there as he gave a slight bow. As he straightened his posture, he looked at the intent eyes fixed upon them. "This way, Ma'am," he said, "Follow me." Reluctantly, the old woman followed, stripped bare by the eyes magnetized by her every movement.

As they walked into a private room, the noise of the men and women began again, muffled by the door they closed behind them. "Thought this would be more suitable, ma'am," he offered, smiling, revealing teeth tainted with black. "Seeing as you are a lady of great esteem, I mean."

Violet's grandmother sucked the air between her teeth. The room was dark and damp. Pungent air, thick within its enclosed walls. The smell was putrid. She wanted their transaction to be smooth, but preferably swift. "Mr. Carson," she began, "I am an honest woman and do not intend to play these games. My granddaughter is perfect for your business. I will provide you with details of where you shall collect her, but I expect our financial agreement to be adhered to prior to your arrival at my home."

Mr. Carson studied the woman. What she required was not what he would usually have agreed to, but he wanted this new attraction. He wanted to have the greatest Freakshow in the whole of England. He smoothed his fingers over his unshaven face as if considering the woman's proposal. "Well," he said, running his tongue over his teeth. He stretched the thick muscle to the back of his inner jaw until it made a short sucking sound. "I suppose I could oblige, seeing as your granddaughter is a sought-after oddity." Mr. Carson squinted at Mrs. Bainbridge, wondering whether he could fully trust her. The woman was mature and, by the way her body gave away her discomfort, he very much doubted she would be there with him if it was just a ruse.

His hand reached inside the hidden breast pocket of his jacket. The jacket was old and worn, but it was obvious it had once been a fine jacket. Perhaps, if Mr. Carson cleaned it, the old woman thought, it would restore the colour and vivacity of the crimson that swam beneath the soot. In his hands, he held a wad of crumpled notes, tarnished with dirty fingerprints. He licked his finger and pressed it on the top note, dragging the corner into a quick, short curl to separate it from the next. He then continued with the same action in a repetitive pattern, counting each one as he did so. Slowly he laid two hundred pounds on the table, counting it again for Mrs. Bainbridge to see, then folded the rest back into his filth-ridden pocket.

Violet's grandmother removed her gloves from her reticule. She did not want to touch the horrendously filthy notes he'd produced, 'but money is money, after all!' she thought. Her steady hands pushed the notes deep into the lining of the reticule where she had deliberately severed the fabric, creating a hidden pocket specifically for this moment. "Thank you, Mr. Carson." she sniffed, standing once again. She slid a folded piece of paper across the table toward the man. "You will need this."

Mr. Carson unfolded the paper. "Ah, yes." he agreed. "I will collect the freak on our travels to our next destination. It will be within the next two days, if that is suitable, ma'am?"

"Quite." Violet's grandmother replied abruptly. "I shall be returning there myself within that time frame."

"Perhaps you would like to travel with us?" The man's eyes glittered with greed as he looked to secure the collection.

The thought of travelling amongst Mr. Carson's show did not appeal to her. By the state of his attire, she knew the carriage he would travel in would not impress her.

"Thank you, Mr. Carson, but I have already arranged my travels. I plan to return home this evening and I cannot cancel." she lied.

The man looked at her suspiciously. "Do not take me for a fool, ma'am," he drawled. His malice cut like a blade as his words scored through the air. "If this address is incorrect, I will find you."

Mrs. Bainbridge reddened at his threatening behaviour. "I assure you, Mr. Carson, I am a woman of my word and I do not take kindly to your threat. I have no intention of misleading you. We both know that you are doing me a great favour by relieving me of my granddaughter. I shall be glad to get rid of the creature! YOU, Mr. Carson... do NOT let ME down!" Her eyes pierced the dark in retaliation for his suspicions of her. She did not take kindly to his disrespect.

The man swallowed. He could see that he had misjudged her strength of character, but as much as it startled him, a wave of confidence in her honesty soared through him. 'This'll be a good week.' he thought, 'A very good week.'

Money crossed palms and words exchanged, Mrs. Bainbridge turned on her heel and strode out of the room. She pulled back her shoulders, looked straight ahead, and walked out of the public house as every pair of eyes watched her leave.

Mr. Carson leaned against the door frame, a wicked smile stretched upon his face. He was feeling most fortuitous.

"Grandmama, where have you been?" Isabelle asked as she kissed the woman's cheek, "We have been most concerned."

"Sorry my darling," Mrs. Bainbridge replied, "I had some business to attend to."

Isabelle's brow furrowed in curiosity, but she thought it best not to question her. She was still a little wary after her grandmother's strange behaviour the previous day and did not want to upset her further.

"You must be famished!" she suggested, "I will get Miss Everleigh to make you some supper."

"That would be most kind. I shall eat before I leave."

"You're leaving?" The woman's announcement surprised Isabelle. It seemed extremely sudden.

"Yes, I am afraid so. Violet needs me." Mrs. Bainbridge lied. "I cannot rely on the nurse any longer and I do worry about the dear girl."

"Yes, of course, Grandmama. Forgive me. I did not mean to be selfish. We have loved having you here. I do hope you will come again soon."

"I would love that." Mrs. Bainbridge floated up the stairs to her chambers, ready to leave this place and be rid of Violet forever.

"Mother, I hear you are leaving us today?" William boomed, as he stood watching Miss. Everleigh lower the bowl of thick vegetable soup and a plate of bread onto the small table.

"Yes, darling, I am afraid so. I need to return to Violet." she replied, remembering her lies.

"Thank you, Miss Everleigh." she smiled. 'That is another I will be glad to be rid of.' she thought as she watched the young maid exit the room. The young women curtseyed and walked past Mr. Bainbridge and onto the landing.

"Will you not consider staying a little longer, Mother?" William asked.

"I'm afraid I cannot, William. Violet needs her grandmother. I cannot rely on the nurse forever."

"I can get old Barnaby to fetch her if you would like?" he offered.

Barnaby stared up the stairs at the mention of his

name. He had just arrived back at the house after several of his usual daily errands. He wasn't sure what his title was in the house, but he had been working there for many years. "It would be no problem, ma'am!" he called out.

"Thank you, William, but there is no need. I must get back anyway. I have booked a carriage that will arrive soon."

"If you insist, Mother, but if you should change your mind, please just let me know." Mr. Bainbridge nodded to Barnaby to relieve him of the suggested duty.

Mrs. Bainbridge tucked the last item into her valise and closed it. "I shall eat now, before the carriage arrives."

"I shall leave you to it, Mother, but do not leave without telling me."

"No, of course not."

The soup was practically cold as it reached her lips. She placed her spoon back into the bowl and rubbed the sides of her head in a circular motion. The day had been hard work, but she reminded herself of what it was all for. Any day now, she would have her home all to herself. She could purchase a home with neighbours like she used to have before the burden of Violet had been placed upon her. 'Once the girl has gone, I will inform everyone that she has simply passed. No one will ever suspect a thing.' she thought as she exhaled. Her plan was nearly complete.

21

A ring of pearl white skin was all that remained of where the ring had once sat. It was as if it had branded her finger as a reminder of their love. She ran the tip of her finger over the smooth skin.

The cabin was cold, and the snow was, once again, thick outside the window. Plump pillows of white rested on the steps. Her clothes were grey and miserable, but the rich purple of the Violet refused to wilt on the table, lifting her spirits. Every time she returned from Emil, there was one additional item of proof that he was waiting for her. The Violet had seemed to act as an invitation, but the book and the mark of the ring could be nothing but evidence of her love's existence. Violet was determined to not lose sight of the hope that burned within her. She would return to Emil, and she would become his wife.

She had lost track of how many days her grandmother had been absent. The days in her world and those in Emil's had fused together. Time confused her now, but she assumed it would not be long before the old woman returned. The thought of it made her head ache and her heart pummel with dread. She had a sweet taste of life without her; a life with people that loved her and wanted her there. The old woman left a bitter taste in Violet's mouth. She was everything she did not want.

As she gazed around the cabin, she made a mental note of additional items she would need to collect from her grandmother's house. She had retrieved most of the things that she thought would be useful. They were perfect to make the cabin her home, yet there were still some possessions that were personal to her she did not want to leave behind when she left for the place for good. She thought of the photo of her parents; the limited books that reminded her of the time she'd had a family. It was unlikely that she would ever read the books again, but they were hers. They would be a perfect personal touch to the cabin until she could, somehow, learn how to stay with Emil in his world.

She pushed the thought aside. The very idea that they may be destined to live apart panicked her. Emil was her future, but she had to think only of the cabin for now. To think solely of him would not help her. She held onto the invisible thread that pulled at her heart, tying her and Emil together.

Violet's stomach growled. The food was all but gone. The cupboards in her grandmother's home were bare. She had no money to buy anymore but, even if she did, where would she buy it? Something inside her warned her not to even attempt the outside world here. She heeded its warning as it persisted. The forest will have to be my source of food, she thought. She had already found apples. There must be other food. She could fetch water from the brook and some vegetables from her grandmother's land when she was not there. Violet pulled her grandmother's cape over her shoulders and headed out.

22

Two lives intertwined, yet so incredibly different, as Mrs. Bainbridge confidently boarded the carriage that would carry her home to the young woman who feared her. Even though the incessant high-pitched tone had irritated her on her journey to London, Mrs. Bainbridge did not care that the man who sat behind her whistled this time. There seemed very little he could do to sway her from her good mood. The old woman was positively beaming at her success.

She clutched her cash-filled reticule close to her stomach. As alone as she appeared in the carriage, she would not risk being separated from the precious and promising two hundred pounds that lay within. Her hand grasped the fabric of the reticule with the strength of a vice. The blood drained from her knuckles beneath her gloves, turning them as white as Lilies. Not even the burliest of men could have prized it from her fingers.

As the sun fought against the evening that was slowly drawing in, the light continued to pour over the land. She watched the world pass outside as the wheels of the carriage rolled continuously over uneven roads. The dips and bumps rocked her upon her seat. Green pastures, trees, and gravel paths created scenery after scenery in the neat rectangle frame of the window. Its beauty was a far cry from the dirt and filth of London. She found it soothing to her eyes. It was a relief to return to what she knew. A respite. Here she could relinquish the mask and declare her anger freely whenever it suited her.

There was just one more step until the old woman gained the life of freedom she passionately desired. The apprehension played havoc with her nerves as she hurried the minutes and hours until Mr. Carson would arrive to collect his purchase.

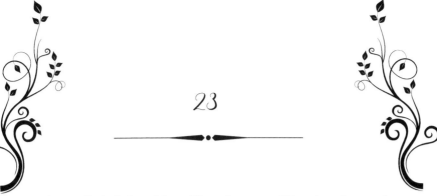

23

Violet unfurled the skirt of her dress, spilling berries and apples out onto the wooden table. The forest had provided well, she thought, as she considered the feast before her eyes. The certain knowledge of her ability to be self-sufficient offered her some comfort.

The berries popped on her tongue. Some sizzled sourly, fizzing over her taste buds, making her shudder, yet others were soothingly sweet. The apples quenched her thirst. The juice flooded her mouth, travelling over the back of her tongue and down her throat. Their fibrous texture filled her stomach, silencing the growl within.

While Violet ate, she pondered whether she should return to her grandmother's home that very evening to collect the last few items that would truly make the cabin a home but, after careful consideration, she decided it would be best if she returned the next day. Foraging for food had tired her. She did not have the strength or heart to return until then. She would collect the last items tomorrow, but for tonight she would rest in the cabin, hoping she would see Emil once more.

Violet dressed and hurried quickly down to the parlour.

She did not knock or wait for an invitation as she rushed through the door and wrapped her arms tightly around Emil.

"Good morning, darling." he beamed, surprised, and elated by her entrance. He drew her in, planting small kisses behind her ear that led slowly down her neck. Her skin shivered at his gentle touch. Her knees, weakened with pleasure.

"How long have I been away?" she asked.

"Just one day this time." Emil replied, "and thank the heavens it was just that because I do not think I could bear any longer."

"Nor I." Violet answered.

Emil's hands slowly ran down the sides of her torso, resting on her hips. His lips soft and hungry against hers, electricity tingling between them.

"Excuse me, Mr. Meriwether, there is someone here to see you." A maid, Violet did not recognize, stood in the doorway. She curtseyed and apologized for interrupting them. Her cheeks were rosy for walking in on an obviously intimate moment.

"Thank you, Clara." Emil called across the room.

"Mr. Meriwether, Miss Violet." The maid bobbed, curtseying again, and left.

"Do not move, soon-to-be Mrs. Meriwether." Emil demanded. Fire burned in his eyes, a devilish grin across his face as he walked backward out of the room, making sure that Violet did not move an inch from the spot she stood in.

Violet trembled beneath her skin, breathing deeply to control the sensations that were fizzing through her body like fireworks. Emil was fast becoming her addiction, yet she knew she must control herself. She told herself that it was because she wanted to be the lady she knew she was supposed to be, but deep down there was something else holding her back. It was something far greater than the opinions of others. It was the opinion she had of herself.

Quickly, she scanned the room for a distraction. She noted the furniture in deep walnut. An oil-painted scenery displayed itself proudly above a drink cabinet. Crystal-cut glass tumblers stood next to a matching decanter and a single bottle of whisky beneath the wooden frame. Wisps of silver curled and coiled in the depths of the midnight blue paper that decorated the walls. The room was elaborate, dark and rich, but what stood out the most were the shelves of books that adorned the walls near the door.

There were so many books, more than Violet had ever owned. Much like the bookshop, Emil's books were beautifully bound with leather. Most had gilded text on the covers, but there were a few without. The gold had crumbled with the repetitive touch of the readers. Those must be the best ones, she thought, for surely they would not have been read so many times and by so many people had they been an unfortunate read.

Her body sat still and calm as she sat with a book open against the palms of her hands. Time escaped her as she dove in and out of the adventures within those pages. She weaved in and out of worlds plucked straight from the imaginations of the author. As her mind spread its wings, she left her worries behind.

Emil returned a few hours later, apologetic and attentive. "I'm so sorry, my love. It was my employer."
Emil had not mentioned his work before this moment, and Violet realized she had not even asked him what he did for work. She looked at him quizzically.
"I am an editor." he smiled, understanding her look of confusion. "Most of these you see before you," he said, gesturing to the shelves, "were edited and published by myself and my colleagues."

Could this man be any more perfect? she thought as she listened to him explain how the books were created so meticulously. Every intricate detail seemed laced together as beautifully as the story within each book. She hadn't ever given thought to the process of such a craft, but to hear the man she loved spill over with the enthusiasm of his artistry added far more value to the book she held in her hands.
"I'm talking too much, aren't I?" he asked, looking at her. Her eyes were intent on his face and every hand gesture he made. He looked down, hiding his embarrassment.
"No!" she exclaimed, "not at all! I love listening to you." Violet placed her book on the small table next to her and rose from the chair where she had been sitting. "Please don't stop." she said. Her hands slipped smoothly into his. His rough skin tickled against her touch as she

moved closer. She knew she should not be doing this. Every move was going against her fears, but there was something about him that silently told her she had nothing to be afraid of.

The heat of Emil's body radiated against Violet's. Between them, a furnace of desire burned. His chest rose and fell in deep, heavy motions. "Violet..." he began. His words failed as the young woman stretched up, her feet flexed and pointed on tiptoes until her face was parallel with his. The pattern of their breathing ebbed and flowed in synchronicity, absorbed in the silence. Both holding themselves back. Emil's fingers brushed over her lips; her breath faltered at his touch. "Perhaps we shouldn't?" he breathed. His forehead rested upon hers, the tip of their noses touching with only a breath between them.

"Not here." she whispered. It was as though some part of Violet had been released, a more confident version of herself. Her hand grasped his as she led him up the stairs. A battle between the insecure version of herself and the one that now held her fiancé's hand fought tirelessly between themselves as she took each step.

"Wait." she breathed as they stood in the doorway, eyes intent on one another. "I'm not like other women."

"I know," he replied, his eyes alight with desire.

"No, I mean my body is different. I'm scared it will disgust you... I will disgust you."

Emil caressed his fingertips along the line of her jaw, tilting her face up to meet his. "Violet, if you were like all the other women, then I would not love you as I do."

"But my spine..." she began, tears pricking her eyes.

"Your spine is a part of you and every inch of you is beautiful." Emil assured her. He leaned forward, lips against hers, sparks of electricity tingling as his hands stroked down the side of her neck and brushed against her collarbone.

"What if I repulse you?" Violet's voice, a whisper at his sensual touch. Her resistance was weak.

"You could never. It is not possible." Emil's hands released the pins from her hair. Gentle silken waves of glorious chestnut brown fell freely down her back and over her shoulders. She gasped as his fingers cupped the back of her head, pulling her towards him. Her eyes closed, trusting him as he walked them both back toward the bed. His foot kicked the door closed behind them.

Violet's dress fell to the floor. Her body trembled with apprehension. She wanted to be with him more than she could say, but her mind kept tugging at her with thoughts that scared her more than she could explain. This was it. This was the ultimate test to see whether the man that excited her, that made her heart dance and thud louder than it ever had, truly could accept her. She braced herself for the rejection but, as she stood there naked and at her most vulnerable, it never came.

Emil's lips planted small kisses, hungrily, along her shoulder. Violet tilted her head, extending the length of her neck. It was an invitation Emil could not refuse. The young woman leaned into his touch. Her soul danced, the flutter of excitement thrilling her. Each tender touch seeped into her skin, filling her soul with desire. Her legs wrapped around his waist as he lifted her. The fragrance of his cologne lit her senses as she nuzzled between his jaw and his shoulder. A masculine rasp escaped Emil's lips as he laid her on the bed and drank in her beauty.

"Dear God.... " he breathed longingly, "Violet, you are divine." Emil lay down beside her, nuzzling into her neck. He gently teased her earlobe between his teeth, scraping against the soft flesh as he pulled away. His touch trailed down her neck and across her shoulders; her flesh, alive with pleasure. His fingers slowly traced the fullness of her breasts. They wandered lustfully down toward her navel, teasing as they circled the inside of her thigh. Violet's body arched with rapture as he explored every inch of her. She shook uncontrollably as the space between them disappeared; their bodies entwined. Her body danced with the motion of the all-consuming tidal waves of ecstasy.

He was gentle, kind, and attentive. Each touch was a reminder of his love for her. He was everything she'd hoped he would be, she thought, as his hands run over her back, followed by a trail of soft kisses of reassurance. She had been terrified to allow him to see all of her; scared that he would fall out of love with her at the sight, but he had made her feel like the most beautiful woman in the world. As she turned over to lay her eyes upon the man she adored, his hand caressed her face. The love in his eyes was undeniable. He will never know how much this means, she thought, as she curled up in his arms and slept.

24

With a click of the latch, the door opened. A breath. A pause. With a click of the latch again, the door closed. Violet stood still, the sound of her breathing loud as she strained to hear. She had just packed the last few items she had collected into the hessian sack, now hidden in the darkness under her bed. The clack of heels against hard stone paced the lower floors, sharp enough to be heard. The sound smothered the ticking of the clock. Violet remained quiet and listened.

A quick succession of thuds from heavy bags gave a short rumble against the floor. A pummel of heavy fists followed suit, pounding eagerly against the damp wooden panels of the front door. The door rattled on its hinges, threatening to come loose, as the footsteps rushed toward the sound. The visitor's incessant pounding sounded desperate, as though they were in danger from a beast prowling the land, but Violet waited silently as she could, her heart competing with the sounds from downstairs. Her grandmother's footsteps had been Violet's only indication of her return, but it was enough to know she was there. It would not hurt her to answer it this once, she thought.

A long, arduous creak of the door upon its hinges silenced the knocking. Mumbles, a bitter twang of the old woman's high pitch tones mingled with a deeper, rough masculine drawl. They held a brief but direct conversation until one set of footsteps turned into two upon the cold floor. They moved, slowly, but surely, towards and up the stairs, getting louder with every step.

Violet pushed her body against the door of her chambers. Her ear pressed against the wood as she tried to listen. Her own breathing melted the edges of each word, dulling them to nothing more than simple, indecipherable murmurs. She held her breath at the indisputable groan of the top step. It sounded out with a warning directly outside the room. What were they doing? Why were they upstairs? Violet backed away from the door, toward the window. Her eyes flitted from side to side, then back to the door. Everything inside her told her to run, to escape any way she could, but there was only one way. Quickly, she fumbled at the window latch. She pushed the bar up to release it from its catch, but it was stuck fast. "Dear God, please help me." she whispered. Panic rose within her as pain struck the heel of her hand, the bar digging into her flesh. She pushed and pushed, but to no avail. Of all the times it could have done this, why now? she thought. Why would it be stuck now? This had never happened before. Her panic turned to bile in her throat as she continued her efforts to escape her grandmother's home for good.

Mr. Carson kicked the door half off its hinges. The wood splintered as it hung desperately against the wall. "There you are." he said, glaring triumphantly at her and licking his lips as if Violet was a plump turkey ready for carving on Christmas day. The sight of her filled him with images of the fame he could achieve. The girl in front of him tantalized his imagination and the bulk of his wallet as he drank in her image. "You weren't lying were you, ma'am" It was not a question but a direct statement to Mrs. Bainbridge. He grinned, his blackened teeth stark against the white as he stepped towards Violet. His heavy boots clomped on the bare floor, accentuating the menacing glint in his eyes.

Violet's eyes grew wide with panic, looking from the beast of a man in front of her to the woman that always failed to protect her. There was no one to save her other than herself. That she was sure of. "Who are you?" she asked. She continued to fumble with the latch of the window, her arms bent behind her back, hiding her actions from the predators in her room.

"Oh, it talks." he mused, looking at Mrs. Bainbridge. "Weren't sure if it would." He sniffed the air like a dog hunting for food. "Cor, it smells pretty too." he remarked, "Not sure that's going to last long, mind". The man laughed at his own joke as if he should have been a comedian rather than a showman of such a despicable nature as he was.

Mrs. Bainbridge stood quietly in the corner, steadily breathing as she smirked at her petrified granddaughter.

"Grandmama?" Violet begged. She didn't know why she had even bothered to cry her name. It was utterly futile to even hope. The old woman had never helped her before. Violet could not fathom what on heaven's earth had made her try to plead with the woman now. Mrs. Bainbridge remained silent, satisfied by the anguish on Violet's face.

Mr. Carson stepped forward and grabbed Violet's wrist tightly. The calloused skin of his broad hands burned her as she twisted in his grasp.

"Let go of me!" she screamed. She yanked her arm backward, but he would not release her. "Please let me go." Her eyes pleaded with him, but he looked nothing but amused at her terror.

The fear in Violet added a certain thrill to the encounter for Mr. Carson. A surge of power flooded his veins as she squirmed at his touch. "Proper feisty one, this." he commented, nodding his head at Violet. "Don't you worry though ma'am, we'll get it trained up in no time." he assured her grandmother.

Violet struggled, relentlessly pulling away from his grip. Her body stooped forward as she planted her teeth into the supple, dirty skin on his arm. She felt the tear as her canine teeth pierced into his flesh.

"Bloody hell!!!" he bellowed. He grabbed her by the hair with his free hand, swinging her round to stand, twisted in pain, in front of him. Her eyes watered as she felt her hair ripping from her scalp. The man would not release his fist as the strands of hair tangled around it and between his fingers. He held on tight.

Violet continued to fight him even as her grandmother placed a damp rag over Violet's nose and mouth. The odour was pungent yet sweet, cloying her airways. Her eyes stung as the old woman pushed it against her face, almost to the point of suffocation. The more Violet pushed, pulled, and cried, the faster the chloroform took effect. Violet slumped to the floor, her grasp on the moment faded as the world slipped silently away.

"Right, I'll be off now." Mr. Carson announced, looking ruffled as he gave Mrs. Bainbridge a look of determination. He shifted Violet's limp body as she lay unconscious over his shoulder. "Per'aps, you'd want to come and see it perform?" he offered.

"I don't think so, Mr. Carson." the old woman replied tartly, "I have had enough of Thorn to last me a lifetime."

Mr. Carson looked confused. "Thorn?" he asked.

Mrs. Bainbridge said nothing more, leaving his curiosity unresolved, and his ears ringing with the slam of the door as she shut it in his face.

Mr. Carson carried Violet away from the house and all she had ever known.

25

Clouds of dark grey ink washed across the sky; a forlorn and angry artist sorrowfully expressing their mood. Spatters of rain fell silently upon the rickety trailer as Violet lay hidden in the dark behind an elaborate, enthusiastic display of colour announcing the arrival of 'Carson's Creatures of Curiosity' to all of whom they passed.

The wooden trailer wobbled and swayed over unmade roads until the smooth cobbles of London offered balance as they returned once more.

Mr. Carson had intended to travel further but, now that he had a new star for his show, everything was different. This one, he thought, would draw in the crowds and make a name for him. Mr. Carson believed Violet would bring him fame and untold riches. He would raise the price of entry to almost double the last fee. It would enforce the rarity of his new curiosity. He would even name Violet after the city itself, 'The Hunchback Of London'.

Violet pushed the palm of her hands against the floor of the trailer. The crumbled soil and grit had scattered across the floor from dirty boots and shoes. It hid beneath the darkness, clinging to her skin and clothes, but she had felt it prickle and scrape against her, scratching against the wooden panels as she moved. Some dirt had even embedded itself beneath her nails. She sucked in her breath as a splinter slid eagerly into and under her skin. Cold, heavy, metal, thick cuffs held her wrists down by her sides while long, cumbersome chains pulled against them. The splinter would have to stay for now, for she could not even touch her other hand. The chains kept them in position, restricting every movement. The odour of the iron shackles enriched the musty scent of the unkempt carriage. Her stomach churned from its intensity as the last lingering effects of the chloroform swamped her mind. Violet leaned against the wall, allowing her eyes to adjust to the dark. A stream of light, no bigger than the prick of a pin, and no brighter than a storm cloud, poked through the gaps in the worn timber frame. She could make out nothing but the chains that secured her to the wall. The trailer looked to be empty, all but Violet herself. Violet curled up on the floor and closed her eyes. She had resigned herself to being trapped for now. She knew she could not escape the powerful jaws of the iron shackles that clasped her... not yet. 'This will take time.' she thought. Her chest burned with frustration, anger, and sadness. Her only consolation was the thread of hope she held on to, knowing that she would do everything she could to return to the cabin... to Emil.

She wasn't sure how long she had been asleep, but when the trailer doors opened, the daylight flooded the wooden box she sat in. A man she had not seen before leered at her. It was a proud, satisfied, competitive leer. His clothes were smarter and cleaner than Mr. Carson's, but she would soon learn that he, too, had the same name. They were brothers. An unlikely duo, to say the least, as she compared their differences. The first Mr. Carson – Reginald - she had the displeasure of meeting, was unkempt. A slither of madness crawled under his skin. He was the name that covered the brash, revolting brand on the side of the trailer but, the second Mr. Carson - Mycroft - could have been mistaken for a gentleman had she not had the terror of knowing the truth.

His eyes glistened with venom as he yanked at the chains, dragging her out of the trailer. Her feet struggled to keep up with her body.

"'Ere Mycroft!" Reginald yelled, "That's our prize possession! Be careful, will ya?!"

"Oh, do be quiet, Reginald." Mycroft Carson drawled, "It's already broken what does a few extra bruises and cuts matter?"

"It'll make us famous. We'll call it The 'unchback O' London!" Reginald announced as his hand lingered in the air, sweeping across the imaginary sign that hung there over their heads.

"The Hunchback Of London? Hmmm... It has got rather a certain ring to it." Mycroft agreed.

Violet listened. The pain seared, red hot, at her heart.

Claws of fire dragged, scoring through the soft tissue. The muscles tensed with the pain as it continued to beat. Tension built within her jaw, crawling down her neck to her shoulders, as she held back her her hot, angry tears of frustration. Her grandmother had given her to these awful men. She had thrown her away like scraps of old, filthy, unwanted food.

The brothers marched violet forward, a metal ring around her neck that matched those clutching her wrists. She was their property, an object, and nothing more. They never referred to her as she, her, or by her name, but simply referred to her as 'it'.

They had already erected the tent with the title 'Carson's Creatures of Curiosities' arced over the entrance.

"If you behave" Mycroft began, "We could make you famous.". His breath was hot in her ear as he rasped the words in a whisper.

Violet flinched, bringing her shoulder to ear to wipe away the sensation, slithering against her skin. "I don't want to be famous." she spat, "I want to go home!"

"This is your home now. My brother and I paid for you. You belong to us."

A fire burned in Violet's eyes as she glared at him. Her furnace of strength, rising to the surface, simmering away. "I do not belong to you!" she screamed, "I only belong to me." Violet punched her fist at the air away from him, tightening the chain between them. The force gave her the freedom to run as Mycroft Carson fell to his knees, but after the first four strides, her feet left the ground as the man pulled the chain, yanking them out from underneath her. Violet's head hit the earth, and the world disappeared.

When the young woman awoke, rust-ridden bars hindered her view. The dry scent of hay tickled her nose as her fingertips delicately ran over the raised scratch marks that were scored down the side of her face. There was dirt in her hair and she no longer wore her dress. Instead, they had dressed her in dark brown trousers, a man's jacket, and a shirt. Violet huddled in the corner of the locked cage wrapped in shame. They had violated her by removing her clothes to replace them with the ones she now wore. They must have removed the shackles when they had changed her clothing, but did not waste any time before returning them to her wrists, neck, and ankles. She didn't need to look, she could feel them. The ones at her ankles hurt the most. Her skin felt sore under the metallic grip. Her bones ached against the solidity of the iron.

The cage that held her could not have contained more than two people at one time, and even that would have been a tight squeeze. This was her prison. The cold of the stone floor penetrated her bare feet. She twisted her body to sit cross-legged; her aching ankles resting on her knees and her feet elevated. Violet rubbed them profusely to warm them. The throbbing pain reverberating in her bones was too much to bear, and she did not care that her feet were dirty.

"Psst!"

Violet looked up. Her gaze had been on the floor until now. She hadn't realized that she was being watched. She turned her head in the sound's direction to see a young man in another cage. Her mouth opened, shocked.

"Yeah, I know." he said, "I ain't the most handsome of men. Guess that's why I'm 'ere."

"No." Violet drew a breath, and continued, "I didn't mean to make you feel like that. I'm just shocked that you are in a cage, too."

The young man's beautiful, deep brown eyes glittered as a smile stretched across his face. "They call me Pip, but that's not my real name."

"What is your real name?" she asked, warming to the kindness that oozed from him.

"It's Will." he replied, "What's yours?"

"Violet, but I'm too ashamed to tell you what they're calling me instead." she muttered.

"Afraid, I already know."

Violet buried her face in her knees.

"Please, Violet," Will pleaded, "Don't let them make you feel ashamed. They are just ignorant fools."

Violet looked up at Will. His eyes were still intent on her. They told her he understood. The pain from his own experiences had blurred and softened his features. They had created shadows against his brown skin. His nose sloped perfectly with utter precision, 'Carved by God's own hands', she thought. The masculinity of his jaw, strong and chiseled. The Carson brothers had shaved his head, all but a patch on his crown to accentuate what they believed was an irregularity, but to Violet, he possessed a beauty that they were unable to see. The Carson brothers had been robbed by their own prejudice.

They had stripped Will of his identity and marked him as a freak, as they would do to her. A sign gently rocked back and forth in the breeze, clanking against his prison, marking him as 'The Missing Link of Evolution.' Violet gasped when she read it. Will let out a half-hearted breath of a laugh. "I know." he said, "I'm not allowed to talk to anyone when the show is on, ya know."

"What do you mean?" she asked him. Her brow furrowed. It seemed such a ridiculous demand for someone to place on another.

"I'm only allowed to grunt."

It was then that Violet's eyes wandered to his clothing. They had dressed him in a suit made only of fur. "Did they..." she started, suggesting to his suit.

"Yes. Apparently, it makes my role more believable." Will's eyebrows raised in mockery of the Carson brothers. It surprised Violet that his mood was not solemn after living in such a terrible situation, but she was glad of his kind nature. She wondered whether she could, one day, find that acceptance or whether this life would hold her in the state of despair that was currently coursing through her veins. Will's words and cheerful nature had calmed Violet. She could not say that she felt happy, but he seemed to have a soothing effect on her.

She would never have wished for a life like this on anyone but, at the same time, she was grateful that he was there with her.

When the Carsons realized a friendship was stirring between Violet and Will, they heaved her cage to the opposite side of the arena.

"Can't 'ave you disruptin' the acts." Reginald declared as the cage hit the ground with Violet in it. "Besides, we need to get you into full character. I chose that suit for ya. Perfec' ain't it?" he beamed. Violet looked at him incredulously. 'Did he really think I would talk with him like we are friends?' she thought. "Ah, going to be like that, are we?" he sneered. His face darkened as he kicked the bars of her cage and walked away.

26

They had painted her face. A white chalky powder smeared across her pale skin, slathered over every inch. Particles of dust settled on her eyelashes, irritating her eyes. With a dark, unsettling brown, Reginald Carson had deepened the colour of her eyebrows. He had worked the colour across her forehead, uniting both brows in a thick scribble of colour. They had pulled her hair back and ruffled it into a mess upon her head. Violet knew that she was not supposed to look like her usual self, but that of a character plucked from a book.

"Perfec'!" he proclaimed, stepping back to have a look at her. "They're going to love ya."

"Do I need to wear these?" Violet asked, gesturing to the shackles.

Reginald Carson threw back his head and laughed. It was a deep belly laugh that mocked her. "You reckon I'm that daft, do ya?"

Violet looked at him more intensely, mustering a look of innocence as she studied him. How was she ever going to escape with those wrapped around her? "I don't understand." she begged.

"Tsk! Acting skills as well." he scoffed, "Got me money's

worth wiv you. You, my 'unchback o' London, ain't getting rid of these." Reginald Carson lifted the shackles, hoisting Violet's arms up, and then dropped them abruptly as if they'd scolded him. Violet's heart plummeted with them.

The crowd gathered around the edge of the arena. The noise was overbearing. Mycroft Carson watched from behind the thick red curtain as Reginald stood, practically salivating over the money that passed through wealthy fingers into the palms of his hands. You would never have known that the brothers had quarrelled that afternoon, both fighting to be the centre of attention. Mycroft had scorned him, reminding him he had not had the chance to perform in London because Reginald had hogged the limelight and made him sit on the sidelines last time. It was his turn, Mycroft insisted, and he would not relent in his belief. Reginald conceded to his brother's demands.

As the lights dimmed, the caged cast members, Will and Violet, remained in their prisons. A hush swept the audience as anticipation grew for the first act. Violet watched as a young woman with dwarfism rode into the arena on the back of an elephant. Her long, thick, ink-black hair cascaded over her shoulders and down her back. She had a small delicate nose and big blue eyes, her lips dusky pink. The young woman, with all her beauty, looked thoroughly regal. All she needed was a crown and Violet would have believed, wholeheartedly, that she was a queen.

Violet's heart fractured as she heard Mycroft Carson ignorantly introduce her as a midget. One, he proclaimed he had rescued. 'More like trapped.' seethed Violet to herself. Her eyes were fierce with resentment. They pierced through the shadows and onto the back of his jacket. The man reached behind him to scratch where she had been staring. It was as though he could feel the heat of her glare upon his skin.

Mycroft Carson circled the elephant, brandishing a whip. Violet noted the fear in the elephant's eyes as he followed the orders under the threat of violence. It was the first time Violet had ever seen an elephant. The animal looked exhausted. His eyes glazed in the monotony of what they demanded of him. She looked at the young woman as she continued to circle the arena. She was leaning forward now, her body close to the elephant's back in an attempt of an embrace, reassuring him as he trembled beneath her. Mycroft's whip ripped through the air and slashed against the elephant's flesh, missing the young woman's fingers by mere millimeters.

The young woman sat bolt upright; her hand remained on the elephant. She stroked him subtly to reassure him she was with him; to show him she cared. Mycroft Carson smiled outward to the crowd whilst his sharp looks of disdain reminded her he owned her. The young woman upon the elephant did not flinch. Her mind wandered elsewhere while the lights glistened on the sadness pooled within the shadows beneath her eyes.

The show continued. An audience oblivious to the anguish and humiliation their jeers inflicted upon the cast. The Carson brothers alight with glee at the crowd's applause and repetitive shouts of encore that rang out under the fabric roof of the tent.

Mycroft turned the key in the lock. The gate to her prison swung open. "Get out." he ordered between clenched teeth. He smiled at the crowd as he yanked at the shackles, forcing Violet to move. Slowly, Violet crawled out. Gasps filled the air as the crowd watched.
"FREAK!" came a loud, burly voice, twisting toward a pitch that did not fit the depth of the tone the man had started with. Violet closed her eyes, trying to free her mind. She wanted to be anywhere but there. As she stood, eyes closed, she held her head high. She would not look at them, but she would not crumble at their ignorance, she thought. But despite the promises and the reassurance she offered herself, the voices outside her thoughts cut like blades through her armour.
"Ladies, Gentlemen, and children!" Mycroft bellowed, "I present to you The Hunchback Of London!"
A blanket of silence washed over the men, women, and children as they gawped at Violet from a distance. She walked reluctantly as Mycroft led her like a beast around the ring, her teeth grinding as she fumbled in her mind for images of Emil. What would he think of her now? she wondered, the cuffs digging into the soft skin on her wrists and shoulders. She pictured him smiling,

reassuring her she was beautiful as he had many times before, but the images appeared marred and as faded as old letters lost to time. Her mind grabbed them as she tried to drown out the chatter that rumbled in her ears. Her throat burned with the fiery heat of shame. She longed to escape the body she had; to leave it there, like old rags, crumpled and broken upon the floor.

A raucous laugh exploded into a chorus of names.

"Hunchback!"

"Gibface!"

"Freeeaaakkkk!"

"It's like that beast out of that book!" another cried excitedly. It was the one time Violet felt relieved at being denied any more books by her grandmother. She did not know the beast of a character the voice had described. Had the author betrayed and humiliated them like she was being betrayed and humiliated? Or had they portrayed them as the person they truly were? She had hoped for the latter. The world was already cruel enough. It did not need words that could inflict pain, over and over again, and would last the length of time.

She felt hollow as she walked in circles several times. Pairs of hands reached out to touch her, checking to see if she was real. Someone had grabbed dirt from the ground and lobbed it at her face. "Open your eyes, freak!" they shouted, but as she continued to circle inside the arena, she refused to give in to their demand.

The night sky grew darker still and, with it, came the bite

of a chill. Reginald hauled Will, still trapped within his cage, toward the exit. He kicked the bars and ordered him to grunt. It was a chance for the departing guests to gaze upon Will and to be reminded of the rarities the Carson brothers had to offer. An attempt to draw them back once again, to another show but, to the young man that sat huddled in the prison, forced to be what the world wanted him to be, it was humiliation at its worse. Will had a life once and it could have been his own, but because he didn't fit the ideals of others, he had ended up in a show that was slowly grinding him down, afraid that one day he may be nothing more than dust.

The wind beat against the canvas and whistled through the seams of the fabric dome that covered them. Reginald had given her a simple blanket, not too dissimilar from the threadbare blanket she slept under at her grandmother's house. Neither kept the cold at bay but, there in London, there was the addition of the damp, cold earth beneath the cage. It rose in pungent wisps and moist fingers upon her skin. Her body sat propped in the cage, cramped and uncomfortable as her spine pressed painfully against the unforgiving bars. She rested her hand between her head and the metal; the shackles tugged against every movement she made and there were many. Try as she might, she found no position that would allow her to sleep.

27

Morning broke, offering little light within the tent. The Carson brothers arrived early and were already setting the cast to work with rehearsals and stage set-up. Violet's stomach ached with hunger, unsatisfied by the dry bread and small amount of cheese that they had left for her. She had squeezed her hand through the bars to take it off the tin plate. She noticed that Will had been allowed to move freely while the London public could not see him, but none of them were permitted to leave the enclosure.

Reginald's incessant yelling at the animals disturbed Violet immensely. His tormenting and scolding grated on her imagination. She could only hear his cruelty as they had left her with her back to the arena and facing the rows of empty seats. He was vicious and uncaring toward them, even more than he had been to her. Violet cupped her hands over her ears, muffling the sounds in bubbles of pressure. She wasn't sure which was worse, whether it was being trapped in the cage or hearing the whines and cries of the defenceless and frightened animals.

Will wandered by her prison. His hand hung low as he dropped another bit of cheese onto her plate.

"For you." he whispered while checking to see whether anyone had seen him.

Violet grabbed it eagerly. "Thank you."

"Stay as you have been and don't fight them. If you do, they may let you out of there as they did with me."

Violet's throat creaked as she swallowed the food and held back the sob that was crashing forward in waves of despair. Will looked down at her. His look was one of understanding. "I know," he whispered, "but it's the only way."

Violet nodded, unable to speak as fat tears streaked through the dirt and white chalk on her face.

"Oi Pip!" Reginald bellowed, "Get away from that!"

"Sorry I got to go," Will whispered down to Violet, "I'll come back when I can."

Will walked away and disappeared behind her. "Can't she come out Mr. Carson?" she heard him plead.

"I'll consider it." Mycroft answered. His drawl reached Violet's ears, triggering the beginning of the strength she knew she must muster.

She exhaled deeply, the dry, brittle dust from the hay biting the inside of her nose. Her skin was tight under the chalk and dirt from the day before. She was exhausted, but she had understood many things in the few words that Will had spoken. If she was to be free from this cage, then she had to play her part. How would she ever leave if they kept her confined behind those bars? Her silence reigned until long after midday. The only visitor she'd had was Will with her food. There had been no word from the Carson brothers. She had hoped it was a good sign. They'd not felt the need to scold or chastise her. She considered they may have forgotten her, but at mid-afternoon the lock to the cage flung open and a pair of dark black trousers and patent shoes stood before her.

Violet slowly raised her eyes to see Mycroft staring down at her.

"Well?" he drawled, one eyebrow raised, "are you getting out or not?"

Violet dragged herself out. The chains were heavy against her pain-stricken muscles and aching bones. As she stood up cautiously, a searing pain tore through the flesh under her ribs. It ripped deep beneath several layers of numbed skin. She looked down, but there was no blood; the pain radiated inside where no-one, but she, knew it existed.

"Come on!" Mycroft barked.

Violet pushed against the heat of the pain as she followed him to the centre of the arena.

"Right," he began, "Tonight we want to show you off." He gestured to a tower constructed of wood. She had never seen it before. It certainly wasn't there last night, she thought.

"It's new... just for you." he announced as though he was waiting for an unbridled out-pour of gratitude from her. "What do you think?" he asked.

It amazed Violet how this man had treated her so poorly, referring to her as an 'it', caging and shackling her, and then, in the next breath, he was asking her opinion. She bit her tongue, remembering Will's advice. "It's lovely." she offered.

"Reginald and I made that."

Violet lowered her eyes as the pride lit up his face. She could not reveal the anger that writhed inside her for fear it would only lead to her being shoved back behind the awful bars.

A large brass bell hung at the top of the Carson brothers' tower. A long, dense rope swung freely from the top as Violet sat on the ledge they had created for her. She was ordered to ring the bell over and over for the audience as they wheeled the tower in circles around the arena. Violet did as she was told, placating the brothers, avoiding her prison for the afternoon.

Violet sat and watched the rehearsals. A woman with excessive facial hair stood under the spotlight. Her label described her as a human dog, the same label attached to the child she held lovingly in her arms. They forced her to raise her tiny infant into the air to show everyone for supposed entertainment. Violet watched as the woman drew her baby back towards the warmth of her body. Her embrace was one of anguish and sorrow as she mouthed the words "I'm sorry, I'm sorry." between planting small, tiny kisses upon her baby's head.

Violet covered her mouth, stifling a gasp when Mycroft stepped forward. He held the woman's other child, no older than four, in his arms with nothing but hair to cover the boy. The young, naked child shivered from the cold. Not a thread of fabric to keep him warm or protect him from the leers of strangers. The light dappled the tears welling in his eyes from fear as he reached for his mama. Mycroft scolded him, heaving him further up toward his shoulder and away from the loving arms of his mother. They did not allow her to hold him or to cover him. The pain in her eyes spoke a thousand words. She was utterly helpless. Violet didn't know how much more her heart could stand. An ache throbbed in her chest, one of empathy for all these people; anger towards their captors; and hatred for those that came to encourage them.

As the woman sat down, the urge to comfort her spurred Violet to hold her hand. At first, the woman flinched but, as she turned to face Violet, relief softened her features. Unsaid words filled the void between them. "I'm Jules." she whispered so that Mycroft could not hear. "Violet." Violet replied.

Jules smiled sweetly as she wrapped a thin blanket around her four-year-old. "This is my son, Steven."

"Hi Steven, nice to meet you." Violet smiled.

The little boy climbed onto his mama's lap, careful not to knock his little brother. He snuggled close into the warmth of his mama, his voice stolen by his shy nature.

28

Emil Meriwether described Violet in intricate detail to the man that sat behind the desk. His brow furrowed as he paced the floor.

"Please, Sir. Please sit down." the man begged, gesturing to the seat. "It makes it very hard to concentrate with you pacing like that."

Emil's movements were slight and agitated as he tried to remain still in the chair. "I'm sorry. I'm just so worried."

"I understand, sir. Now, I've drawn who I think you are describing, but I'd like you to have a look and give your honest opinion."

The man held up a detailed and precise portrait of Violet. Emil could see that he'd described her well. "Yes, you have captured her perfectly." he exclaimed.

"How many copies would you like, sir?" the artist asked, tucking the pencil behind his ear.

"As many as you can manage." Emil bit his nails profusely, once again taking strides across the office.

"I'll put this on the printing press. I must warn you, sir, that it may take a while."

"Thank you. If it's alright with you, I shall wait."

The man nodded and left the office, taking the

illustration of Violet with him.

Time stretched to its full capacity as Emil paced repeatedly, back and forth in the office. It was all he could do to bide time without losing himself to his emotions. The minutes and hours dragged like feet wading through thick, sticky treacle. This day did not differ from the previous one or the ones before that. All Emil could do was hope that tomorrow would be a better day. He was fraught with worry for the woman he loved, but there was a part of him that somehow knew she was still alive. He could not explain how he knew just as much as he could never explain how he had met Violet for the first time or how she kept reappearing and disappearing overnight.

Mystery had shrouded each part of Emil's life with Violet so far. When people asked, he would swerve around the truth with more reasonable and believable scenarios. Ones that would make sense. The actual truth would only inspire doubt in Violet's existence, and then the world would give up on her. He would not allow them to do so.

As Emil trundled home with an enormous pile of posters cradled in his arms, passersby mistook the dark shadows beneath his eyes for exhaustion. It had been months since he'd held her in his arms and the emotions weighed heavily on him. Work colleagues had encouraged him to take time away to rest, but he could not bear to pace the hallways waiting. Rosie's promise to fetch him, should

Violet show up, was a comfort, but that day was yet to come.

Emil stood outside on the street, his forehead resting against the cold wood of the front door. He took deep, soothing breaths and plucked fragments of courage from deep within. A silent prayer fluttered across his heart as he knocked. The door opened slowly to reveal only Clara. Her face was ashen with regret, for she could not give him the joyful news she knew he longed for. She could not lift his spirits with news of Violet's return.

"It's okay, Clara." Emil offered, "You do not need to be afraid to open the door to me."

"So sorry sir." she muttered, "I just hoped that I would have good news for you, but we have not heard from Miss Violet yet."

"We will find her." Emil said confidently. A promise made for his benefit as much as Clara's. A simple thread of hope he would not release.

Rosie traced her fingers over the paper, pinching it between the hard surface of the table and her touch, strengthening the crease into a firm fold. She and Emil had been busy preparing the portrait copies for delivery the next day. She marvelled at the artist's attention to detail, especially since he had never seen the girl in person. It pained her to see Emil in such despair. He had not attended any functions since Violet stopped coming, and he had barely touched his meals. She wished she knew how to reach young Violet, but it was a mystery to all. There wasn't much she could do to help the young couple other than to assist Emil now, hoping his work would bring Violet home.

Rosie placed her hand gently on the back of Emil's shoulder. "Per'aps we can put her picture in the newspaper?" she suggested.

"That's a grand idea!" Emil beamed, "We shall take one to the London paper tomorrow when we deliver the others."

"There's that smile." Rosie said, patting his hand, "I was starting to think we would never see it again. You must remain hopeful, Emil. That young lady needs you. I know she'll be doing all she can to find you again."

"Do you really believe that?" Emil asked.

That moment reminded Rosie of the small boy she'd first met many years ago as he'd greeted her at the door of his grandmother's home. Such a hopeful, optimistic boy, despite his parents abandoning him so openly at such a young age. A haunted look swam in his eyes but, behind it all, there was a small glimmer of hope like the rays of the sun breaking through the clouds after a turbulent storm. "Yes, duck." she offered, "I really do."

Rosie prayed that their effort would not be in vain. But like Emil, she also knew that Violet was out there somewhere, and she hoped it would just be a matter of time before she returned. She silently vowed to herself that she would do all that she could to help the young man find her again.

29

Dark clouds threatened the late afternoon with heavy rain and storms. The wind smacked against the canvas with fists of fury.

"That's all we bloody need!" Mycroft raged. "At this rate, no-one will show up."

His mood was unsettling. Violet stood back. She did not want to be put back in the cage. Mycroft turned on his heel and glared at her. He held up his cane, pointing at her face.

"You!"

Violet swallowed, frozen to the spot.

"Well, get over here." he growled.

One thing she had learned in the few days she had been captive was that you did not ignore the Carson brothers. She stepped forward.

"That's it... and you!" Mycroft was now pointing at Jules. "Leave that thing there." he barked, his teeth clenched, like a hound ready to attack. Jules reluctantly passed her baby to Will to look after him and his little brother, then stepped beside Violet. She squeezed Violet's hand.

"One more..." Mycroft squinted his eyes and scanned the people. "Perhaps two then." he sneered, pointing his cane at two young men. "Two for the price of one, eh?"

Reginald snorted from the far side of the tent as if his brother had cracked the most hilarious joke. "Hah! That's a good un!"

The young men stepped forward. Identical twins – Christopher and Miles - walked forward together. Their slender bodies joined at the hip and waist. Halos of sandy blonde hair softened the sharp edges of their jaws and cheekbones. Olive skin and warm amber eyes, like the waning days of summer that stretched into autumn. Both young men nodded at Violet as she smiled at them reassuringly.

"Come with me." Mycroft ordered, "I've got a job for you."

Violet, Jules, Christopher, and Miles had been standing on the podium for hours before the first people arrived. A sign hung from the stage. The words "Strange People", displayed for all to read. Each pair of eyes slid up from the large font, covering every inch of their bodies. The onlookers' faces crumpled in disgust, as if they were perusing a row of gowns smeared with animal waste.

Violet shivered. They had tried to huddle together for warmth, but Reginald had threatened to withhold their meals if they did not stand up straight for all to see. He had laughed when he mentioned the word straight to Violet. Another ignorant joke that he assumed was highly amusing, she'd thought.

Women and men looked up at them as they passed,

fingers pointing. A group of young boys threw the pebbles they'd collected from the sides of the paths. A pebble the size of a shilling struck Jules at the side of her head. The way she maintained her composure whilst the blood trickled slowly from the wound surprised Violet. "This is what normal is for us." she whispered. "Our lives are not ours in this world, but I hope the next one will be beautiful."

Her words caught Violet off guard. There was an air of forgiveness for those who had mistreated her and her children, or maybe it was that of acceptance. Violet wondered whether she could ever find that feeling in her heart. It concerned her she too may one day just give up, relent to the unkindness and the cruelty, as if she deserved it. No, she would never, she told herself, because the day that happens she would be letting her grandmother and all those like her win. "Wouldn't you ever want to get away from here?" Violet muttered under her breath, just loud enough for Jules to hear.

"Of course. I never wanted this life, nor did I want to bring children into the world that would have to live as I do, but I have never had a choice. There is nowhere for me to go now. I must stay and protect my children." she replied.

Violet nodded. She could understand that, and she respected it, but before she would concede to this life of torment, she would do all she could to escape.

Mycroft's plan to draw in the crowds had succeeded and,

as the last citizen took their seat, Violet, Jules, Christopher, and Miles stepped down from the stage outside. The cold pinched at her muscles, restricting them. Her body shook with repetitive shudders as she walked under the canvas dome.

Reginald shoved them in succession to keep walking. Violet wanted to yell at him. The shackles were still weighing heavy around her ankles. The skin was sore from the friction as it rubbed against the rust-raised edges. Violet refrained from releasing the anger bubbling inside her. If she wanted to be free of them, she would have to make them believe she would not try to escape. She would have to convince them she was happy to stay. The very notion was ludicrous. It was the absolute opposite of how she felt. How they ever believed that any of them would be content to be humiliated night after night, left her in utter disbelief.

The clank of her chains attracted the eyes of many. Whispers and sniggers filled the dome. Their stares were excruciating to bear. Once again, she closed her eyes, looked inward, and drowned them out.

Reginald did not lock her behind the iron bars when they eventually stopped behind a poorly hung curtain. It hung heavy. The folds bagged under the odd and inadequately spaced brass rings with no cornice to hide their mistakes. "Get yourself up there." he demanded, pointing to the newly built tower.

Violet climbed the old worn ladder that stood propped

against it. Even with Violet's tiny frame, the ladder swayed against the insecure structure of the tower. She did not know how it coped with the weight of the large brass bell at the top or how it could withstand the weight of her for as long as the Carson brothers had hoped.

Her legs rested against the tatty edges of the last rung of the ladder. Violet shifted herself onto her knees into a small compartment where they ordered her to stand. The wood was roughly cut; large splinters pointing up like needles in different directions. She had been lucky with the last one she'd endured as it had found its way out from under her skin without the aid of the Carson brothers, but these would have caused far more damage, she thought. The trousers she wore were a barrier between her skin and the sharp miniature daggers of wood, but her hands were being pricked and jabbed with every movement, no matter how slight.

When she finally settled, her body balanced against the rocking of the slapdash carpentry efforts of the Carson brothers. Mycroft bellowed an order for her to take hold of the thick, rough rope that swung silently above her head. She grabbed at it with both hands, careful not to elbow the wooden walls that closed her in. There was a single glassless window, large enough for her to see the audience and for their watchful eyes to fall upon the entertainment they viewed her to be. Nausea rumbled in her stomach. She would fool them, she promised herself. She would be an actress for however long it took until they released her from her shackles.

As the wheels from the cart holding the tower rolled over the hat-strewn floor, Violet tugged down on the rope with both hands. Her stomach muscles clenched as she pulled the rope against the weight of the brass and pressed her feet hard against the single plank of wood beneath them. Her leg muscles fought against the rocking motion as the bell drowned out the names that rang out from the crowd. She wondered whether the Carson brothers knew they had saved her from the crowd's torment or whether it had been just a fortunate coincidence. Violet bathed in the depth of the resounding, singular, repetitive note.

Will sat huddled in his prison as the departing guests poked and prodded through the bars. He grunted on cue as demanded of him. Violet watched as small hands rocked the tower beneath her while parents cheered them on. Children giggled and contorted their bodies trying to imitate her. Invisible fingers with long nails pinched at her heart. There was no way that this would get any easier for her, she thought.

Beyond the crowd, a man stood behind the children, simply staring. His eyes were pools of ink, as black as coal. His tailored coat drew him in at the waist. The tails flowed over his narrow hips and blended into his trousers. His silk waistcoat and top hat glistened in the light as he peered from under the hat's brim. Violet shuddered under his glare. His look was not like those who delighted in her difference, it was the look of a predator. She shifted back into the tower, squeezing herself into the shadows that pooled in its depths. Her blood curdled in her veins as cold as ice, the image of him etched in her mind.

"Oi!!!" bellowed Reginald Carson, running up to the crowd. They had cocooned the tower, with Violet inside, in a neatly packed circle of warm, jostling bodies. "Get away from that! Took me bloomin' ages, that did."
'Typical!' thought Violet, 'Worried about the tower and not the person sitting in it.' Reginald Carson's words eradicated the image of the wolf-like man from her mind, but she knew she could not forget him entirely. Flames of determination flickered in the man's eyes. A chill in her bones warned her of his return.

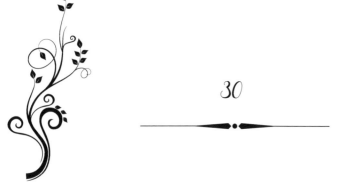

30

———— ◆•◆ ————

"That's it." Emil sighed, "Every house has received a copy of Violet's portrait."

"Not quite. We still have that meeting to attend." Rosie offered.

Emil's optimism was fraying at the edges. He was trying desperately to maintain hope, but where it had once been in buckets, it now was just a small handful. "Come on, duck." Rosie said as she gestured to the carriage, "You can't give up. Who knows, she could be 'ome any day now." The old woman smiled deeply at Emil. Her eyes twinkled with sadness at his breaking heart.

"Let us hope, dear Rosie... let us hope." Emil muttered.

Both parties relaxed back into the soft leather of the seats as the wheels flicked and splayed the gravel caught within their spokes. The soft crunch of the grinding grit beneath them and the gentle clop of the horses' hooves filled the void. Emil straightened the last few of the portraits on his lap. "Where are you, my love?" he mused, releasing a long, exasperated sigh.

Mr. Franklin leaned back in his chair, inhaling deeply

through a large, fat cigar perched between his thumb and his forefinger before releasing small circular puffs of sweetly scented smoke. "What can I do for you today?" he asked in his broad and deep American accent.

Mr. Franklin tried to figure out the young man that stood only two feet away from him. When he had packed up and moved to England from the States, they had not described men as young as this one to be so lacking in life and lustre, but this one was just that.

"I would like for you to print this portrait in your newspaper." Emil stated. He did not want to ask because if he asked, he would allow them the opportunity to refuse.

Mr. Franklin stared at Violet's image. "Why, she's a pretty young thing, sir. Is she your sweetheart?"

"She is my fiancée." Emil corrected, "and she is missing."

A mist of sadness clouded Mr. Franklin's eyes. He understood why this young man had looked so forlorn. "Say no more … err…"

"Mr. Meriwether… Emil Meriwether, sir."

"Say no more, Mr. Meriwether. This pretty lady will be on the front of the paper tomorrow morning, first thing."

Emil grabbed the man's hand and shook it profusely. "Thank you so much, Mr. Franklin. I can't tell you how much this means to me."

"Oh, I think I have a fair idea, young Emil." he smiled, "Perhaps, if we could let London know a little more about your fiancée then they may even help you look for her?" Mr. Franklin raised his eyebrows, waiting for Emil to agree.

"What would you like to know?" Emil asked.

Mr. Franklin gestured for him and Rosie to sit. "First, let's have a nice cup of tea, shall we?" Before Rosie or Emil could answer, the man had called for his secretary to bring in tea and cakes.

"Thank you, Mr. Franklin, that's very kind." Rosie smiled.

"My pleasure ma'am." Mr. Franklin dipped the quill of his pen in a full pot of ink and poised himself, ready for the answers he expected would flow from Emil's mouth.

"What's the young lady's name and where is she from, Mr. Meriwether?" he began.

"Her name is Violet Hall."

"Where is she from?"

"Well..."

Mr. Franklin's eyes raised from the paper. His brow furrowed at Emil's stuttering response. "Perhaps we should have a little drink. It'll steady your nerves." He raised a bottle of whiskey and splashed it into a teacup, handing it to Emil. Mr. Franklin's cheeks were flushed red, leading Emil to believe that he'd been at the bottle already that day.

Emil swallowed hard as the liquid sloshed against the back of his throat, hot and bitter. The sting of the alcohol zipped back and forth under his skin as he fought back the need to shudder. "Thank you, Mr. Franklin." he said. The teacup clinked against the saucer as he placed it back into the neat, smooth dip at the centre.

"Now where were we?" Mr. Franklin said.

"Violet is from London." Guilt rose in Emil's throat for lying, but the truth would have destroyed any chance of the newspaper printing the portrait.

"Ah, that's right. Has she lived here very long?"

"No, only a few weeks."

Mr. Franklin scraped his top teeth over his bottom lip as he dipped the quill in the pot of ink again.

"Do you know where she lived before?" he asked, poised and ready for in-depth details of the missing woman's life.

Even after one lie, Emil was anxious and exhausted. Lying was not a trait that he wished to participate in. "I'm afraid I didn't ask."

"I see." Mr. Franklin smiled wickedly, waggling his eyebrows at Emil. "Too busy getting to know each other, were we?"

Emil blushed. "Something like that, Mr. Franklin."

"Ah, don't be so embarrassed, Mr. Meriwether. I was a young man once, you know."

Emil smiled and lowered his eyes from the man, halting the conversation in its tracks.

After several more questions that required nothing but the truth, Mr. Franklin shook Emil's hand and promised him that Violet would be on the front cover of the newspaper early the next morning and in every home in London.

"Thank you, Mr. Franklin. This is truly very kind of you."

"Not at all, dear lad. Let's hope we can return Miss. Hall to you as soon as possible. I'm an old romantic at heart and I do so love a happy ending." he beamed.

Outside the office, Emil relaxed his shoulders and stared up at the sky. "I'm so glad that part is over, Rosie."

"Me too, duck." she replied.

"I feel awful, having to deceive him."

"What were you supposed to say?" she chuckled, "Well, I'm not entirely sure where Violet is from. She just turned up in my house out of nowhere?" she mimicked. "If you'd done that, Emil, we would have all been carted off to the asylum, and then we'd never have a chance of finding our Violet."

"Yes, sadly, that is the truth." Emil agreed, "and I don't think those grey gowns the asylum residents wear are really our colour, do you?" he grinned.

"Definitely not. They're much too dreary." Rosie laughed, lifting her skirts above her feet as they boarded the carriage for home.

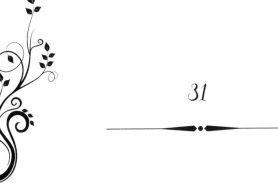

31

Violet could not tell whether the chill in her bones came from the glare in the man's eyes or whether there was an illness lurking within her body. The penetrating chill of the iron bars dug into her shoulder as she tried to find a position of comfort against them. Every slight movement or shift in her position was fruitless. They all resulted in further discomfort and pain. If she could sleep, then perhaps she could find her way back to Emil. If she could tell him where she was, then maybe he could get her out of there. There couldn't be that many by the name of Carson's Creatures of Curiosity, surely? she thought.

With just a thin layer of skin and her hair as the only cushion between her skull and the bars, Violet tried, in earnest, to sleep. One hour passed into another and then another until the drowning tug of sleep pulled her under.

The purest black, darker than the night itself, was all she could see. No voices, no colour, just a long resting void. Violet exhaled, deflated by Emil's absence. Was it because she was too far away? Did she not sleep well enough? She did not understand why she could not reach him. Everything inside her cried out for him.

The ebb and flow of heat and cold, swallowed her fears. Her brow moistened with sweat. The ache in her bones from the discomfort of the bars where she lay, intensified as the throbbing, pulsing thrum of the fever vibrated through them. A dizziness stirred the room before her eyes. At the slightest movement, her stomach churned in a whirlpool, rising and falling with every breath. Violet closed her eyes, trying to restore a feeling of balance. Shivers relentlessly rattled up and down her spine without rest.

"Wakey, Wakey!" Reginald pounded his fist against the iron bars. "You wiped that bloody paint off ya, again?" he moaned, "That stuff costs money, ya know!"
Violet hadn't forgotten her attempts to get the brothers' trust, but it was getting more and more difficult each time. The more they treated her like she was nothing more than excrement ground into the soles of their shoes, the more she fought not to retaliate. "Sorry." she said, "I must have wiped it off in the night. I'm not feeling very well."

Reginald dismissed her excuse for the face paint as he gave her a sideways glance. "Ah, I ain't got time for none of that 'I don't feel well' malarkey." His face stilled, stern and adamant. "You need to earn back what I paid for you and then some."

His words were not unexpected, but they had made Violet curious. "How much did you pay my grandmother for me?" she asked, as she crawled out of the cage, her limbs heavy and weak.

"Never you bloody mind. That is the business of real folks, not for the likes of you." he sniffed.

She didn't persist. She'd had many years within the grasp of her grandmother's ignorance to tell when to refrain from pushing the subject. Ignorance, she had learned, was the behaviour of fools, and those that were uneducated in real life and the realities of the world they lived in. They were too afraid of what they did not understand, so, rather than try to learn, they cast those with differences out. It was extremely sad, she thought, and definitely hard to be one of those at the knife edge of their closed minds but, nevertheless, it remained the absolute truth.

Her thoughts had helped her to muster a little sympathy for their lacking, but as she looked at Reginald Carson, those sympathies died in a single breath. This man and his brother had gone above and beyond ignorant, diving straight into a dangerous and cruel world.

Violet rehearsed as they expected her to. Resentment had become exhausting. It wasn't helping her, she realized. She pushed the anger aside as she trudged up the tower for the fifth time that morning. Exhaustion folded around her shoulders as sickness secreted from her body in beads of sweat. At the top of the tower, everything swayed. Her vision blurred as the rope swayed back and forth out of her reach. Nothing defined its edges, not even her own hands as she tried to adjust her eyes.

"What on God's earth are you doing?!" yelled Mycroft as he watched her. "Grab the bloody rope!"

Violet tried again, but she just couldn't align the rope with the length of her arm to grab it. When she thought she had it in her grasp, there was no sensation against her skin. Mycroft cursed under his breath as he stomped to the ladder.

"For heaven's sake!" he seethed, climbing the first ten rungs to peer into the small box where she sat. He grabbed the rope then, forcing Violet's fingers open, he shoved the coarse fibres of the rope against her soft skin. His face grimaced at Violet's sweat that now clung to his skin.

"Reginald!" he bellowed.

Reginald ran quickly to his aid. "What is it?" he panted.

"Get this thing clean, will you?!" Mycroft ordered, wiping his soaked hand on his trousers.

"It looks alright." Reginald looked confused by his brother's request.

"Yes, well, it probably would by your standards." Mycroft's eyes travelled the length of his brother's body from his toes to his head and back down again, snarling in disgust at the filth that clung to his clothes. He looked more like a chimney sweep rather than a showman, he thought. "Do I have to be the only one that appreciates hygiene in this place?"

"Tsk, what flumadiddle." Reginald muttered as Mycroft glared at him. "Alright, alright. Get yourself down here, me 'unchback. Let's give ya a wash then for my brother's delicate sense of smell."

Violet didn't have it in her to feel anything more than she did as she listened to those words. She wished she could just curl up in a ball and sleep but, perhaps a nice warm bath would be all she needed to revive herself, she thought. Violet climbed carefully down the ladder, keeping her eyes closed and using only her sense of touch to guide her.

Mycroft's face was puce as he held back his intolerance of his brother. If he had been as wealthy and fortunate as the filthy urchin, then he would be the one to reap the benefits of 'Carson's Creatures of Curiosity.' It would refer to his name rather than his brother's. He was the intelligence behind all that the show had to offer, but still, here he was, the hired help, he fumed quietly.

Reginald pushed Violet out into an open area. Gravel crunched beneath her worn soles. The icy blast of air cooled her glistening skin. Shadows pooled in the depths of her sunken eyes as she stood shivering while the man sized her up. Surely, she was supposed to be inside to bathe, she thought. Her head drooped at the discomfort of his look.

Reginald heaved at a long flat heavy ribbon made of leather. Brass studs dotted down its centre; a metal attachment protruded at the end. Before Violet could ask what the thing was and where her bath would be, water fired from its circular jaws. The painfully cold liquid pelted at her skin in a relentless stream of power. She ground her jaws as a mixture of the force and temperature stole her breath and burned her skin. She gasped for air as the pain behind her eyes cut like blades. Her legs trembled furiously as fist after fist of water bruised her skin. First in the chest, then the stomach. Sprays of water stung her face. Reginald walked around her, hose still active in his hands, and the strength of the water knocking her back repeatedly until she could no longer feel her skin. The last blow of water took her legs out from beneath her.

"Bloody hell! I ain't got all day. Besides, you're going to make my brother angry." Reginald's fingers dug into her arm as he yanked her weak, drenched body from the floor. Violet's stomach cramped violently. The tightening of her muscles pulsed up her torso, reaching her throat as she heaved, hurling the contents of her stomach at Reginald's feet, missing his shoes by a mere centimetre. Instinctively, the man jumped back.

Inside the tent, Reginald caught Mycroft's attention. He refrained from shouting as it would only cause mayhem amongst the other acts. Mycroft huffed loudly, tsked, then exhaled in a drawn-out, extended, and exaggerated breath as he walked toward his sibling. "Carry on rehearsing!" he bellowed furiously back to the acts, their curiosity peaked by the expression on Reginald's face. "What is it?!" Mycroft blustered, "Can you not see that I am busy?"

"Don't you forget who owns this place!" It was a rare

occurrence that Reginald would remind Mycroft of that fact, but when he did, he would always come to regret it. He knew Mycroft had been the brains behind it all, as well as the attraction that lured in the ladies. Reginald scowled at that thought. He couldn't understand what Mycroft had that he didn't.

"Oh, I do not forget, dear brother, but if you would prefer, I can just leave you to it?"

Reginald erred on the side of caution as he lowered his tone and apologised for his outburst.

"Very well, I shall stay. Now, what was it that is so important?"

"It's shitting through its teeth." he blurted, nodding his head and gesturing outside.

Mycroft pushed back the curtain as its corners flapped back and forth from the wind. His distaste at his brother's foul use of slang screwed up his defined features as he poked his head out into the open. A strangled whisper of a moan squeezed at the back of his throat as he looked at Violet and the puddle of vomit at her feet.

"Putrid." he snapped. One hand gestured as to shoo her away and the other pinched his nose. "Clear it up and help that creature."

"Should we get the doctor?" Reginald suggested.

"And waste good money?... Good heavens, no. Don't be ridiculous."

"Well, what should we do?"

"I suppose its role is not exactly arduous or really in need of a rehearsal today. Let it rest for now, dry off, and then it will play its part tonight."

"Good thinkin', Mycroft. I'll go lock it up."

32

The strain of the bars against Violet's body was excruciating. It was the worse pain she had ever felt. Every fibre of her muscles clung to one another, afraid they would rip beneath her flesh if they didn't. The pain roared, searing in tremors. Her skin screamed as the damp, cold clothes rested against it.

She had been drifting in and out of consciousness since Reginald Carson had turned the key to her lock. Snippets of voices and conversations could be heard as the darkness wavered. Her eyelids fought to stay open. Eventually, the pain she was in didn't matter anymore as she gave in to sleep.

Darkness. Nothing but darkness and then the stark reality of day as the light played havoc with her eyes. Her vision resembled that of fractured glass, each shard tinged with a rainbow hue. It was not pretty but hindering. Visions of objects and people around her, distorted. The pain in her head throbbed. Her cheeks were warm with an unhealthy heat, elevated over time.

Loud, argumentative voices reigned above her; the Carson brothers, conversing and bickering about what to do with her. Violet listened carefully, not wanting them to know she could hear them. Her eyes remained closed, pretending to sleep.

"We need to get a doctor!" Reginald barked. The hay flew up in the air as his foot hit the ground in a frenzied temper. Violet lay there, silently amused at the concern the man portrayed. It was new, but she was not a fool. The man only cared for his investment and what he would lose if something happened to her.

"It is an expense that we cannot afford!" Mycroft bellowed in retaliation.

"For someone who finks he's so astute, you ain't exactly clever, are ya?." Reginald retorted, "If we lose it, we will lose far more money than if we 'ave to get it 'elp."

Mycroft sniffed, his breathing stiff and agitated. He stared at his brother, lips pursed and eyes burning with frustration at being corrected. He desperately wanted to say something that would prove he had been correct all along, but there was nothing he could say. "Very well, brother." he spat, "Get the doctor. You clearly paid far too much for this thing, otherwise you wouldn't be so insolent toward me!" Mycroft kicked the bars of Violet's prison and stormed off.

The doctor was a tall, stout gentleman. His movements were leisurely as he walked into the tent. "Where is the patient?" he enquired. His eyes met Reginald's, over the rim of his glasses, when he could see no sign of someone that needed his attention.

"She's there." Reginald pointed to the cage at the man's feet. He stared at Violet, trembling and trapped in tight-fitting rusty shackles.

The doctor's chest puffed out, his jaw rigid, and his eyes ferocious with disgust. "Why, sir, is this young woman trapped like an animal in a cage?!"

"It ain't a woman doctor. It's a beast." Reginald stated.

"I do not care what you call her, sir, but I do ask you this... Would you would be as callous with an animal as you have been with her?"

Reginald's eyes roved across the arena at the poorly kept animals that struggled tirelessly under the threat of Mycroft's whip.

"Do not bother to answer that." the doctor blustered, infuriated at the man. "My first orders are that you get this young woman some clean dry clothes, somewhere comfortable to lie down, and something warm to drink. Do you understand?"

Reginald was speechless at what he viewed was nothing but audacity from the doctor. How dare he tell him what to do? He decided he would not argue with the man. If a heated outburst met with Mycroft's ears, it would only serve as a prompt for his brother to say, "I told you so." and he would not let that happen. "Mycroft's head is already big enough as it is." he muttered.

"What did you say?" the doctor snapped.

"Oh, not you, sir." Reginald grovelled. "I was just thinking about my brother. I will do just as you say."

Reginald dragged in several large bales of hay and placed them side by side, creating a large surface for Violet to lie down upon. Next, he placed two large hessian sacks over the top as a sheet. The doctor made a grumbling noise at the back of his throat. A look of disbelief on his face.

"It ain't perfec', I know." Reginald smiled, baring his lack of hygiene in the cracks and cavities of his teeth. "But it's all we 'ave, what with travelling and all."

The doctor remained silent, disturbed by the man before him. "There!" Reginald exclaimed as he presented the makeshift bed he'd made for Violet. "Will that do, doctor?"

The man sighed. "That will have to do. Now, tell me this, Mr. Carson, how, exactly, is my patient to dress in that?!" The doctor pointed at the cage as Reginald scurried like a snivelling rat toward the lock.

"Yes, of course, doctor."

As the lock clicked open, Violet pushed her shoulders against the small door, careful not to catch the shackles against the bars. Her skin was raw beneath the rusted iron. She could not see how much, but she could imagine. Any knock against them now would only cause further complications. A gentle hand guided Violet to her feet. The doctor stood next to her, his face filled with concern.

"Thank you." she rasped. Violet had not realized how sore her throat was. She hadn't had to use her throat until then, but now a long sharp sting seared inside with every movement.

"The clean, dry clothes, Mr. Carson?" The doctor's eyebrows raised upon his stern, accusing face.

"'Ere they are." Reginald placed the clean clothes on the hay bed and stared at Violet.

"Perhaps the young lady would like some privacy?!" The doctor was practically purple with rage. 'How on God's earth did this buffoon manage to function?', he thought.

"I keep tellin' ya doctor, it ain't a young lady. It's an 'it'." Reginald spoke slowly, as if the doctor did not understand what he was telling him.

"Mr. Carson, do not patronize me. I implore you to heed my instructions and give this young woman some privacy while she changes into the new clothes."

Reginald Carson rolled his eyes at the doctor but relented. He released the shackles from Violet's wrists, neck, and ankles. "Don't you go getting any funny ideas." he threatened as the chains crashed against the floor, then turned his back on Violet while she changed into the dry clothes he had found.

Violet's spirit lifted. The doctor's kindness towards her had pleasantly surprised her. Perhaps he would take her away from here, she thought, as she inspected the new clothes. They were identical to the ones that she was already wearing, but they felt much heavier against her aching body. They must have been spare clothing they'd already put aside for her, she thought, sitting fully dressed on the makeshift hay bale bed. She couldn't tell if the clothes had warmed her. Her body was indecisive whether she was hot or cold, but the feel of the softer hay bales beneath her was divine. She would never have believed that she would describe a hay bed as divine, but after spending nights on the ice-cold floor, she appreciated the comfort it offered.

"Are you decent, Miss?" the doctor asked Violet, his back to her.

"Yes, doctor." she croaked.

As the doctor turned, the rage that reddened his cheeks drained into a lily white. Rings of blood wrapped around Violet's neck like a choker, and around her wrists like cuffs. The shackles had twisted, tugged, and turned with every movement against her skin until it tore beneath them. Traces of pus festered, igniting the infection that had begun to ravage her body.

"What have you done?" the doctor growled. Anger flickered in his eyes as he stared at Reginald Carson. "Do not bother to answer. I shall tell you what you have done. The reason this young lady is poorly is that you have shackled her like the beast you believe she is. Look at her neck, her wrists!" he scolded, pulling back the sheet to reveal her ankles. "And her ankles!"

"They don't 'urt the tigers or the lions." Reginald sniffed, annoyed by the doctor's accusations. "Ain't had this problem before. Must be its own fault."

The doctor inhaled to cool his temper. "Mr. Carson, if I am to help this young lady..."

"It." Reginald corrected.

"If I am to help this young lady," the doctor repeated, "You are not to replace the shackles on her. Is that understood?"

"What if it runs away?"

"I won't!" Violet burst in weakly, seizing her opportunity. "I promise I won't."

Reginald eyed Violet suspiciously. "Hmm, alright doctor, you have a deal. Besides, I paid good money for it to some old biddy who says she was its grandmother."

"How interesting." the doctor rolled his eyes sarcastically. "May I treat my patient now?"

"Do what you need to, doctor." Reginald declared as though he wanted to save Violet, but both she and the doctor knew better. They knew he was merely trying to save money and his reputation.

Violet did not get the chance to say farewell or thank the doctor. Intermittent fatigue had stolen snippets of the day from her, and still, it wanted more. The kind doctor had cleaned and bandaged her wounds. She wondered whether she would come to regret not seizing her chance to beg him to save her.

The excited chatter of guests filled Violet's ears as she lay upon the hay bales at war with sleep. Sleep had engulfed her body as she lay silent in its grasp, but it had left her mind alert to the world that carried on without her.

The noise was loud, Violet thought, as she listened. Too much noise for people that were far away from her. Fingers poked at her body, focusing on her back as she lay helpless.

"Remove your fingers." hissed Mycroft, "It is not to be touched. Do you not see the sign?!"

The eager crowd drew back. Many a disgruntled father's face glared at Mycroft for scolding their children. "See here," grumbled a scrawny man with a thin line of black hair above his lip, "We have paid good money to see this creature." The man pointed at Violet, then jabbed his finger into her back. Violet let out a weak moan at the man's touch. His fingertip poked her skin. It was sharp and bony, like the rest of him.

"Sir," Mycroft seethed, "You do not pay to touch, you pay to observe."

The man backed away, guiding his sons with him. His thin body was rigid and haughty. His cane bashed against the floor to emphasize his dislike for Mycroft Carson.

Violet opened her eyes a fraction to appear as though she still slept. She peered at the men confronting each other over who had the right to touch her or look at her, as though she was something to be possessed by others. Either they had drawn a crowd or she had, she couldn't tell, but it gathered around her in a closed circle. She was on display like an exhibit in a museum. Even in her poor state, the Carson Brothers were determined to reap the benefits of their investment. Violet closed her eyes tight, humming under her breath, suffocating the drone of onlookers.

The evening was horrendous. Violet lay there, eyes closed and silent, being pawed and prodded by strangers' fingers. The show lingered to music and the guffawing and gasps of many. She kept still on her stage of hay, frightened that she would alert Reginald or Mycroft to her conscious state. They would make her perform. It was bad enough performing when well but the thought of performing when she felt so ill was one she could not bear. Violet remained steadfast in her act until all that remained was the silence of an almost empty tent.

There was an eerie silence between each breath. A sense that she was being watched pushed against her chest, her body too weak to move. The darkness shielded her eyes. She waited for them to adjust, but they refused to do so. A scrape of grit between the floor and the soles of shoes broke the silence. Violet gasped. Her heart galloped in her chest like a thousand horses fleeing for safety. She pushed her hands against the hay bales. Sharp prickles of the dried grass clawed against her palms as she heaved her body into a sitting position. The noise came again, this time a little closer. She paused, suffocating in the turmoil of her fear.

Long spindly fingers ran through her tangled, unwashed hair. "Hmmm… we will have to do something about this." A deep, masculine drawl vibrated in her ear. The noise coiled around the fear that twisted and writhed in her stomach, pulling it tighter and tighter. As another set of feet shuffled into the tent, she tried to call out, but her voice got as far as the hand clamped over her mouth, and ceased behind a door of cold fingers.

"Time to leave." the man hissed like a snake; his arms cradled her. His fingers were rough and pinching into her skin as he lifted her off the hay. The fear overrode the retaliation that boiled inside her and Violet slipped into the darkness of her mind once more, oblivious to the danger the figure carried her towards.

33

He was there. She was there.

"Emil!" Violet called loudly, "Emil!"

Emil's head was in his hands. His body hunched over his desk. Rosie stood behind him, a sadness swimming in the pools of her eyes.

"Give it time, duck. It's only been a day since they printed the newspaper." Rosie gently squeezed Emil's shoulder to offer comfort.

Emil's palms dragged over his face, pulling at his features. Agony flushed his face while Violet looked on in dismay. "Emil!" she called again, "I'm right here. I'm in front of you."

There was no recognition of the cries that flooded the room. She howled in distress as his eyes failed to see her. The man she loved didn't know that she was trying to communicate with him. She wanted to tell him she was doing all she could to return to him. She wanted to assure him she would keep trying, no matter how long it would take. Suddenly, panic struck Violet. What if it was too late? What if she was dead? She stared at her hands. Her breathing quickened, fear cutting into it, staggering its fluidity. The pale skin of her hands was opaque with the transparency of smoke yet perfectly formed. Her arms, an extension of the same. Tendrils of colour emanated from her body's outline. It would take just a simple breeze and she would drift away. "This can't be happening!" she whimpered, 'This can't be true. Emil!!!' she cried. Violet's arm stretched out towards the man she loved and then he was gone.

"Good morning." It was that voice again. Was he death? Is that why he had taken her? Violet's fingers roamed the flat surface beneath where she lay. Linen, cool, and dry against her skin. The overpowering, ashy scent of tobacco filled her mouth and nose. She coughed, expelling it from her body. The fever had broken. Fear of the unknown replaced her exhaustion. Slowly, she opened her eyes to face the voice that now haunted her existence.

A man looked down at her. She had only ever seen him one time, and she remembered it vividly. His eyes were just as dark, perhaps darker still, as he stared down at her. A malevolent glint pulsated in his irises. His sharp, defined features were almost piercing. 'He could be death.' she thought as she cowered under the spindly tower of a man. He seemed to read her mind as an angular, wicked smile stretched his features.

"Where am I?" she said. "What I mean is, am I dead?"
The thin, beady-eyed man threw his head back and laughed. Each breath he drew into his lungs vibrated like rough stone scraping across wood. "No, you are not

dead. Far from it, in fact."

His amusement annoyed Violet with the added insult of a limited answer. "Where am I, then?" she asked again. "Why, you are here." he replied, his hand upturned and gesturing to the room. Its four walls boxing them neatly inside. "This is where you shall live now." he added, "I will make you a star!"

"What do you mean?" she asked, trying to get the man to explain, but he simply turned around and sauntered out of the room, locking the door behind him. Violet untangled her legs from the sheet and ran to the door. Her small hands clutched at the knob, twisting and turning it as she pulled at the door to open it. It would take much more than what she could offer to release her from this new jail.

Her plan was to escape the Carson brothers' claws. At the circus, she'd had some idea of where she was. They had even released her from the shackles and her cage. It had given her a surge of hope of finding her way back to the cabin and Emil. Now, though, she knew nothing about her captor, his location, or what he intended for her but, what troubled her more than anything was the pain she'd seen in Emil's eyes. It had nearly broken her. 'Most people would probably just surrender,' she thought, 'but I'm not like most people.' She would not dwell on it and plunge herself into melancholy, but use it as her reason to try harder to get home. 'Besides,' she thought, 'How far could I have travelled in one night?'

❖

Supper time came and went, but no visitors or food to satisfy the hunger that scratched her insides. The tension in her head cracked and snapped against her skull as she tried to ignore her body's need for nourishment. Her tongue was dry with thirst.

Violet knocked on the wooden door from the inside of her room, then pressed her ear firmly against it, listening for signs of any movement outside. A steady clomp of shoes thumped upon the dark wood panels of the landing that stretched in front of her room. Impatience echoed in the rhythm of the footsteps. Constant, agitated pacing back and forth. "Hello?" she called again. The pacing stopped. They had heard her, she thought hopefully. Even so, they chose to ignore her.

"Please, can I have some food?" she pleaded, "I haven't eaten for days." Nothing again, but this time the footsteps beat against the wood, the volume decreasing as they moved further away, then disappeared. Violet settled back onto the bed, noting her new surroundings. She could not deny that the room was indeed an improvement of what the Carson brothers subjected her to, but she had no doubt she was once again at the mercy of a wicked man. A depressing darkness burdened the room. A musty odour lingered on every piece of furniture. Dust lined the wooden chest of drawers. Violet traced her finger through it, revealing a vibrant, lavish chestnut-stained wood. The lacquer highlighted the intense shades of red and copper in its pattern. It broke the dull depth of the shadows that leered over her. The copper shade was a reminder of how her hair once glistened in the sunlight. What was once glossy and healthy, now hung dull and matte. She longed for the warmth of bathing; to feel hot water, pour gently over her hair, and wash away the grime that knotted the strands in clumps of filth; and for the chance to feel clean.

An hour later, a light tapping on the door interrupted her thoughts. The familiar click of a key turning in the lock warned her to move back into the shadows, afraid of who would enter. A young maid stood with a tray in her hands. A bowl of soup perched on the top with two thick slices of buttered bread. "Here you are, miss." she said, as she placed the tray on the small table at the side of her bed. "Master is out, but the butler said you were hungry and we can't have that."

The maid seemed nervous, Violet thought. She wondered whether it was because she'd hidden from her or whether it was because she knew what her master was up to. Either way, she did not know, but she could find out if one part was true. Violet stepped out of the shadows and into the dim room, standing before the young maid. The maid gasped. Her face was ashen as she looked at Violet, but it was not a look Violet understood. She had understood the looks of disgust, horror, and repulsion, but this look was one of fear. "Please don't be scared of me." Violet pleaded.

"Oh, I'm not scared of you, miss." the maid breathed.

"Then what is it that frightens you?" Violet asked, stepping closer.

"N-nothing, miss. Don't you pay any attention to me, miss. My ma says I can be a bit daft sometimes. I'd like to tell you she was wrong but I'm afraid she's not, miss." the young maid rambled.

Her rambling concerned Violet immensely as she listened. A secret buried itself in the maid's words, but she was too afraid to reveal it. "Well, I best be going, miss." the maid declared. She knew Violet had questions, but she could not answer them for her. "Don't let that soup get cold, miss." The maid hurried out of the room and locked the door behind her.

The maid's frantic breaths sounded through the door as she rested her back against it on the other side. "Dear God, please not again." she prayed.

34

Emil had risen early. Fear and worry for Violet had disturbed his sleep. There was still no word of her. Nobody had offered even a scrap of information that may lead him to her. His nerves were in tatters. If it had not been for the unexplainable tug in his chest that told him she was alive, he feared he would stumble easily over the edge into utter despair.

"Good morning, Rosie." he yawned, stepping down from the last stair. "Is there any post?"

"Afraid not, duck." Rosie looked as disappointed and downhearted as Emil, even though she had tried so hard not to reveal her fears. It would only drag him down further, she thought.

Emil nodded and headed towards the parlour with the newspaper tucked neatly under his arm.

Violet curled up in a ball as the sun shone onto her face. The warmth of the light against her eyelids confused her. Yesterday, it had been suffocatingly dreary in that room without a window. After the maid's reaction to her, she didn't dare to look up. She had tried to analyze what the young woman may have been hiding, but her thoughts rapidly descended into darkness as she dug deeper into what it could have meant. No, she decided, she would not open her eyes to look. That man would most likely be leering at her, studying her. Her heartbeat filled her ears. The pumping of her blood, like fists pounding against a wall.

"Violet?" The voice was soft, tender, caring, and familiar. "Violet, is that you?"

Violet took a deep breath as she slowly uncurled her body. Glorious sunshine drenched the room as it streamed through the window. She was no longer in the dark confinement of her chambers, guarded by her captor.

Arms of a soft chair held her in its grip, cushioning and protecting her as she fumbled to focus and find her bearings. Clarity of her surroundings, found in those sparkling green eyes she knew so well, as they softly gazed down at her. "Emil?" she murmured. Violet's body shook. She wanted to believe she had returned to him, but the fear of losing him all over again was unbearable.

"Yes, darling, it's me." Emil gazed at her trembling body. The way she curled in on herself told him she was trying to protect herself. Her clothes were filthy rags, and her hair showed the cruelty she had suffered in every knot and tangle within it.

Violet felt ashamed of the dirt encrusted on her clothes, her skin, and her hair. Even her face left traces of her humiliation as powder remained in smudges of grey. There was soil and grime on her hands. Fingernails broken and chipped. 'What must he think of me?' she thought. Her throat ached as she let out a sob. Emil fell to his knees in front of her. Her emotions were raw as he held her tight. He did not care about the dirt on her clothes. His heart fractured as her body heaved with unbridled tears of anguish. The young woman he held was slowly breaking, and he didn't know how to save her.

The warm, luxurious water from the bath prepared for Violet wrapped itself around her waist. Her lower half, submerged blissfully in its comfort. The steam rose, filling the air with the inviting aroma of lavender, and drifted over the stench of her torment.

"I'll wash these." Rosie muttered to Violet as she collected up her dirty clothes. Her voice reduced to nothing more than a whisper by the pain reflected in the young woman's eyes. She couldn't bring herself to say the next part, although they both knew she was only washing them in case Violet had to leave again. Rosie hurried from the room as tears pooled in her eyes.

Violet sat upright in the bath; her knees bent in front of her, her arms curled around them. The plumes of steam left small puffs of moisture on her face as silent tears tore rivers through them. She breathed in the orange scent infused with lavender. A vibrancy mixed with the stillness of the calm she had longed for, but there was still a fear that wriggled like a parasite in the pit of her stomach. How could she stay? What did she need to do to never go back there?

Sensing her troubled mind, Emil knelt at the side of the bath. One arm reached out, dragging up the soaked cloth from the water. As he held it up, a waterfall cascaded down her back, relieving the muscles that ached there; the ones that reminded her why they had treated her so cruelly.

Both were comfortable in each other's silence as Emil waited, biding his time until she was ready to talk. "How do I stay here?" she rasped, turning her head towards Emil. "How am I ever going to stay with you and be your wife? I keep going back there and I don't know how to stop." Violet's voice cracked with the agony of not having the answer they needed.

Her hope was slowly disintegrating into a fine powder. She was petrified of the man she knew she would have to return to. He terrified her more than the Carson brothers ever had. How had she been so unfortunate to have jumped from a nightmare and straight into one that appeared much worse? She knew long before she'd spoken to the maid that the man was evil... but she feared to what extent that may be.

"We will find a way." Emil replied, trying to keep his voice confident.

"You can't possibly know that." she sighed, "Even as we speak, I can feel the grip that world has on me."

"World?"

"What else could this be?" Violet's eyes looked longingly at him for an answer that would make sense. "One minute I am in one place and the next I am here. I do not travel here via foot or by carriage, but by the means of sleep. Perhaps you and all of this are just a beautiful dream?" she wondered.

"I am as real as you are." Emil stated. He would not allow her to doubt his existence and simply disappear from his life. "Do not doubt that. I fear that if you do, you will not return. Perhaps your trust and belief in me are what bring you home each time. You must believe that I am real. Feel me, flesh and bone." Emil offered her his arm so that she could check for herself. Violet's hand shook as her fingers touched his warm skin, his pulse thudding in assurance at his wrist. Every beat reminding her he was real.

"There is all the proof that you need. I exist. I am as real as the love that I feel for you." Emil leaned forward and kissed her, "and as genuine as that kiss."

"Whatever happens, Emil," she said, her voice fighting to be heard, "I will always keep trying to get back to you. I will never stop, I promise."

"And I promise, I will be right here waiting for you." he replied.

35

Violet gasped. The air was thick with dust, causing her to cough. Her fingers skimmed the fabric of her clothes. She was a prisoner again, wearing the rags she had worn for days on end.

Her skin was no longer taught with filth. Her hair was soft with a sweet scent. Violet felt more like herself as she pushed back the covers on the bed. Thanks to Rosie, her clothes were clean and pressed. It was something she would have to explain to her captor, but she hoped he had not paid enough attention to notice the difference.

"Why is there no window in here?" she called out, frustration of her continual imprisonment bubbling inside her. Surely, they could hear her. She needed that maid to tell her what she was so afraid of.

"What's all this commotion?" The tall, slender man stepped into the room, angered by her outbursts. "I have welcomed you into my home and you persist in making an extreme amount of noise. You are frightening my staff."

"I didn't ask you to bring me here, you just took me!" she spat. Violet clenched her fists, her face reddening as her fingernails cut into the palms of her hand. The pain kept her alert, reminding her she had to fight.

Something shifted in the man's black eyes as his irises revealed their sharp ice-blue tones. "I believe we have got off on the wrong foot." he offered.

He was like a snake, simply shredding his outer layer revealing something brighter underneath, but Violet knew something was lurking deep within him. Something poisonous and malicious. She did not trust him. Violet took a step backward, bumping into the bed.

"Oh dear, are you alright?" he drawled, "Do be careful. There are so many things in this house that could do an untold amount of harm." His eyes narrowed, swallowing the blue.

"I'm fine." she replied meekly. Her knees gave way and folded, lowering her into a sitting position on the bed. The man's proximity was far too close as he bathed her in intimidation.

"My name is Marcus Claydale, and you are?"

"Violet Hall." she replied, keeping eye contact. "Why did you kidnap me?"

"Kidnap you?" Mr. Claydale laughed in his awful stretched, mocking rasp, "I did not kidnap you, I rescued you." he corrected her.

"Then why did you lock me up in here?" Violet softened her gaze. There was more to this man, she thought, and in the most frightening way. She could almost smell the danger on him.

"For your safety, of course. There are far too many unsavoury characters walking the streets. I do not trust them." Marcus Claydale walked up to the far wall and pushed his body against the wardrobe. It slid across the floor, screeching until it reached the far corner, revealing a window that had been hidden by its vast structure.

"There, that's better." he crooned.

It wasn't a large window, but Violet was relieved to see beyond the walls of the room. She could see the tops of trees. There was so much nature outside the house. This wasn't London anymore. "Where are we?" Violet asked nervously.

"Right back where you started."

Violet paled at his cryptic clue.

"I have known you for a long time, Violet, or should I call you Thorn? Don't worry, that was just a little joke. I have watched you work under that beast of a woman, your grandmother." he began.

His words tumbled around in her mind, chipping away at her first impression of him. Maybe this man wasn't who she thought he was. Maybe she had imagined it. She felt her shoulders relax.

"I have walked every day I have lived here, and I have seen you work tirelessly on the land, and I have heard her incessant, torturous screams of abuse. Perhaps I should have said something earlier, and for that, I apologise but, when I saw those hideous Carson brothers drag you from your home, I knew I had to rescue you. I set out to find you as soon as I could."

Violet was shocked by what he was telling her. She could not remember ever seeing him. She did not remember seeing anyone pass her grandmother's home while she was there, but, as she looked out of the window, there was no denying where she was. Hope stood tall in the distance. Her cabin, hidden by the forest just waiting for her to return.

Why had he not saved her earlier? She realized that there was quite a distance between his home and her grandmother's, but surely that would only aid him rather than hinder him? It didn't matter now, she thought, shaking off the questions. What's done is done.

"I have somewhere I can go, Mr. Claydale." Violet beamed. The pull of the cabin was more persistent now than it had been in London. The thread between her and Emil, more taught.

"You do?" a single silver eyebrow arched up in curiosity as Marcus Claydale looked to Violet for more details of this place she mentioned. As far as he was aware, the only place she could go was to her grandmother's home. Surely, she wouldn't wish to return there, of all places, he wondered.

"Yes, I do not wish to trouble you more than I have already." Excitement soared through her body. She had waited for this day for what seemed like forever. It was her chance to find a way to live her life with Emil, as his wife. It was all she wanted. Everything was working out. Perhaps she wasn't so unfortunate after all?

"You are no trouble at all, dear. I insist you stay a little longer."

"But, really, there's no need..."

"You will not leave!" he snapped, taking Violet by

surprise. Mr. Claydale cleared his throat and straightened his cravat. "What I meant to say is that you need time to recover. It is not wise for you to leave so soon." he smiled, "Now get some rest and I will get Nellie to bring you your breakfast."

Violet remained silent as the man turned his back on her. His intentions confused her. One minute he had seemed to care for her welfare and in the next, he seemed only to want to possess her.

Darkness returned to Marcus Claydale's eyes as he turned his back to her. A wicked smile sharpened his features. The girl is going nowhere, he growled in his mind as he walked confidently away.

Breakfast arrived, along with the young maid. "Morning miss." she bobbed. "Master said you were hungry. I've bought you some toast and eggs." she smiled. Violet was relieved to see her. They were about the same age, Violet thought.

"What's your name?" Violet asked. She would like a friend here, she thought.

"Nellie, miss."

"I'm Violet."

"Pleasure, Miss Violet." replied Nellie bobbing quickly again.

"Nellie," Violet began, "I..." Before Violet could continue, Marcus Claydale bellowed for the maid.

"Must go, Miss Violet." she muttered and hurried nervously out of the room.

Violet chewed absent-mindedly on the food that was left for her. The way the maid responded to the man's call unsettled her. Her master frightened her. Why was she so scared of him? Violet resolved to find out.

Meals came at regular intervals for the rest of the day, but not by Nellie. A single, masculine hand passed the tray through the door. The only other part of the body that she was privy to was the man's arm. He hid the rest of himself beyond the gap.

The boredom of being alone was excruciating. It made her think of Will. He would think she had just left them all there. She wished she could tell him that it wasn't true. The only comfort she had was the view from her window. It looked like she could reach out and touch the forest from where she sat, but what was the point of wanting to be there if she was locked up like a prisoner? And why did this man lock her up if his only intention was to rescue her?

When supper arrived, all it did was make her mind sluggish, her body limp and heavy. She assumed it was because of the stress of it all, but as she sucked in a cool breath of air at the window, not even that seemed to revive her. The feeling was overwhelming, as though there had been something more than just food upon her plate, she thought. The pull of slumber, strong and victorious as her mind gave way to the dark.

36

"Ah, Violet!" Marcus Claydale greeted her, "I see you are up. I hope everything is satisfactory." His words were more of a statement rather than a question. He did not leave time for an answer, rendering Violet silent. The man held out his arm for her to take, "Walk with me, Miss. Hall."

Mr. Claydale led her through the corridors. They were much brighter than her room. A pattern of ivory and gold filled the walls. It was a welcomed contrast to the dark box of a room where she spent most of her days. Portraits of the man himself adorned the walls alongside, what she presumed were, more portraits of his ancestors. Each member of the Claydale legacy was similar in appearance. The eyes of each one followed her every movement. Each face conjured darkness. They appeared malevolent and fierce. Their images played havoc with her ability to decide exactly what kind of man she was walking with. It was as if there were two sides to him. Each side, entirely opposite to the other. They could not have been any more dissimilar. Violet's brow creased in confusion.

"Mr. Claydale..."

"Please call me Marcus." he smiled. "All these formalities

are not necessary. This is your home now."

"Marcus," she corrected herself, "Well, that is what I would like to talk to you about."

Marcus stopped. A bolt of anger shot up through his chest, resting in his throat, swirling in a ball of fiery rage. His body, upright, rigid, and still. Shadows loomed over their heads, ready to strike. Violet stopped next to him, surprised by the sudden change in him and the light. "Are you quite alright?" she asked.

Marcus inhaled deeply, swallowing his rage. His body relaxed back into his walk as the shadows retreated. "Yes. I do apologize, Violet. I believe I have a migraine. Please forgive me, but I will have to leave you in the very capable hands of the maid."

Nellie's face paled as he shot her a warning glare that did not fail to meet its mark. "This way, Miss." Nellie beckoned, leading Violet down the stairs and into a small library. Nellie appeared to be in a rush as she headed straight through the library and through the door on the other side.

"I can't keep up with you, Nellie." Violet puffed.

"Quickly, Miss." she called in a whisper, her hand waving frantically, gesturing for Violet to follow.

Both young women stood in the open. The cool breeze and the warm sun kissed Violet's skin. Her chest heaved as the clean air filled her lungs. If she had missed anything about her grandmother's home, it was this. Nellie grabbed hold of her hand and pulled her forward. "Not here, Miss." she whispered. A rasp of warning shaped her words as she pulled Violet out of sight.

"What is it, Nellie?" Violet asked, her eyes wide with fear.

"You are in danger, Miss. The master is not a good man." Nellie warned, confirming all of Violet's suspicions.

"Then I must leave at once."

"You can't, Miss. He will know."

Violet swallowed hard at what she was hearing. What exactly does this man want with her? "What can I do?" she begged Nellie.

"Please, Miss, don't panic. The master will hear you and there's no telling what he will do to both of us. I am telling you because I want to help you. I think I know a way we can get you out."

Violet searched the maid's face for any deception, but she could not find any. "What can we do?" she asked, steadying her breathing.

"First, Miss, you must act like I haven't said a word to you. The master must never know that I have warned you."

Violet nodded as she wiped away a tear of frustration and sat down on the bench. Nellie sat beside her. Both faced away from the house, their faces hidden. "What will he do to me if I cannot get away?" Violet asked nervously. She wasn't sure that it was wise asking, but the question was the loudest one in her mind, demanding attention.

Nellie bowed her head and stared at her hands. "There was another one like you here, Miss."

"What do you mean, like me?"

"Different, Miss. I don't mean to be rude but, you know."

Violet knew. She understood the maid spoke only with kindness. "Carry on..."

"She was a lovely lady, Miss. Beautiful like you, Miss. She had big brown eyes and her hair, Miss... It was a rich ebony silk. She had dots all over her face, Miss, like the angels had kissed her over and over again. I reckon they did, Miss, she was such a kind woman. My ma would have said she had a heart of gold. I bet she did, and it would have been the most glorious gold, miss." Nellie twiddled her fingers, aware that she would have to divulge so much more than she had already.

"What happened to her, Nellie?"

"The master married her, Miss. He told her he loved her. If you had seen them together, you would have believed it too, miss. Miss. Lily, that was her name, always worried what people would say, miss, because she had one arm shorter than the other. That was her difference, you see. But the master assured her she was beautiful as she was. And she was, Miss. But the master didn't see that in her. He was tricking her. He had other plans for her, Miss." A tear rolled from Nellie's eye and coursed down her cheek, splashing onto the cotton of her dress in dark patches of grey. "He didn't love her, Miss. She should never have married him. He told everyone that she went back to her family, miss. But her body is displayed in a museum. He sold it to them, Miss."

Violet gasped at the revelation.

"Poor Lily, Miss, she wasn't even buried like everyone else. What of her soul, Miss?"

"Are you saying..." Violet lowered her voice further, "Are you saying that Mr. Claydale killed her?"

"Yes, Miss." she sobbed.

"How do you know?" Violet was searching for something, anything, that may offer her an alternative to what this young woman was telling her.

"There you are. Enjoying the sunshine, I see. Can't say I blame you." Marcus Claydale stepped confidently into the garden to join them. His migraine simply vanished without a trace. It baffled Violet as she struggled with what Nellie had told her and the inconsistency of the man.

Nellie discreetly wiped away her tear and inhaled. "Yes, sir." she said, getting to her feet, standing tall, "I thought Miss. Violet would like some fresh air."

"Splendid idea." Marcus beamed, looking from Nellie to Violet. There was no trace of their earlier conversation, just two women who were basking in the garden's beauty.

"I'll get back to work, sir." Nellie bobbed, as she glanced at Violet, a silent plea for her not to repeat what she had said. Violet gazed back, offering a tiny nod that only Nellie understood.

"It's glorious out here, isn't it?" Mr. Claydale smiled, his eyes squinted a mere fraction as he waited for her reply.

"Yes, quite splendid." Violet replied, keeping her voice steady.

"I've decided that it would be most inhospitable for me to keep you locked up any further. Of course, I did it for your safety at first, you understand?"

Violet nodded to portray agreement.

"But you must remain here, Violet. Your grandmother knows you are no longer with the circus and she has men out looking for you."

Violet looked at him, fear dancing across her expression. She could not decide who was more terrifying, Marcus Claydale or her grandmother.

"Yes. I see." she whispered. Violet had much experience pacifying her cruel grandmother, the Carson brothers, and now she must do it again but with Mr. Claydale. She needed to find out what happened to Lily.

Mr. Claydale spent the afternoon at her side. His manners were most charming, she mused, but not charming enough to make her forget what she had seen and the potential danger that lurked behind those striking eyes. His words were full of silent demands, controlling. Violet suppressed her reactions. To be locked up again would not help her at all.

The evening meal was in an awkward, unbearable silence. His piercing eyes studied her from across the table. Vulnerability crept over Violet's body like a cloak of shame, unable to remove her from the situation.

"What do you do, Marcus?" Violet asked, shifting his gaze from her back to her face.

"I'm a doctor of sorts." he drawled.

"Doctor of sorts?"

"Yes, I have a passion for oddities."

Violet inhaled sharply at the glint in Claydale's eyes, unintentionally inhaling the piece of meat in her mouth. It lodged in her throat, startling her, as it blocked her airway. Marcus Claydale rose from his seat and walked casually to her side, where he hit her hard on her back until the meat dislodged and she could breathe again.

"Thank you." she coughed, "I thought I was going to die." Violet let out a nervous laugh as the man said nothing. He continued to stroke her back, his fingers trailing over the curve of her spine, following every inch of its path. Violet shuddered at his touch. Her insides froze as his energy gripped and twisted them into knots. Willing him to remove his hand, she shuffled awkwardly in her seat.

"I do beg your pardon." he droned, moving away from her. His eyes were hungry with intrigue. "I just find you deliciously fascinating."

Those few seconds had told her all she needed to know.

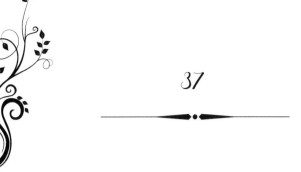

37

The next morning, Violet was still reeling from the way Mr. Claydale had acted over their evening meal and the words that he had said. What kind of man refers to someone as 'deliciously fascinating'? she thought, shuddering as she remembered the look in his eyes. She had absolutely no doubt that this man's intentions were barbaric.

Nellie brought a breakfast tray of toast and eggs to her room after Violet had feigned a headache. She could not face sitting across the table from Marcus Claydale while his eyes bored into her very being.

"Morning, Miss." Nellie gave a quick smile. There was an air of tension after their conversation yesterday.

"Morning, Nellie." Violet replied, "I need to talk to you."

"Not now, miss."

Nellie curtseyed and hurried backward out of the room to reveal Mr. Claydale standing there. Violet's breath hitched in her throat, wondering whether he'd heard what she had said to Nellie, but then surely that wouldn't matter because she'd hardly said anything at all and nothing that could reveal what she knew. Still, his eyes were vibrant with suspicion as he entered the room.

She maintained the ruse of the headache she'd informed him of earlier, laying down on the bed, trying her best to look pained.

"I just wanted to check on you before I leave today." Claydale said, "Nasty business, headaches, aren't they?"

Violet nodded, trying not to meet his curious gaze. Silence hung between them as Violet closed her eyes, hoping he would leave quickly.

"Well, I shall go then." he sniffed. He had never failed to win over a woman with his charm, yet it would seem this one was not charmed so easily, he thought.

"Goodbye." Violet said quietly, just enough for him to hear. She loathed saying it as much as she loathed him, knowing that he would take it as a sign that she thought well of him. How delusional he was, she thought.

Violet wandered the corridor by herself, hunting for Nellie in every room. She had waited a few hours after the master of the house had left in case he had employed people to watch her. She had to keep to the pretense.

"Nellie!" she called, in a rasping whisper, "Nellie!"

Nothing but the sound of her boots on the wooden panelled flooring. They were new boots. A gift from Mr. Claydale, along with a clean wardrobe of dresses and bonnets. For those, she was extremely grateful, but she was not that easily dissuaded from her suspicions of him. His eyes had burned their image into her mind. When she closed her eyes at night, she could still see them. His spindly, prodding fingers that buried into each vertebra as if tracing a route on a map, had scarred the memory of her skin. The man did not realize that there were no number of dresses or material possessions that could erase any of it.

Violet, eventually, found Nellie in the parlour. She was tending to the grate, sweeping out the ashes of many a cold evening.

"Nellie, you're here." she exclaimed as relief filled her. Violet gazed around the room, making sure they were alone. "We need to talk."

"Yes, Miss, but we must be careful, Miss. The walls have ears, Miss." Nellie glanced at the door that led to Claydale's study. "Would you like me to show you the garden again, Miss." she said, her voice raised for anyone that may be listening.

"That would be lovely. Thank you, Nellie."

Nellie guided Violet to the farthest side of the garden, where it would be safe to talk.

"The master told you he was a doctor, didn't he, Miss?" She looked intently at Violet.

"Yes, but I fear he is not a good one. He told me that curiosities intrigue him." Violet replied.

"Yes, Miss." A look of knowing passed between them. "I can prove it, Miss. I will show you where he does his work, Miss."

"Although I do not doubt you at all, I would like you to show me so I can see just how intrigued he is in 'curiosities', as he calls us."

"I don't think like that, Miss." Nellie offered, her cheeks flushed with embarrassment. "I only work here for the money, Miss."

"It's ok, Nellie." Violet reassured her. "I know this isn't your fault."

"I will help you escape, Miss, but we have to be careful. He is a very astute man, Miss." Nellie glanced back at the house. This time, Violet spotted the butler glaring at them both. She raised her hand and waved at him, adding a broad smile to shake the man's confidence as to his beliefs in what they were up to. He stepped back into the shadows of the building and disappeared.

"Oh, well done, Miss. I wasn't sure how I was going to explain that one to Mr. Thompson."

"Is that the butler's name?"

"Yes, Miss. He and the master are as thick as thieves, Miss."

"I see. Are there any others we should be careful of?"

"I'm not sure, Miss. I keep to myself, you see. Best not to trust anyone, but you can trust me, I promise."

The fear in Nellie's eyes was all the proof that Violet needed. She knew it wasn't easy for her to be taking on such a risk. "You don't have to help me, Nellie." Violet said, "I don't want you to get into any trouble on my account." Violet was worried about what Claydale would do to Nellie if he ever found out that she had helped her to escape.

"I want to help you, Miss. I've written to my ma and told her I'm coming home soon, so when we get you out of here, I will be leaving too."

"Are you sure you want to do this?"

"Yes, Miss, absolutely."

Violet followed Nellie around the side of the house until they came to a door she had never seen before.

"Quickly." Nellie pulled Violet inside.

The room had an odour that stole her breath, sour and thick with chemicals. Both women covered their faces. Nellie covered hers with the lower part of her apron, and Violet covered hers with her handkerchief.

"Sorry, Miss, but I have to close the door, or someone will catch us."

Violet nodded and stepped further into the room, allowing Nellie to move behind her and close the door.

The walls were of dark stone, glistening with damp and mould. A constant drip chipped into the silence. A long table sat in the middle, padded with a thin mattress. Leather straps at the sides and the feet. There was no mistaking what that was for.

On the shelves sat glass jars filled with murky liquid. Objects floated inside each one. Violet could not quite recognize what they were under the clouds that spoiled the transparency.

At the far wall, there was a desk piled high with paperwork and in the middle a book laid open, a pot of ink with the point of the quill rested inside. Violet moved around the table, careful not to spill the ink. She wanted to inspect what Claydale had written. It was more than words. Diagrams with labels filled the pages, and in the middle, the man had drawn her image. Violet fell back into the chair, causing it to screech on the stone floor.

"Miss, please!" Nellie whispered pleadingly. Violet looked terrified by what she had seen. It ignited a flame of guilt in the maid. "I'm so sorry, Miss, I just don't want us to be caught." Taking Violet's hand, she led her back out of the door and into the light of day.

Violet eased herself back against the wall of Claydale House. Her body trembled violently with shock; her face, as white as a ghost, drained of any hope. Nellie took Violet's hands in hers, trying to warm them. "Let's get you inside, Miss, before you get a chill."

"What is the matter with her?" barked the butler. His glare was harsh and accusing.

"She's still not too well, Mr. Thompson. I'm going to take her back to her room so she can rest." Nellie answered in the strongest voice she could muster.

"Quite." the man agreed, "You know that the master needs her in good health. Now hurry along."

The two women held on tight to one another as they made their way up to Violet's chambers. Violet trembled in Nellie's grip as she pushed the door open. The young maid assisted Violet to her bed and removed her boots. "Please don't fret, Miss. I know what we saw today was horrific, but I promise you, I won't let him do to you what he did to Lily. I have a plan, Miss. I do. Really, I do."

The warmth of the covers slowed the tremors of her body as Violet's eyes met Nellie's. "What plan?" she asked hopefully.

Nellie pushed down on the bed, rising from her knees. "I've got some laudanum, Miss."

"What are you going to do with it?" Violet asked. Panic rose as bile burned in her throat. She swallowed it down, chastising herself. Sometimes you have to play people at their own game, she thought. If this man was going to kill her, what other way is there?

"From tomorrow morning, Miss, I will be adding a little to his tea, miss."

"Surely, he will notice, Nellie?"

"We can only hope he doesn't, Miss."

38

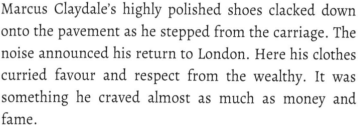

Marcus Claydale's highly polished shoes clacked down onto the pavement as he stepped from the carriage. The noise announced his return to London. Here his clothes curried favour and respect from the wealthy. It was something he craved almost as much as money and fame.

"Would you like me to wait, sir?" The driver of the carriage leaned over and waited for the man's reply.

"No, thank you, Thomas. Just give me a few hours."

"Yes, Sir. I'll see you later on."

As the horses began their slow canter upon the cobbles, they led the carriage away, leaving Mr. Claydale staring up at the entrance of the museum. He pulled down the cuffs of his coat, neatly, and straightened his top hat. The world would see him as a true gentleman - his artistic deception, while his insides were nothing of the sort.

The heels of his shoes resounded off the marble flooring. A particular beat like glorious music to his ears. The museum held a special place in the man's heart from a very young age. Each display held such wonders, and in three, they had printed his name on a small plaque.

They were recognition of his hard work, his genius, and his loyalty to the establishment.

He smiled at the cadavers. Their lives drained from them too early. "Ah, Lily." he breathed, "Still ever as beautiful as the day I last laid my eyes on you."

He had saved them, he thought. There they could be loved and admired by many, whereas, if they still breathed, if their hearts still pumped their infernal beat, society would have cast them aside. The very same people that gazed at them now in awe, admiration, and wonder. Marcus Claydale had paused them in time for all to see. He believed he had given them purpose.

"Ah, Marcus!" boomed a deep voice. "I received your letter. I must say I am most intrigued as to what you have for us next, sir." The museum curator shook Claydale's hand enthusiastically.

"Mr. Jenkins, a pleasure to see you again. Yes, I do indeed have something rather delightful for you." Marcus replied.

A look passed between the two men. "Shall we discuss this in my office, young man?" Mr. Jenkins led Marcus through the displays and up the stairs to his office. "Come in, come in." He beckoned for Claydale to sit as he clicked the door shut behind him. The museum director poured two glasses of brandy and passed one to Claydale. "Now, tell me more, Marcus."

"What would you like to know?"

"How did you come to be in possession of this cadaver? Was it in the asylum trash? There must be a few excellent finds there after the freak shows have no use for them, eh?"

"No, that is not where I found her." The corner of Claydale's mouth tilted into a smirk. A single flame ignited from the fires of hell danced in his eyes. Mr. Jenkin's caught it and mirrored it in his own.

"I say, Marcus, you are a sly old dog. What did you do to make her trust you?"

"I'm not sure that she does yet, but she has no choice because I rescued her from the Carson brothers."

Mr. Jenkins rolled his eyes at the mention of Reginald and Mycroft Carson. "Bumbling buffoons. Bet she wasn't too difficult to procure with those two squabbling all the time."

"I have to admit that I did come into some luck, but I have a doctor to thank for that."

"Please, tell me more." Jenkins lowered himself into the leather seat opposite Claydale and sipped on his brandy, eagerly awaiting more details.

"The exhibit in question had been wearing shackles, so maybe I do have to thank the Carson brothers for that part, but when she became ill because of them, the doctor demanded that Reginald Carson unshackle her and give her somewhere comfortable to sleep. It was easy pickings. I simply picked her up in the middle of the night and took her home."

"You told her you rescued her, didn't you?" Jenkins asked,

his face red with the thrill of Claydale's devious nature. "That, Sir, I certainly did."

Mr. Jenkins threw his head back and guffawed. "You, Marcus, are an utter genius. What is her oddity?"

"I assure you, this one is truly a rarity. The Carson brothers were trying to gather attention, referring to her as The Hunchback Of London."

Mr. Jenkin's face glowed with greed. "We shall give her centre stage of the museum." he proclaimed. He could already hear the jingle of coins as he imagined her form mounted for all their guests. "People will come from miles around. This will truly put us on the map!"

Claydale smiled victoriously, knowing that he could ask for considerably more money than what he had before, but there was one thing he wanted so much more than riches. He wanted fame, his name to be displayed in large font, not the small pathetic mention he had now. He wanted to be noticed, for the visitors to pay attention to the man that found her. "There is the subject of a price." Claydale said, interrupting the museum director's wayward imagination.

"Yes, of course. What were you thinking? Obviously, we will pay you handsomely for someone so magnificent."

"There will be no need to pay more than my usual price. I will take the same as I have for every other cadaver. However, there is one thing I would like in exchange."

"Anything at all..." Jenkins breathed. Excitement dripped off his face in beads of sweat.

"I would like for my name to be displayed much more

generously than you have done so thus far."

"We can definitely ensure that happens, Marcus."

"On all of them." Claydale finished. His eyebrow rose as he looked upon the man.

"All the cadavers?"

"Yes, or I shall take my exhibit elsewhere."

"No need for that, Marcus. We shall make your name much more visible on all the cadavers, I swear." The man was almost begging now. It pained Claydale to see the man snivel. The respect he'd had for him slowly dissipated at the sight of his hungry little eyes.

"Very well, she is yours."

Jenkins composed himself under the scrutinous look of Claydale. His cheeks were scarlet with embarrassment at his behaviour. "How long do we have to prepare for the arrival?" he asked. His voice was calmer and more professional than just a few minutes ago. The desperation blanketed by a deep gruff tone.

"You shall have her in a week."

"Perfect. We shall make the necessary preparations."

The two men raised their glasses, toasting to their upcoming success dependent on the arrival of a lost and lifeless Violet.

Violet raised the blanket over her head. Her heart pounded violently in her chest as she listened to Marcus Claydale outside her door.

"Does she suspect anything, Thompson?"

"No, sir, not a thing. You have been most astute. It is as it was with Lily and Alfred, sir." the butler replied.

"Good, good."

"Would you like me to prepare the room, sir?." drawled Thompson.

"No, thank you, Thompson. I feel it is too early yet. She has to trust me. I have my suspicions that she is not quite at that point yet."

"Very good, sir."

Violet heard Thompson's feet shuffle away down the corridor. There were no other footsteps, just deep heavy breaths and the key turning in her door. Marcus Claydale had locked her in again. Violet closed her eyes and thought of Emil; of her promise to find him again. She prayed, and she prayed as her tears wet the pillow and sleep embraced her in its warmth.

39

Violet wandered the darkness of her dreams, relentlessly searching for Emil. Her thoughts plagued the void, sealing the boundary between their worlds. Their voices were her only connection, a tether between both their hearts.

"Emil?" Violet called out.

"Yes, Violet?"

"Why can't I see you?"

"I don't know, my love, but I can see you."

Violet felt the warmth of his breath upon her neck, the touch of his hands upon her hips. "I'm right here, Violet." he whispered.

"I need you." she sobbed. Her heart broke at his touch. "I just want to be with you now."

Emil's arms wrapped around her. "If I could break down the wall between our worlds and meet you in yours, I would. It tortures me that I cannot! I would make those that have hurt you pay for what they have done!"

There was anger in his voice as he pulled her closer to him. She found comfort in his warmth. It was the first time Violet had heard Emil speak with such tenacity. "There is a maid here who says she will help me escape."

she sniffed, wiping away her tears. She wanted to give him hope. His belief in the maid and that she would escape would reassure him, she thought.

Emil lowered his voice, "It is not the same."

"But it is something." Violet offered, her voice begging for confirmation that she would be okay.

"Yes, you are right. I'm sorry. Do you think she can help you?"

"Yes, I really do." Violet could feel the distance growing between them. Emil's voice sounded further away. "I think I have to go now." she muttered, "Wait for me."

Violet awoke to panic. A falling sensation beheld her as she flailed her arms, searching for purchase of the mattress to save her. Her eyes snapped open to find herself back in the confines of Claydale's makeshift prison cell.

The night outside the window crept away as the sun rose in the distance. She exhaled, relieved he had not taken her in the night despite Thompson eagerly suggesting to do so. There was a kinship between the two, one that made Violet's blood run cold. She would be vigilant of both men, she promised herself.

Nellie pocketed the small vial of Laudanum in the apron of her dress. The pitter-patter of her soft shoes along the corridor echoed her heartbeat as fear coursed through her body. Her conscience was sharp, prodding, and poking at her thoughts, but there was no room for her conscience in this matter. It was either Violet, or the most wicked man she had ever known. Claydale was an evil, delusional man. Violet was a kind-hearted, gentle young woman that did not deserve to be subject to the master's sick and twisted fantasy. She couldn't deny that what she had to do petrified her. The man could easily dispose of her if he ever caught her. He did not hesitate to drain the life out of poor, sweet Lily and goodness knows how many others. She shuddered at his wickedness. What Nellie did not know was that she would not rest in the museum where his other victims were but deep in the grounds of Claydale House, discarded as a mere inconvenience.

The tea slopped on the tray as her petite feet carried her, and it, toward the master's chambers. It splashed her fingers, scolding her for being so clumsy. She paused and took a breath. What was the point of doing all this, she thought, berating herself, if there is no tea to add the laudanum to? He would not drink it freely, of that she was certain. Nellie's steps were slower as she continued the rest of the journey. The liquid merely sloshed in the teacup, but every drop stayed within the boundary of its shape.

Nellie rested the tray on the table at the side of the room. She stood over it, trying to hide it with her petite frame. Her back turned to Marcus Claydale as she gripped the vial of laudanum between her trembling fingers and slipped it from the pocket of her apron.

Limiting her movements, she added several drops of

the liquid to his tea, followed by a splash of milk and two teaspoons of sugar. She stirred it, praying the laudanum would not mar the flavour of the tea. Quietly, she placed the vial back into her pocket again and took two deep breaths, readying herself to turn to the master. As the tightness in her chest softened, she turned. The teacup glided through the air, held only by her fingers. They trembled slightly as she placed the hot liquid in front of Claydale.

"Here you are, sir." she muttered, curtseying and backing away.

Claydale noted the quiver in the maid's hand. "Are you alright, Nellie?" he asked, "Your hands are shaking."

"Yes, sir, just a little tired, that's all. Didn't get much sleep, sir." Nellie surprised herself with her quick answer. Perhaps this wouldn't be so difficult after all, she hoped.

"Make sure you get a good night's rest tonight. I have some important business to attend to, so I will be needing Thompson in a few days. There will be additional duties for you until I have completed my work."

"Yes, sir. Of course, sir." Nellie bobbed, keeping her eyes down. She felt only bitterness toward this monster, who hid behind the ruse of kindness. She would not allow him to see that burning anger within her.

When she had first worked at Claydale House, she thought the master was a good, kind, and generous man. It wasn't until the death of Lily that she doubted what kind of man he was.

Lily had appeared perfectly well. A vibrant woman whose laughter could fill the room and the hearts of all those who were in it. She and Nellie had formed a bond. She considered her a close friend, as close as a sister. Lily told Nellie, in the last week of her life, how the master was acting peculiarly. She told her how he had been paying close attention to her shorter arm, measuring it and such. It had made Lily extremely uncomfortable, but she didn't know how to express such an emotion, verbally, to the man who was supposed to love her.

He talked of infinite fame and admiration of her, but Lily wanted neither of those. She had not even asked or hinted at them. His new behaviour baffled her. She had become afraid of him. The life that Lily wanted was one of love, happiness, and laughter. He had promised her that when they had first met. She'd wanted to believe that he had meant his words, but as the days went by, she wasn't confident of her trust in him. A week later, Lily vanished. She hadn't said goodbye and Nellie knew she would never have left without doing that one small gesture.

She would never forget how black Claydale's eyes appeared the day after when she had asked him where Lily was. He'd offered an unlikely explanation; something about family illness, but Lily did not have any family. They had rejected her for her difference as a baby. Thompson had corroborated Claydale's story to the full, of course, but his word meant nothing. Their words made very little sense.

Eventually, Nellie took it upon herself to explore Lily's chambers and the rest of the house, even venturing into the rooms that were strictly forbidden. It was then that she stumbled upon Claydale's hidden room of horrors.

Claydale's book of studies, lain open on his desk in the dark, dank room with Lily front and centre. A scientific sketch of her body spread across two pages, as though she was nothing more than another one of his experiments.

Nellie's breath staggered as the grief of Lily's loss squeezed at her heart. She would never let that happen to Violet... Never.

"Will there be anything else, sir?" she asked.

"No, that will be all." Claydale replied, "Actually," His voice dragged across the air, pausing the maid's movements. She turned slowly to meet his gaze.

"Yes, sir?"

"Send Thompson in. I need to have a word."

How long does this laudanum take? she wondered. She hoped it would be soon. "Yes, sir. Right away, sir." Nellie hurried out of the room to find the butler.

Violet wandered the small area of her room. The wait for Nellie to arrive was making her fret. What if they had caught her? What then? What would happen to Nellie? How would she escape? Nellie was late. Violet believed that she would soon create a moat around her bed if she paced any longer. She stilled herself on the bed. Surely, a soft mattress would soften her moods, she thought, but her anxiety at the maid's absence rushed through her in strong violent waves of worry.

"Where is she?" she whispered. Her words mingled with the secrets that bounced off the room's dreary walls. Every word she said, every movement she made, would etch upon the memory of Claydale House and remain long after she had gone. It unnerved her as to how she would come to leave there but she quieted the negative thoughts as they begged to be heard.

Violet sat up. She was too restless to just be still. The ball of her right foot rested upon the hard floor, causing her leg to bounce repetitively on the spot as her stomach tightened with nausea. Violet got up and moved to the window, her foot released from the incessant rhythm it had been locked in.

She took large gulps of clean country air through the open window and closed her eyes, listening to the chirrup of the birds outside. It made her think of the one that led her toward the cabin in the forest. She wondered whether he was one of those birds who sang so sweetly. Did he know she was behind the glass, and was he waiting for her to return? She liked to think he was. The thought comforted her as she eased back into a relaxed state.

"Morning, Miss."

"Nellie!" Violet beamed. She peered quickly into the corridor to see if they were alone, then closed the door behind her. "Nellie, sit down, please." Violet gestured to the bed. "You look terribly pale." Violet was relieved to see the maid, but the lack of colour in her face alarmed her.

"Yes, Miss. I've never done anything like that before, Miss." the young maid's eyes swam with guilt.

"Nellie, you don't have to do this, you know? I can try to get out some other way." Violet did not like to think that this young woman was risking everything for her.

"No, Miss. There is no other way. The master is a cruel man, Miss, and the butler, too. You can't do this alone." Nellie's cheeks flushed with determination. "Besides, Miss, it's nothing he don't deserve, Miss. Especially after what he did to Lily."

"I just don't want you to get hurt on my behalf, Nellie. I couldn't live with myself."

"You won't be living though, will you, Miss? I mean he will make sure of that won't he?" Nellie shook her head at the thought of how terrible her master was. She wondered why she had not left Claydale House earlier, when Lily had disappeared, but, if she had, then who would there be to help Violet now?

"I mean it, Nellie, when I say if you find yourself in any danger, you must stop. I do not want you getting hurt. You have been such a good friend to me. People like you are very rare in my life, Nellie. I will never forget what you have done for me, whether you follow it through to the end or whether you must stop because it's too dangerous." Violet's gaze was intense. She wanted Nellie to know that she meant every word.

Nellie nodded, "I think of you as a friend too, Miss." she smiled, "I'll be back as soon as I can. We will make the final plans, then." With that, Nellie left Violet alone.

40

The room swayed before Marcus Claydale's eyes. How long had he been asleep? He tried to stand, but his body swayed against the room as he tried to stand straight. His feet shuffled back against the chair, the weight of his body shifting it from underneath him and, as he fell, his body hit the floor. "Thompson!" he slurred, "Thompson!"

Thompson was never far from the call of Marcus Claydale. He was a devoted servant to the man. The staff referred to him as a snivelling rat, yet he liked to think that he was loyal without fault.

Thompson did not associate with the staff at Claydale House. He believed they were beneath him and that Mr. Claydale was far more in his league than those who merely washed pots, made beds, and cooked food. Of course, the staff simply rolled their eyes at him and thought him thoroughly deluded. Where Thompson believed he was Claydale's wingman, the rest of the house saw him as his fool.

"Sir!" Thompson called as he entered the room.
"Over here, Thompson." Claydale held up his arm so that the butler could see him.

"Oh dear, sir, whatever happened?"

"I thought I would enjoy a mid-morning snooze on the floor." he replied sarcastically.

"Very droll, sir." Thompson retorted. "Let me help you up."

Thompson heaved Claydale into the chair that had slipped backward.

"Thank you, Thompson."

"Should I get the doctor, sir?"

"No, thank you, Thompson. I believe I am just a little worn out from the excitement of yesterday and the journey to London. Perhaps you could help me to my chambers so I can rest?"

"Yes, of course, sir."

Claydale draped his arm over the shoulders of the butler as the butler scooped his arm around the back of his master's ribs. Together, they swayed up the stairs like two drunken friends returning from a night out. Beads of sweat dripped down Thompson's back, sealing the gap between his skin and the fabric of his shirt. Claydale had put all of his weight on the man, but he was determined to get his master safely to the room.

When Thompson released Claydale's body onto his mattress, he sighed heavily and wiped his brow. The feeling of his clothes forming another skin on his flesh was uncomfortable. When his master looked to be sleeping, he crept away.

"Nellie, what are you doing here?" Thompson eyed the

maid suspiciously.

"I've come to clean the master's chambers, ain't I?" she retorted. The man's lack of manners crawled under her skin. He is delusional, she thought as she kept her eyes locked on his, unwilling to back down and refusing to bow to his power-hungry ways.

"That won't be necessary. The master is asleep."

"Really? At this hour?" The maid knew that this was the sign she needed. The laudanum was working. A thread of excitement at her success so far tickled her insides.

"He is unwell." Thompson sniffed, looking down his nose at Nellie.

"Have you called the doctor then?" Nellie asked, raising her eyebrows. Her voice had risen to an assertive tone that did not seem to perturb the butler in the slightest.

"No. I asked Mr. Claydale, but he said that he did not want me to. Not that it is any of your business." he barked.

Nellie held her breath. She would not relent to the rush of air, her lungs wanted to exhale in relief. 'If the doctor visited the master, surely, he would know that I had tampered with his tea.' she thought.

"Right, I'll see to the others then." Nellie proclaimed, beginning to walk away.

"Before you go." Thompson began, stopping the maid in her tracks, "I require you to make sure the master is taken care of. It will be your duty to serve his meals, etcetera, etcetera." The butler revelled in his power.

The way he emphasized the letter T in etcetera was

nauseating to Nellie, however, she would allow him to have his moment. His assumption that he had irked the maid simply by giving her extra duties had worked in Nellie's favour. He had inadvertently given her the access to Claydale that she needed.

"Pompous old fart." she muttered under her breath.

"I beg your pardon?!" Thompson boomed.

"I said, yes, sir. Must dart. As in rush, sir, you know?"

Thompson squinted at her. "I hope that's all you said."

"What else could I have said, sir?"

"Get back to work." the butler sneered.

Nellie nodded, then walked away, smiling.

"The master has already taken to the laudanum, Miss." Nellie whispered as she entered the room. She held a bundle of dark velvet like a baby in her arms and dropped it onto the bed. Carefully, she separated the items.

A cape draped over the mattress like a luxurious blanket. Its dark shade of grey against the thick, soft fabric and fur lining reminded Violet of a turbulent winter storm.

"I hope you don't mind me saying, Miss, but that hood will disguise you and your shape. I'm not saying there's anything wrong with your shape, Miss..." The maid twiddled her fingers, blushing.

Violet chuckled, "It's okay, Nellie, I completely understand, and I am truly grateful."

"My ma says I don't always have a great way with words, but I never want to hurt anyone, especially you, Miss."

"You haven't and could never, I assure you." Violet smiled.

One large silver candlestick pressed its weight against the fabric of the cape, pushing it downward into the bed. "Nellie, what is this for?" Violet asked. The confusion etched in a deep pinch between Violet's brows.

"Well, if someone tries to attack you, Miss, you can clonk 'em on the head with it, Miss." A spark of mischief twinkled in Nellie's eye. Violet was glad to see it. She had thought she had stolen the young maid's happiness, but to see that it was still there pleased her.

"Well, that will certainly knock them out for a while." Violet laughed, "And this?"

"A reticule for you, Miss." The small bag flopped, hiding its true shape. Violet was relieved by how small it was. The heaviest item so far was the candlestick, which she wasn't sure she could ever bring herself to use how Nellie had suggested.

"I put some money in there in case you need it, Miss." Nellie said, pointing to the reticule, "I had some money saved. It's not much, but I reckon it's enough if you need to get further away."

"But what about you?" Violet asked. "Won't you need this?"

"No, Miss. My family will be waiting for me, Miss. They have all that we need, so don't you go concerning yourself with me. Your need is much greater than mine, Miss."

"Thank you, Nellie. You have really thought about this, haven't you?" Violet felt choked with emotion by the maid's kindness.

"Now don't you go getting all soppy on me, Miss." the maid gently remarked, "You'll have me sobbing in a minute and then the master will know something is going on."

Violet wrapped her arms around Nellie. "We're actually doing this, aren't we?"

"Yes, Miss. We are."

Claydale rambled from inside his chambers. His mind stretched toward the waking world but, no matter how much he tried, it was outside of his grasp. The suffocating, downward pull of the laudanum was his worthy and unbeatable opponent.

"See that... my name. It was me. My Lily... so beautiful." His voice slurred into the hallway as Nellie listened. The heat of the steam that rose toward her already flushed face only added to her discomfort. She despised the anger and hatred she felt toward the man, but she allowed it to consume her. For now, she would use it. It gave her the willpower and the driving force to do what was necessary to free Violet.

With a gentle rap of her knuckles, the maid knocked on the door. "I've bought you some tea, sir." She didn't bother to wait for his approval to enter his chambers. "Thought it might make you feel a little better, sir."

Nellie picked up the tea laced with laudanum and held it to Marcus Claydale's lips.

"I don't want it!" he growled. His hand flopped toward the

cup, knocking it from Nellie's hand.

"Bloody man." she flustered quietly, then refilled the cup with the same concoction before wiping up the spill at her feet. She tried again, but this time she guided his own hand to the cup.

The man's fingers curled loosely around the handle as Nellie scooped her hand underneath the base of the teacup itself. She watched as he poured the golden liquid into his mouth and swallowed. His mind was in another place altogether.

"Would you like anything to eat, sir?" she asked.

"No thank you, young lady, I couldn't eat another morsel after that divine meal." he mumbled.

"I don't know what you just ate, sir," the maid smirked, "but I will be sure to give the cook your thanks." 'Dreams are peculiar things.' Nellie thought, 'He's never normally that grateful when the cook prepares his meals.'

Nellie's legs trembled as she rinsed the teacup, removing any traces of the laudanum. She gathered all the dirty crockery and arranged it onto the tray, then carried it back to the kitchen. 'I'll pay Violet a visit after,' she told herself. 'I need to remind myself why I am doing this.'

41

Mycroft Carson wedged himself into the seat next to his brother. He had barely spoken to the man for days now.

"Mind me leg, will ya?!" Reginald barked. He was sick of his brother's silence. After all, he hadn't just let the thing leave. He elbowed Mycroft in retaliation at the memory of the blazing row they'd had when they'd realized their act was missing. His words still bothered him.

"Mind my ribs!" Mycroft growled. His eyes bore into the side of Reginald's head as if he could make the man's brain, or lack thereof, explode with one meaningful stare.

"What you lookin' at?" Reginald asked, wiping the heat of his brother's breath off his face.

"I'm not entirely sure!" Mycroft retorted.

"Yeah, bet you think you're funny, don't ya?"

Both brothers were purple with fury. Mycroft's colour was more visible on his clean skin whereas Reginald's colour brewed beneath the usual filth that stuck to him.

"No, I do not believe that I am funny." Mycroft began, "What I believe is that my brother YOU are an absolute buffoon." he spat. "Two hundred pounds... I repeat two hundred pounds... thrown away, just like that, because you didn't think to safeguard it!"

"Technically, I wasn't supposed to safeguard two hundred pounds. It was the act I was supposed to safeguard." Reginald argued.

Mycroft's face dropped with exasperation and annoyance, "You know exactly what I meant."

"We should pay the doc a visit. We could rough 'im up a bit and get our money back that way." Reginald suggested. His face was alight at what he believed was a genius idea, waiting for his brother to agree.

"What we should do, dear brother," Mycroft growled, "is pay the grandmother a visit, don't you think?"

"Well, I guess it's one idea." Reginald looked to be meandering over his brother's plan as if Mycroft was waiting for his approval, "Or...."

"Oh, do tell me, brother, what genius plan you have now. I'm so intrigued." Mycroft snarled, holding the reins of the horses in his firm grip as he imagined them to be his brother's neck.

"No need to be sarcastic." Reginald mumbled, "Let's go see the grandmother then."

"What a splendid idea. I'm so glad that we agree on something for a change." Mycroft slashed the reins through the cold air and snapped them down over the horses' backs with the sound of a whip.

The night brought the ice-cold stream that weaved within the winds as they sped out of London. It would be at least two days before they even reached the old woman who so desperately wanted rid of her granddaughter. Surely, she could not have agreed to take it back in, thought Reginald.

Although there was no use arguing with Mycroft, he would only have some other patronizing quip to lacerate Reginald's ego with and he was already bruised enough from the ones he'd received so far. 'No, I will let him look at the thing's grandmother's home. Be it on him if we have a wasted journey.' he thought, smugly.

42

"Where are you?" bellowed Claydale. His clothes were all crumpled from curling in the heat beneath his blankets. "Thompson!"

The butler hurried from his room in his nightclothes, startled by his master's outburst. "I'm here, sir!" he flustered, holding out his candle to light the way in front of him.

"We need to get started with our plan!" Claydale slurred, bumping into the wall.

"Be careful, sir. You will fall."

"Hush Thompson. You will wake the staff." Marcus Claydale's eyes were bright but vacant.

"Quite right, sir." the butler said, noticing his master's incoherence.

"Now, let's kill Lily, shall we?" Marcus bellowed. "She'll look simply delicious for eternity!"

Thompson's face turned puce as he held his flame up, lingering it back and forth to see whether anyone was in the corridor with them. He would hang for what he and his master had done, his mind blustered. With his other hand, he wiped over his neck to rid him of the phantom sensation of the noose that may, one day, be his demise.

The butler raised his voice. "Lily left you, sir! Don't you remember?" He hoped that the rest of the household staff would hear him correct Claydale, putting to bed any suspicions they may have and buffing off the master's madness as a result of the fever that ravaged him.

Claydale put a finger to his lips. "Oh, yes! I remember!" he shouted. His volume matching Thompson's, "That's right!"

"Let's get you to bed, sir." The butler sighed and rolled his eyes at the master's inability to function. The man led him back to his chambers, silently praying that Claydale had not signed their death warrant. 'This is why he needs me', the butler thought, 'He would be nothing without my help.'

"Morning Thompson." Nellie smiled as the man approached. His lack of sleep deepened the grey, slightly wrinkled folds of skin beneath his eyes.

"Yes, quite." the man sniffed. He studied her face for any signs that she may have heard the night's commotion, but if she had, she did not reveal it.

Nellie bowed her head and hurried past him. She wanted to be the one that took Violet's breakfast to her. By the time the maid reached the kitchen, she was gasping for air.

"You been running?" laughed the cook.

Nellie leaned against the door as her breaths slowed from rasps to a steady flow. "Wanted to give Violet... her... breakfast."

"Not met her yet. What's she like?" the old woman asked. Her eyes glittered grey against her soft white hair as she eagerly waited for Nellie to describe Violet.

"I think you'll like her, Mrs. Grange. She's a bit like Lily." Nellie smiled sweetly at Lily's memory.

"Ah, dear Lily. So sad, she and Mr. Claydale didn't last. Wonder where she is now?" Mrs. Grange pondered.

Nellie didn't want to tell her what she knew and, clearly, the woman never heard the master and Thompson last night as she had. "Who knows, Mrs. Grange? We can only hope she is happy, eh?"

"Yes, love, you're quite right. Best get that breakfast to the young lady before it spoils." The cook nodded to the tray as Nellie lifted it and carried it out of the kitchen.

"I won't be here tomorrow, Miss." Nellie announced as she sat next to Violet. "I have to make sure I have everything I need before we leave."

Violet nodded, digesting the information. "But don't you sleep downstairs?"

"Sometimes, Miss, but when I can, I stay at my Ma's, like tonight."

"Oh." Violet looked thoughtful.

"I'm not leaving you, Miss, I promise. I will be back the day after tomorrow because it's then that I want us to leave." Nellie held Violet's hands in her own, "I will get you out of this, Violet."

It was the first time she had called her by her first name, and Violet listened to it ring out like a soft tinkle of a bell.

It was as though her name had solidified their friendship. "Thank you, Nellie."

"You shouldn't get any trouble from the master, as I've added some of the stuff to his brandy." she said, patting the pocket of her apron. "Old Thompson's taken it upon himself to make sure Claydale gets his usual tipple throughout the day." Violet noted a change in the maid's mindset. The determination in her eyes and the tone of her voice were profound, she thought, and extremely reassuring.

"Silly, pompous, old fool hasn't got a clue that he's helping us." she giggled, "That stuff, and the alcohol, should see him sleep for days, and by the time he wakes up, we'll be gone. Now, you stop worrying and eat your breakfast. You're going to need your strength for when I return." Nellie beamed and walked out of the room.

Violet walked to the window. There was no way she could eat anything with the influx of emotions she was feeling. She would be leaving any day now. She could find her way back to the cabin. The thought thrilled her, but terrified her at the same time. It wasn't as though she could simply walk out of the front door and be on her way like any other human being. Goodness knows what or who she would have to confront to free herself from this prison and what if Nellie got hurt? Large, thick fingers of concern for her new friend's safety wrapped around her insides, twisting and pulling at her gut.

"Is everything to your satisfaction, Miss." Thompson

stood at the door, his body filling the frame. His eyes were haunting, Violet thought, as she met his look. He was not concerned whether she enjoyed her breakfast, he wanted to make sure that she hadn't run away.

"Yes, thank you." she replied. "I apologise. I'm just not very hungry this morning." Violet nodded to the untouched breakfast. Thompson's expression baffled her. She couldn't understand why he almost looked fearful.

"Is there any reason you have lost your appetite, Miss?" Thompson's throat bobbed as he remembered Claydale's rather loud confession of sorts to the real reason Lily had vanished.

"I don't think so." Violet lied. "I think I just need to have a walk outside if I am permitted?"

"Yes, of course, Miss. The master is poorly today so, should you need anything, be sure to let me or Nellie know." Thompson bent a little at the waist in a bowing gesture, shuffling backward out of the door, leaving her to her morning.

As the butler walked back through the corridor, he tried to analyze whether he believed the girl knew more than she'd let on. How could she? he thought. Someone like that could not possess such intelligence. He smirked confidently at Violet's apparent oblivion to what lay in store for her.

Violet sat still on the bench outside in the garden. The

breeze was much colder now than when she had left her grandmother's with the Carson brothers. It seemed the autumn was losing the seasonal battle, once again, with winter being the victor. The tall evergreens shielded her from whatever lay beyond the garden. They were walls of bark and dense foliage. It may have felt like another prison, but at least this one had a better view. She scanned the trees for gaps in which she could escape, but there were none. How could she leave anyway, she thought, after everything Nellie had risked for her? She couldn't desert her kind-hearted friend like that. She would be patient. It was only another couple of days and, as Nellie had said, the laudanum had incapacitated Claydale. The man couldn't do anything, even if he wanted to.

"I was just thinking of you." Violet said, turning to Nellie as she sat down beside her.

"I hope it was good thoughts, Miss." she smiled. "I came to see you to tell you that I'm going to go back to me Ma's in a bit. I'm going to tell them I feel a bit poorly, then they'll believe me when I tell them I can't make it in tomorrow."

"That sounds sensible." Violet replied thoughtfully.

"Told 'em, I wanted to get some air. That should be enough to convince them, eh? Right, time to get my mighty poorly face on." Nellie did not give Violet the chance to say anything else as she left her sitting in the garden. Any distraction could cause the young maid to lose her nerve.

"See you soon." Violet called out, to which Nellie eloquently practised her coughing skills.

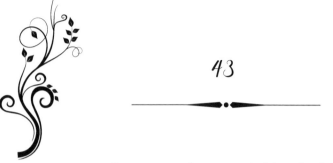

43

"Get out of my way, Thompson!" blared Claydale as he pushed past him. The man's eyes were transfixed by something or someone unseen.

"But, sir, you're not well."

"What rot! Can't you see I'm fighting fit?"

It was true, Marcus Claydale seemed physically better. He walked better, albeit with the odd stumble, but the way his voice drawled, like a marble rolling over rough ground at snail speed, alerted the butler to the master's need for further rest.

"Lily, I'm coming!" Claydale called, his words falling loosely off his tongue.

"But sir!"

Claydale threw his fist into the air. The pressure of the air in the gap between his fist and the butler's chin blew across Thompson's face in a whisper. "Take that, you old fool." Claydale scoffed, believing he had struck the man, "Always thinking you are equal to me. You're nothing but hired help. Tsk!"

The master's words struck harder than any fist could have. He was his equal. No money could ever be the measure of his intellect, the butler thought. 'Violet would soon be the display of all displays in the museum, and the achievement would belong to them both. The master does not know what he is saying,' the butler consoled himself, 'His brain is wracked with fever. When he is better, he will be glad of my help. That is what equals do.'

Thompson laid his hands on Claydale's shoulder without a single word, turning him on the spot. He pushed him gently into the master's chambers as the man continued to spit threats and throw weak punches, as if he had just entered a drunken brawl in the streets.

Thompson found Violet in the library. His mood was still sombre, crushed by the master's words.

"Afternoon, Miss." Thompson displayed his teeth in a weak and strained smile that did not meet his eyes. "The master is still out of sorts. We feel it may be best if you return to your room, where we will bring your evening meal."

Violet looked at him, questioning whether or not she was safe, but he mistook it for concern for Claydale. "He will be fine Miss, but I'm afraid the fever is causing him to see things we may not be able to see. It will be safer for you to return to your room."

Violet left the library and made her way back to her room as the butler suggested. She was sure that he was not worrying for her long-term safety, but perhaps holding off the inevitable until Claydale was well again. Either way, she did not care to bump into the man at all. She held on to the hope that she may never have to see him again.

Thompson knocked firmly on Marcus Claydale's chamber door. He was desperate to hear kinder words from the master, ones that would soothe his fractured ego.

"Sir, I wondered whether you would care for your usual brandy?"

There was no reply from the blanket-covered body shape. Thompson crept closer, not wanting to make the master angry at his intrusion. The covers revealed nothing of Claydale, but Thompson was too afraid to pull them back to check on him. The man had already bitten him verbally, and any more of that would make him regret his part in the master's art. Instead, he poured a single glass of brandy and left it on the side for Claydale to sip when he wanted to.

Marcus Claydale was not beneath the blankets. He was tired of Thompson's snivelling. He thought the man utterly pathetic. 'It was him', he thought, 'He has been lacing my brandy.' How else could he be feeling so delirious? The butler was trying to take the glory for his finds; for his Lily and now for Violet. 'I will not allow it!'

"Now where is she? What room did I put her in?" Marcus Claydale caressed the corridor walls with his hands as he fought to maintain his upright position. Why couldn't he remember where she was? "Damn you, Thompson, I can't think straight."

Claydale could only think of one place she may be, but

that was Lily's room. Surely he would not have put her in the same room. It would have been an insult to Lily's memory. The man leaned against the wall, running his hands through his tangled mass of hair as he searched the house in his mind for Violet. "Ah, yes. I remember now." he exclaimed quietly to himself, "But, first, there is something that I need."

"There it is. Why are there three? I'm sure there was only one." Marcus stared down at the syringe neatly placed on the tray in the basement. He marvelled at how there appeared to be more of them, but he could only feel the one. "Clever, Thompson, but not clever enough. You can't stop me." he sniggered as he wrapped his fingers around the syringe and stomped heavily out of the cold basement and headed to Violet's room.

Claydale's shoulders bashed against the walls of the narrow corridors. Vases and trinkets crashed to the floor. Their beauty burst into shards of porcelain, scattering at his feet. 'I'll just buy more.' he thought without a care in the world. 'By the time I have finished with this little specimen, I will be famous, rich beyond my wildest dreams.' He kicked the fragments away, sending them skidding further along his path.

"Oh, Violet!" Claydale called eerily. The whisper of his menacing voice blew under her door, sending shivers of fear down her spine. His footsteps were out of rhythm as they smacked against the cold floor. She searched the room for an answer to keep him away from her, but there was nothing. 'This is it,' she panicked, 'I will be gone by the time Nellie returns and she will never know what happened to me.'

Violet's heart beat so loudly that she believed it would explode from her chest. It knocked against the inside of her rib cage and filled her ears as though no other sound existed. Her pulse pumped in her neck as she crawled under the bed to hide and wait. She hoped Claydale would be too incoherent to notice her there.

The door smashed against the wall with the strength of a man possessed. "Oh, Violet!" he sang, extending her name until it was just two separate notes. She watched him from where she hid as he swayed at the force of the laudanum that still coursed through his veins. "There you are." he rasped, as he fell to his knees grabbing at Violet's ankles from under the bed. "Ah, look at you. You thought you could hide. But you have no need to escape from me. I'm going to save you. You will be famous; loved by so many. Surely, you would want that?" he asked, slowly dragging her writhing body out from the darkness.

The strength of his laudanum fuelled grip surprised her as she fought against him. "I don't want to be famous. I want to leave!" she screamed. Violet's legs kicked furiously, knocking Claydale sideways as she cried for someone, anyone, to help her.

"Nobody is going to save you now, dear." Claydale sneered, as he crawled towards her on his hands and knees. Violet sat herself up against the edge of the bed so their faces were almost level. She pushed her feet repetitively towards him as he prowled closer. A glimmer of light reflected off the syringe in his hand. She hadn't noticed it there before, but there was no mistaking it now. His eyes were as black as tar. There's that face again, she thought, the one she had first seen, the one that haunted her. The malevolence in his eyes, drank the colour of his irises as the monster riled up from within him.

Without thinking, Violet raised her leg and foot straight up in the air and brought it crashing down on Claydale's hand and the syringe. He let out a bloodcurdling cry of pain as the syringe spun across the room.

"You little..."

"Sir!" Thompson stood in the doorway, staring at Violet huddled against the bed and his master cradling his hand in pain.

"I had to," she rasped, "he was hurting me." Violet pushed the syringe under the bed, out of sight. She did not want Thompson to know that Claydale was ready for her to die now. She wanted him to believe that he had gotten lost and confused.

"Are you okay, miss?" The butler could not have been, or looked, less disinterested than he did at that moment.

"Yes, thank you. He thought I was called Lily." she lied, thankful to know some details of his past.

"I see. Let me get the master back to his room, Miss. I will make sure that he does not bother you again."

Thompson heaved a shocked Claydale from the floor. He was staring at his aching hands in disbelief at what Violet had done. "I will see to that too, sir." the butler added.

Thompson did not reveal to Violet, he'd seen her kick the syringe under the bed. Her indiscreet action had only drawn his attention to it. He realized what the master's intentions were. He blamed Claydale's apparent illness for his lack of judgement and sloppy attempt. 'I could help him with the girl, I suppose,' the butler thought, taking in every factor of the situation, 'but what then? The master is in no fit state to carry out what is necessary. No, this will have to wait.' Thompson would not help him in his foolishly timed endeavour. He hoisted Marcus Claydale up, dragging him from the room with his feet scraping over the wood. As the door clicked shut, Violet exhaled. Nellie's return could not come soon enough.

44

The butler turned restlessly underneath the twisted blankets of his bed. His mind, a turbulent storm of the day's events diving, swooping, and weaving amongst the terrible words that were spoken. Anger stirred inside him at the obvious disrespect Claydale had shown him. He tried to console the resentment, reminding himself that the master was delirious. Claydale was a man of honour, he told himself.

The anger in his heart ebbed and flowed like the waves of a restless sea. There was nothing he could tell himself that would make the master's words disappear from his anguished memory. There was only one thing he could do, the butler decided; he would just have to prove himself. The perfect means to satisfy his own need to be seen and heard and, if Claydale thought so little of him, he would be sorry, for his equal would have shown him how capable he truly is.

"Go easy on the coffee, Thompson." Mrs. Grange smiled. She'd always had a soft spot for him, even if she did think he was far too set in his ways.

Thompson said nothing as he poured himself another.

"Rough night?" she asked, noting the tiredness that dragged his skin down into a solemn expression. Thompson merely grunted, placing his knuckles on the kitchen table, pushing his body up from the chair.

"If anyone needs my services today," he grumbled, "they will have to find another. The master has instructed me to carry out more important duties."

"How can he have?" the cook's brow pinched with confusion. "He can barely think straight, let alone make sense of what he wants done."

Thompson's lips thinned in frustration as he kept his back to the woman. "Are you implying that I am being untruthful, Mrs. Grange?" he asked.

Mrs. Grange felt the tension from across the room and decided it was best not to push the subject. "No, not at all, Thompson. I was just wondering."

"Don't wonder." he snapped, marching out of the kitchen leaving the woman stunned and rosy-cheeked.

Thompson's legs were heavy as he trudged up the stairs to Claydale's chambers. The coffee had not helped him at all. The only driving force the man had was his desire to prove what he was capable of to the master.

Marcus Claydale wasn't nearly half the man the household was accustomed to, as he lay there sprawled on his stomach, one arm dangling off the side of the bed. The stagnant air seemed to cling to the butler and fill his nostrils, making it harder for him to breathe. He pushed open the window to the chambers, sucking the cool morning air into his lungs and feeling them expand. It was crisp and invigorating. It was the perfect remedy to pull him out of his sluggish state.

Feeling revived, the butler turned on his heel and determinedly scowled at Claydale in his sorry state. He poured the master's usual brandy into the glass and left the room. He did not want to wake the man because he would only hinder his plans.

The malevolent contortion of Claydale's face and the sharp lines of his warped, vengeful sneer haunted violet's dreams. When she woke, she did not feel like she had slept at all. The absence of Nellie added to the angst that festered in her mind and knotted her insides. She just had to get through this one day, she reminded herself as she forced spoonfuls of porridge down into the pit of her turbulent stomach.

As she made her way down the stairs toward the library, Violet kept a vigilant watch for any signs of Claydale. The gloom in the corridors was thick and creepy as she tiptoed carefully, keeping to the carpeted floor. She stopped and held her breath several times over, her breathing too loud in her ears, drowning out everything else.

The rooms were empty except for a murmur of a deep voice that she assumed was Claydale in his chambers. She did not have the strength of mind to risk approaching, so she carried on down to the library, where she hoped she would find a book to occupy her mind.

None of the books measured up to the one that Emil had bought her. Dust lay thick on the tattered corners that jutted from the shelves, undisturbed for what looked like decades, albeit the few enormous books dedicated to science. Oval imprints broke through the layers of dust, revealing the path of wandering fingers. Fingers that belonged to those of a scientific inclination seeking more knowledge. Violet shivered, imagining what horrors the pages had revealed to the wicked mind of Claydale.

The winter sun poured through the glass into the library. The dust motes basked in its splendor. They seemed to dance before her eyes, drawing her attention beyond the four walls of her nightmare. She forgot all about the books and followed the warmth of the sun.

A rabbit, white as snow, hopped across the lawn and disappeared into the neatly pruned hedgerow. She envied its freedom. Violet hugged herself against the wintery breeze. It gnawed at her skin, igniting the involuntary shiver as her muscles tensed and trembled. But knowing that she may never see the outside again, she remained as still as possible in the cold, her body slowly becoming numb with her emotions.

A rough, warm hand pressed over her lips. The palm lay flat against her face, sealing her airways. The man clamped her between the force of his hand and his body as he stood behind her. He remained quiet as the sharp pain of a needle pierced her neck.

Violet kicked and screamed against the man's hold on her. Time slowed with her movements, her skin felt thick and heavy like it didn't belong to her. She became nothing but waves of thoughts and fears bundled inside a casket of lead as she looked out at the world moving around her. She watched the trees move further in the distance as the man dragged her still body backward. Her mind willed her head to turn to see him, perhaps beg for her life, but it would not move. She was utterly helpless.

Beads of sweat dripped down the back of Thompson's shirt as he hauled Violet's limp body across the lawn. The cold air revived his determination as it licked against his face, cooling him. This was the beginning of a journey that could only prove his worth to the master, he told himself. It had been simple. The girl could not have made it any easier as she stood outside, staring into nothing. Everyone was on the other side of the house seeing to their duties so they could not hear the girl's boots scrape along the gravel path as he led her to the basement door.

Dropping her body to the ground, steering her head away from the wall, he fumbled with the keys tied to a chain at his hip. He selected a large gold key and rattled it in the lock until he heard the familiar click. Violet could see that it was the butler that had rendered her body the victim of paralysis. His eyes shifted from side to side, beads of sweat moistening his skin, as he struggled to grasp the handle of the basement door.

She couldn't ask him why he would do that to her. Her tongue lay heavy in her mouth, dormant and devoid of sense or ability. Surely, Claydale hadn't asked him to? she thought. But, then again, the man had tried to the day before, so perhaps he had.

Thompson shifted out of her line of sight. The noise of his feet scraping over the loose chippings on the path, sounded as he moved to a position behind her head. On cue, her shoulders rose off the ground, revealing the garden again as he slowly dragged her into the darkness.

Violet's body clunked against the steps in time with the butler's movements. He turned his head to measure the distance between the heavy weight of Violet and the table at the centre of the dark room. His back ached as he bent over her, but he was determined not to relent to the fatigue that slowly crept over him. 'Once she is on the table, I will rest then and not a minute before.' he thought.

Thompson tightened his stomach muscles and pulled back his shoulders as he prepared himself to lift the girl. He bent at his knees, scooping one arm below her spinal curve and the other under the bend in her knees. He growled like a beast as he balanced the weight of his upper body and Violet against the strength of his legs and hauled her up onto the stone-cold table. His breathing, shallow from exertion as the palms of his hands pressed into the table, supporting him.

The butler could feel the young woman's eyes watching him. They were unnerving, but soon remedied as he placed the large leather strap, which was meant only to secure her head against the table, over her eyes.

There was nothing but the sound of leather rushing through buckles and pressure against the thick, cushion feel of her numb wrists, waist, thighs, and ankles. An orchestra erupted inside her body as Violet's heart punched against her breastbone and her breathing rasped in incomprehensible fear. She waited for something. She was susceptible to anything and everything that the man standing over her wanted to inflict upon her body. A tightening wave of apprehension flooded her insides. All she could do was wait.

Thompson removed the strap from Violet's eyes. The girl's breathing was silent, and her eyes showed no sign of recognition. The butler placed his hand over her slack jaw, feeling the heat of her breath against his skin. He didn't know why he was relieved that she still lived because it would be only temporary, but still he could feel the tension in his shoulders disperse as the moisture settled on the back of his hand from the droplets of her warm breath.

He lowered his tired body into Claydale's chair and perused the open book. A diagram of the human body splayed across two pages. 'This one is like Lily,' he thought, 'but she does not have the shorter limb as she did.' He ran his finger over the neatly sketched curve of the spine this girl had, like Violet. He admired the intricate lines and artistry of Claydale's illustration of the young woman's form. He could not confess to holding the same depth of fascination that was evident in the master's work, and the wording he used was most confusing. 'Perhaps I am out of my depth here,' he wondered. 'Time will tell, but he will see my worth now that I have prepared her for him.'

Gathering his strength, Thompson tugged at each leather strap to be sure that they were tight. He could not risk Violet freeing herself. He hurried up the steps back into the open air, locked the door, brushed his clothes down, and continued with his day.

45

"You needn't bother with Miss. Violet's meals anymore." Thompson announced the next morning as he entered the kitchen, "She has left the master."

Mrs. Grange raised her eyebrows at the butler in surprise. "Not again? Oh, that poor man." she crooned.

"I know." the butler replied, "He has been rather unfortunate in his escapades of the heart."

"Does he know yet? What with him being ill and all."

"No, I have not had the chance to inform him yet, as he is still resting."

The cook nodded thoughtfully. "Perhaps I'll give you his tea now and you can take it to him?" she smiled, "If you're not busy like?" She added, remembering his instructions the previous morning.

"Very well, Mrs. Grange. I shall."

"Is that for Violet, sir?" Nellie asked as she entered Claydale House. The butler stopped in his tracks. He hadn't expected the maid to return so soon.

"She has left the master." he slurred, slackening his jaw to remove any telltale signs of his deception.

Nellie frowned at the butler's announcement. It was an

obviously wicked lie, and she knew it, but she had to think of Violet so continued the role of being oblivious to his and Claydale's deeds. "Did she say where she was going?"

"And why, Nellie, would she tell us?"

"Well, she might've done." she began, "I thought maybe she'd left like Lily did, because of family, y'know?" Her eyebrows raised and her eyes widened, animating her look of curiosity. The temptation to put the butler at unease overwhelmed her.

His reaction did not disappoint. Thompson swallowed hard as a quick flash of guilt glazed his eyes. "This time we do not know where she is and do not bother Mr. Claydale with your incessant questions." he sniffed and walked up towards Claydale's chambers.

Violet was either dead or trapped, she thought, praying that she was not too late. "May God forgive you because I never will." Nellie seethed under her breath, watching Thompson enter the master's chamber.

"Morning, sir!" Thompson exclaimed.

"What time is it?" Claydale groaned, pulling his blanket over his head.

"It is breakfast time, sir."

"I'm not hungry. Leave it over there." His voice was still slurred a little, but Thompson noted that his speech was faster, and he seemed more like his usual self.

"You must eat for your strength, sir. I have something to show you. I believe you will find most useful."

"This better be good!" barked Claydale as he pushed his body up the bed into a sitting position.

Thompson shuffled, nervously, on his feet as he prepared himself to confess what he had done to Violet.

"Well, spit it out." Claydale hissed, "I have a terrible headache."

Claydale's mood only added to the regret that was mounting in the butler's mind. It was too late, he thought, he couldn't just let the girl go. "I've prepared the girl, sir!"

"Excuse me?!" The laudanum dulled the ferocity behind his eyes. "Did I just hear what I think I heard?" he rasped, clutching his head.

"Yes, sir, I thought I would help you."

Claydale prodded the centre of his forehead, where the pain pulsed. He was now sitting on the side of the bed, his elbows resting on his knees. "Dear God, what have you done, Thompson?"

"I'm sorry, sir, I was just trying to help you." the butler whimpered like a child.

Thompson wished he could turn back time and undo everything he had done. He scolded himself for being so rash in his decision. He hadn't proved himself capable, yet rather the opposite.

"Stop blathering, Thompson. I assume you hid her from prying eyes?"

"Yes, sir."

"At least that is one aspect to be grateful for." Claydale pinched the bridge of his nose. "Where is she?"

"In the basement, sir, on the table."

Claydale rose to his feet. He was still wearing the same clothes as he'd worn the first day he had taken to his bed. His body reeked of sweat and sleep. His hair tousled in a nest of silver-grey upon his head. He clawed through the mess with his fingers, his mind ruffled by the butler's admission. "If I am to be successful, they must not find her..."

"No-one will find the girl, sir. I have been very careful."

"Quiet!" Claydale roared. "If it hadn't been for your meddling, I would not be in this mess."

Silence flooded the room as Thompson waited for Claydale's next words.

Nellie scrubbed angrily at the dirt in the carpet. The mud of a man's boots imprinted deep into the fibres. The odour of stagnant water and mould wafted up with every swipe of the brush bristles as they splayed against the floor. She knew exactly where that rancid odour was from. Her stomach twisted into knots as she imagined Violet down in the basement, cold, alone, and scared.

Violet wriggled in the grasp of the thick straps that held her body against the hard table. Her spine throbbed as the pressure of the dense wood pushed against it. Her skin moved from side to side over her vertebrae as she writhed to escape the ache.

The pitch-black of the room stole her sight as it swallowed her in its jaws. She inched her head from side to side under the force of the leather strap across her forehead as she searched for fragments of light to relieve her of her desperation to see again.

There was nothing but her sense of touch and sound to help her now. She would have to try to escape with the only tool she had, her strength. Whatever the butler had injected in her, its essence slithered like a wisp of smoke through her veins, hindering her abilities. The more she twisted her limbs, the weaker she became. Frustration grew as she felt the buckles dig into her skin. Thompson knew what he was doing when he had strapped her to the table. He wasn't taking any risks and, as Violet lost the battle against the restraints, it showed. Violet's eyes pricked with tears of anger as she relented to their strength. She wouldn't give up. Time is all she needed. She would find a way.

The master's bellow of frustration boomed out into the corridors of the house. He was livid at Thompson, the maid noted. His words were sharp and panicked, which could only mean that Claydale was not happy with what Thompson had done to Violet.

She'd heard the butler whimpering his apologies and reassuring him Violet was still alive. His voice grated on her ears, but the words offered her the hope she'd longed for.

Claydale swung the door of the chambers against the wall. The force chipped at the paint, which crumbled to the floor.

"Sir, where are you going?" Thompson called.

"Stay out of my business, Thompson. I don't pay you to stick your nose where it's not wanted!"

The butler backed away with a mixture of anger, resentment, and shock. The master had always needed his help in these matters. How dare he talk to him like that? But to attempt to appease the man now, could lead to far worse things than Claydale's wrath. Thompson sat down on the bed and placed his hands on his neck. The ghost of a noose, his ultimate fear, tightened around it, halting him. He would not intervene now. He would wait.

The butler watched the master tumble out of the door while he poured the laudanum-spiked brandy into an empty teacup and gulped it down, followed by another and then another.

Nellie pushed against her stiff knees and climbed to her feet. Claydale was up and, by the sound of his slurred shouts, was on his way to find Violet. She hid in the nook under the stairs and waited patiently for him to pass. At first, his steps sounded laboured and slow, then they tumbled quickly in succession, followed by a groan. The man had fallen the last few steps. Nellie stopped herself from tending to him. She had to remember that from that moment, she would no longer help him ever again. Claydale crawled back toward the stairs and pushed himself up against them. The fall hadn't been enough to stop him, Nellie thought, as she pushed herself further back into the shadows. She held her breath as Claydale ambled closer. The man was all over the place, she thought. She watched and waited until he put some distance between them, then followed him quietly down the hall and toward the library.

Nellie did her best to avoid the spots on the floor she knew would alert him to her presence, but she hadn't known about the one by the fireplace. She ducked behind Claydale's reading chair and braced herself for the confrontation. The only sounds were his clumsy footsteps proceeding on his mission.

As he passed through the library into the garden, she crept out and followed him to the basement. Claydale's fingers looped around the ring of keys and held them in front of his face. He swayed as he tried to focus on the one for the basement door. When his fingers finally connected with the correct one, he placed it in the lock and turned it.

Nellie watched from behind him as he stood at the top of the stairs. Anger burned in her stomach, as hot as lava. The heat rose as she caught sight of her helpless friend strapped to the table, Violet's eyes pleading with her.

Claydale looked at Violet, then turned to see what the young woman was looking at. As he did, Nellie's foot kicked out in front of her and impacted with his body. Claydale rocked on his feet briefly, his fingers grappling at the air for something to hold on to, but the weight of his upper body tipped him over. His eyes were wide as he fell backward, glaring in horror at the maid, realizing what she had done. The side of his head cracked against the basement wall, followed by a single snap of the neck as he reached the floor. Claydale was dead.

46

"Nellie..." Violet whispered from the table where she still lay captive. Her limbs were tight against the flat, rigid surface. "Nellie?"

The maid stared in horror at Claydale, his body twisted and broken. She trembled furiously at the realization of what she had done.

"Nellie..." Violet tried again but, this time, a little louder. The urgency in her voice prompted Nellie to look her way. The young woman stared, bewildered and distressed. All her emotions echoed in her now ice-white complexion. Her eyes were wide, stark with the guilt threatening to drown her.

"Nellie, I need you to help me." Violet begged, seeing her friend's obvious distress.

Nellie nodded, portraying her understanding of what needed to be done. Her body was heavy under the shame of her crime. She dragged her legs, maneuvering around the man's lifeless body, inching toward Violet. The rigidity of her steps made her movements awkward and slow.

Nellie glanced down at Claydale. Her stomach tensed in waves as she caught sight of the sharp angle of his neck, the deep purple-blue skin that stretched over it. The spasms in her stomach travelled upward until they pulsed in her throat, making her wretch.

"Nellie, I need you to be strong for me, just for a little while." Violet pleaded. Their eyes met.

A look of helplessness poured from Violet into Nellie, reminding her why she was there. It vanquished her regret, at least for the present moment, spurring her on.

Violet watched as Nellie regained her wits. Her body appeared to have broken free of the hold that Claydale still had on her, even in his death. She placed her hands on the first leather strap at Violet's ankle.

"This may hurt." Nellie said, "I'm going to have to pull these tighter to release the clasp. I'll be as gentle as I can." she promised.

"It's okay, do what you need to." Violet replied quickly. Taking a deep breath, she braced herself for the sharp pain that was about to come.

As Nellie pulled, freeing the metal from the punctured hole, Violet clenched her teeth. They ground together as the leather ground against her skin. It pressed deep, as though it was trying to reach her bones. She breathed in through her nose and out through her mouth, releasing the pain in silence every time she exhaled.

Wrists and ankles now free, Nellie stood at the top of the table assessing how to rid Violet of the last strap. If she pulled at it like the others, she did not know what damage it would do to Violet's skull. She could not risk that. Instead, she wriggled and shifted the strap backward in slight movements until it looped over the top of Violet's head and slid off. She was finally free.

Violet rolled slowly onto her side and sat herself up on the edge of the table. Her neck felt stiff, a pain pulsing at the base of her skull. Her spine throbbed against the numbed skin on her back.

"You'll have to stay here until it's dark." Nellie muttered, her eyes flitting from Violet to Claydale and back again in repetitive motions. "We can't leave in the daylight; They will see us."

"But the butler will come for me, surely?" Panic rose in Violet's voice.

"I don't think he will," Nellie replied. "He and Mr. Claydale had words. I've never heard the master shout so loud. Thompson will be licking his wounds for the rest of the day, but I will make sure that no-one comes here, I promise. Trust me, Violet, please?"

"I do."

"Good. We've come so far; we can't give up now. I've got to get your cape and reticule, too." Nellie brushed herself down as if brushing away the man that lay dead at her feet. She glanced around the basement, noting the only light came from the doorway, so she lit a candle and placed it on the desk. The flame glowed in an extended orb across the walls and tabletop; Claydale's body blanketed in the shadows.

"I'll be back this evening." Nellie said, squeezing Violet's stiff, cold fingers, "Be ready." she whispered as she walked up the basement stairs. With a click of the lock, she shut the basement door and was gone.

Nellie turned the latch quietly on the library door and made her way across the rug to the other side of the room. She placed her ear to the gap in the door and listened. The house was deathly silent. She hoped it was a good sign. She had to find Thompson before he found Violet. He was the only other person who had the key to the basement, and he would soon wonder where Claydale was.

Nellie crept up the stairs, her lips thinned, trying not to breathe too loud. Her feet padded softly on the carpet, then froze at the top step. A loud rumble vibrated from the master's chamber. A sense of unease at her assuredness and relief, that it could never be Claydale again, chilled her.

The door creaked in a whisper as she pushed it back slowly. Thompson lay asleep on the master's bed. An empty tumbler tilted over his open hand as a thin trickle of brandy dripped, in time with the man's heartbeat, onto the floor. He had drunk the laudanum, Nellie realized with relief. The decanter was empty, all but perhaps one more glass. He would sleep for the rest of the day. The maid walked backward out of the room and locked it. He would never find Violet, even if he did wake, she smiled to herself.

47

Reginald Carson scraped his sleeve over his stubbled chin and dragged it over his mouth, wiping away the ale that spilled from his lips. "'Ow long is this going to take?" he grumbled, slouched over the dust-covered table in the dimly lit inn.

"Not much longer, brother." Mycroft retorted, "May I remind you whose fault this is?"

"Bloody hell, Mycroft, like I need reminding! You've been making sure I won't forget for the whole of this pointless journey!" Reginald Carson's brow furrowed in deep, dirt-ridden lines. "How long is not much longer, anyway?"

"We will be there by nightfall." Mycroft rolled his eyes at the sight of his useless brother. 'One day, I will not need your money.' he thought begrudgingly, 'I will have my own money. I will be in charge!'

"What you scowlin' at?" Reginald squinted his eyes at his brother, trying to focus, looking for a change in the man's expression. "There! You're scowlin' like I thought!"

"Just drink that ghastly ale of yours and we can get moving." Mycroft sniffed.

Nellie had not heard another sound from Thompson all

day and none of the household staff had even questioned his whereabouts or even Claydale's. By the time the evening had rolled around, she was exhausted. She had been running solely on the adrenalin that continually flushed through her in waves as she pictured the broken, decaying body in the basement. Its twisted neck contorted with her insides as she tried to make sense of the plans she had for the hours ahead. The nausea it created was hideous and uncomfortable. She craved to be as far away from the life she knew there and then, as she could be, but she would not abandon Violet.

"Goodnight, Mrs. Grange!" Nellie called from her chambers. She sat on the bed, fully clothed, a small bag in her hand, and waited until she knew it would be safe.
"Goodnight, love!" the cook called back. "Sweet dreams. See you in the morning."
Nellie smiled sadly. She would miss Mrs. Grange. The woman had been like a second mother to her in her time at Claydale House. She whispered a small prayer to keep the woman safe and to keep her and Violet safe, too.

As the soft breathing sounds of Mrs. Grange whispered through the corridor, Nellie silently, and sadly, said goodbye.

The silver moon spread across the night sky in smudges of grey and blue. Stars punctuated the cloudless black sea over their heads. Violet breathed in the crisp, cool air in quick breaths. Her lungs were like fists as they tightened to its caress.

"Are you alright?" Nellie whispered, her arm draped over her shoulder.

"I think I was down there too long." Violet replied, pointing down into the pool of black that filled the basement. She shivered as the winter chill pinched her skin.

"Let's get you warm." Nellie released the cape that was draped over her other arm and wrapped it around Violet's quivering body. She tied it securely at the front, covering every inch of the top half of Violet's dress. "Here, take this." The maid offered Violet a scarf. "Wrap it loosely over your mouth and nose to warm your breath. It will help your breathing. My ma does that when she struggles." she smiled, knowingly.

"Thank you." Violet whispered.

"We've just got to get out of here." Nellie took Violet's hand.

Keeping as close as they could to the walls of the building, she led Violet to the front of the house.

"Wait here." Nellie whispered. She walked over to a large plant and submerged her hand and forearm into the thick leaves. "There you are." she breathed as if she was talking to another.

Violet couldn't see what Nellie was holding. The maid's hand had disappeared with the item under her cape, showing only a slight bump in the folds of the fabric.

"It's your reticule." Nellie smiled, handing it to her. "I could only carry your cape earlier, so I left it in the plant. The money is still there."

Violet thread her wrist through the handle of the reticule and pulled the scarf away from her mouth and nose. Her breathing had slowed and the heat of her own breath against her face was stifling. "Thank you, Nellie. I don't know how I'll ever..."

"We must be quick Violet." the maid interrupted, "The fewer people see of us, the better."

"Yes, of course."

Quickly and calmly, the two young women burst from the Claydale estate onto the lonely country road, their hearts pattering inside their chests. Plumes of white mist puffed into the night air with every panicked breath as they ran. The sound of their boots beat upon the earth, carrying them further toward their intended destination.

Violet did not have time to wonder what would happen when she showed up at her grandmother's door. Perhaps the old woman would assume her a ghost. Her fear would allow Violet to stride in and collect her small hessian sack beneath her bed. Violet had a newfound strength. She would not hide from her grandmother, nor would she back down. Tonight would be the night her life would begin.

Nellie lightly tugged on Violet's arm as they reached her grandmother's land. She was bent over, hands propped on her knees, panting, trying to get her words out for Violet to hear.

"My ma's just over there, see?"

Violet looked toward where Nellie pointed. A woman almost identical to Nellie, all but her age, smiled kindly and waved.

"You can come with us." Nellie offered when she finally got her breath back. "I've already told Ma about you. We'll keep you safe."

Violet waved at Nellie's mother. A brief hello and goodbye at the same time, then turned to the friend she had grown to love and the one she owed her life to. "I have to go." she said. "You have done more than I can ever repay you for and you will always be the best friend I've ever had."

"But..."

"Listen, if I go with you, they will always follow you. You will never be able to forget what we did. I will be your constant reminder."

"You wouldn't be, honestly you wouldn't."

Despite Nellie's kindness, Violet knew it was just that. She wrapped her arms around her friend and held her close. "Thank you for everything." she whispered in her ear. "Take care of yourself."

Nellie wiped the tears from her eyes. "You take care of yourself, too, Miss. Violet. I will miss you so much." the young woman sniffed into her handkerchief.

"As I will miss you, dear Nellie." Violet's breath staggered with the ache in her chest as she squeezed Nellie's hand lightly. Her fingers loosened their grip and let her friend's hand slip from hers as she turned and walked down the path to her grandmother's house.

48

Violet did not feel as brave as she did when she and Nellie fled from Claydale's House. Perhaps it was because she was alone now, or maybe it was because she was about to face the person she feared most of all.

The tired wooden door in front of her looked as withered as her gumption was, as she thought of the person and the memories that stood beyond the daunting barrier. She could just leave the last few items there, lost forever, she thought.

Had it not been for that photo, she would have walked away happily. The single photo of Violet and her parents had kept her company since she was eight. It was her sole reminder that she had been loved once in her life; she'd had a family. She was afraid that she would forget their smiling faces and the adoration in their eyes as they gazed at their daughter, young Violet, on her father's knee.

Before Violet could procrastinate any further, her knuckles rapped on the door four times in succession. There was no turning back now. She was met with silence as she tried once again. After a few minutes, Violet pushed back the door. The house was deserted, cold, and dark. 'She must have left,' Violet thought, as she ventured in further. The echo of her grandmother's absence flooded Violet with relief.

The silver light of the moon lit the kitchen as it watched her in her quest. Its presence was comforting, distracting her from the creaks of the floorboards beneath her weary feet.

All the furniture, except the table, had vanished. The house was now just a husk of history, full of scars and bruises that would always remain a secret lost to time. No-one would ever know who she was, she thought as she climbed the stairs. She thought of the cabin, her heart praying for Emil to be close by. With him, she would have a life, the life she craved.

Just one more step and she was in her old room. Nothing had changed. Her grandmother had not bothered to take any of it. 'Why would she have?' Violet let out a short huff of a laugh at her thought, 'To her, it is worth nothing. That's why she let me have it.' But there was that one thing that meant the world to Violet, and it was still there, as though it had been waiting for her to return.

Violet pinched the photo between her fingers and wiped away the dust. "There you are." she smiled lovingly, "I've missed you." Carefully, she tucked it inside her reticule. Violet disregarded the other objects she'd packed in the hessian sack. She would manage perfectly fine without them. Her body was too tired to carry any extra weight. It was time to leave.

"This is it." she whispered to the room, "I won't be..."

The door slammed against the wall downstairs, snapping Violet from her farewell. She could hear rumbles of masculine voices. Two men bickering. Two tones that were unmistakable and terrifying.

The Carson brothers barged into the house. "Where are ya, you ol' bat?!" Reginald hollered. "We want our money back!"

"What are you doing, you buffoon?" Mycroft scolded, "Can't you see the place is empty?" Mycroft gestured to the lack of light and furniture as though he was handing his brother the last piece to a simple jigsaw puzzle that the man just could not fathom.

"Oh... yeah, I knew that." Reginald sniffed. "Anyway, so much for your clever idea of coming all this way to look for our 'unchback. She ain't 'ere either."

"Yes, well, that is obvious!" Mycroft snapped. The burning pink of his face paled in the moon's haunting light.

"What are we going to do, then?" Reginald asked. He placed his fists onto his hips, perched on the slight curves of his waist above them, and waited.

Violet had heard enough. She inched the window open. The idea of having to jump from such a height had always terrified her, but her reluctance cost her dearly last time. She would not fall into the same trap twice.

The window was narrow, leaving little room for her body and the sheer bulk of her petticoats. Quickly, she removed them and let the thin fabric of her dress flow down over her bare legs. It was colder, she thought, but freeing. It was much easier to haul herself up onto the window ledge, from where she then dropped to the earth outside.

"What in darnation was that?" Mycroft asked. His eyes pierced the dark as he stared at his brother.

"It weren't me. I ain't eaten anything dodgy today." Reginald replied.

"Does everything boil down to your bowel habits?"

Reginald grinned at his own inward joke.

"Listen, you fool!" Mycroft snapped.

Reginald and Mycroft held their breaths and listened. Their eyes darted back and forth as if searching the air in front of them. There was another cluttering sound of timber against stone.

"There!"

Mycroft and Reginald fled from the house toward the sound.

Violet grimaced as she waded through the wood. She hadn't noticed it in the shadows. She would have to run. There was no way the Carson brothers didn't hear her crash like that, she thought. Picking up her thin skirt, Violet's feet took over her body. They drummed against the soil. The wind rushed at her face. There was freedom in her movement that fear had released. She had never run this fast in her entire life.

There were those voices again. They were out there in the open with her, calling her by the name they had given her. She would not and did not stop as she met the forest edge. She was so close now.

Reginald Carson pointed at the figure in the distance. "There it is!... Get it! Cooey! 'Unchback!"
Mycroft looked up and then back at his brother. "What in the heavens is that?" he asked, staring at the pistol in Reginald's hand.
"What do you think it is?" Reginald asked sarcastically as they continued to run toward Violet.
Mycroft huffed; he was struggling to breathe. There was no time to pry further, and he did not have it in him to talk sense into the man.

A bird swooped over Violet's head in circles, welcoming her home as she gathered speed toward the babbling brook. The bird's dark silhouette spurred her on as she heard the men shout for her attention. 'I am not that foolish to turn to your demands.' she thought, defiantly.

Her feet kicked at the dirt. The crunch of the fallen autumn leaves no longer heard. She had missed the beauty of the season, but now she knew she would see another.

Mycroft Carson crooned, "Stop hunchback or we will shoot!". His voice, closer now, alerting Violet's senses to her body. Her lungs burned as the air rasped in her throat. She had let her thoughts interject her body's response and now she was struggling.

'Keep going!' she urged herself. The brook was so close now. She could hear the trickle of the water calling for her to cross. The bird cawed over her in the sky, encouraging her; telling her she could do this.

As her foot sunk into the ice-cold depths of the brook, Reginald Carson squeezed the trigger on the pistol. A burst of sound released the bullet. It soared through the forest at an overwhelming speed. A ghost to the eye but not to the touch as it pierced the air.

Such malice and ferocity met with such a simple sound as a gentle thud could be heard in the distance.

49

The sound smacks against the back of Violet's head. It is sharp, but there is no pain. Her world moves before her eyes at the tremendous speed of galloping horses, hurtling over open fields. Everything rushes past her in visible bursts of wondrous colours. The wind is smooth and calm, softly curving against her body. She is floating, held aloft by invisible hands.

There is a tug at the thread between her and Emil. It is the strongest it has ever been. She can feel the pull at her heart in time with its steady pulse. Everything begins to drift at a calming speed. The picturesque image of the forest melts slowly, dripping like the wax of a candle. Its flame flickering gently.

The changes occurring before her, around her, and within her mesmerize Violet. There is an unearthly beauty that she cannot portray in words. Shimmering orbs surround her; stars pulled down from the sky as if to greet her. They hover beside her, watching expectantly. What they are waiting for, she is not sure, but they are warm and comforting.

Where the cabin once stood, another world unfolds in silence. She feels no sadness as the last piece of wood drifts away. The world is bright and clean now.

There are books and furniture; voices speaking her name...

A man steps forward. He is familiar with his peridot green eyes and his ink-black hair. The warm smile that illuminates his kind face pulls her towards him. He is looking at her in the way that he always has. Violet can feel her lungs expand as she begins to breathe again at the sight of him. Her heart swells, erasing the last fragments of pain.

She can feel the warmth of his skin as he takes her hand and pulls her towards him. "There you are, Violet." he whispers as he pulls her in and nuzzles into the rich chestnut waves of her hair. As he moves to look at her, his hand cups one side of her face. She leans longingly into his touch. The sparkle of a joyful tear trickles down her cheek as he brushes it away with his thumb.

In the quiet of their embrace, there is an unsaid assurance that she would never have to leave him again. Violet did not know how she knew, but only that she did, and with it came a peace she had never known before. "I'm finally home." she breathed.

The End

Printed in Great Britain
by Amazon